HER AIM IS TRUE

The cabin was closer now.

Bullets from all sides of the basin stung the air around Stryker. He thumbed off a fast shot at the Apache by the corral post. Another miss. Behind him Hogg was firing steadily but didn't seem to be scoring hits either.

The Apache stepped away from the corral and drew his Winchester to his shoulder. He and Stryker fired at the same time. The Indian's bullet crashed into the bay, and Stryker cartwheeled from the saddle, landing hard on his back in a cloud of dust.

A man who is thrown by a galloping horse doesn't get up in a hurry. Stryker lay stunned as bullets kicked up startled exclamation points of sand around him. Finally he raised himself into a sitting position. Feet pounded to his right, coming fast. The Apache, grimacing in rage, had grabbed his rifle and was readying himself to swing a killing blow at the white officer's head.

A shot.

The Apache went down, screaming, half of his skull blown away. Stryker turned his reeling head and saw a woman standing at the cabin door, a smoking Sharps still to her shoulder. . . .

Ralph Compton

Stryker's Revenge

A Ralph Compton Novel
by Joseph A. West

BERKLEY
New York

BERKLEY
An imprint of Penguin Random House LLC
penguinrandomhouse.com

ISBN: 9780451228871

Signet mass-market edition / February 2010
Berkley mass-market edition / August 2023

Printed in the United States of America
15 17 19 21 23 22 20 18 16 14

The Immortal Cowboy

This is respectfully dedicated to the "American Cowboy." His was the saga sparked by the turmoil that followed the Civil War, and the passing of more than a century has by no means diminished the flame.

True, the old days and the old ways are but treasured memories, and the old trails have grown dim with the ravages of time, but the spirit of the cowboy lives on.

In my travels—to Texas, Oklahoma, Kansas, Nebraska, Colorado, Wyoming, New Mexico, and Arizona—I always find something that reminds me of the Old West. While I am walking these plains and mountains for the first time, there is this feeling that a part of me is eternal, that I have known these old trails before. I believe it is the undying spirit of the frontier calling, allowing me, through the mind's eye, to step back into time. What is the appeal of the Old West of the American frontier?

It has been epitomized by some as the dark and bloody period in American history. Its heroes—Crockett, Bowie, Hickok, Earp—have been reviled and criticized. Yet the Old West lives on, larger than life.

It has become a symbol of freedom, when there was always another mountain to climb and another river to cross; when a dispute between two men was settled not with expensive lawyers, but with fists, knives, or guns. Barbaric? Maybe. But some things never change. When the cowboy rode into the pages of American history, he left behind a legacy that lives within the hearts of us all.

—Ralph Compton

Chapter 1

Excited, apprehensive, no one wanted to wait until morning. It was the witching hour, dark, but the bandages would come off now.

The desert wind threw itself at the adobe wall of the hospital, rattling the timber door and the windows in their frames. Blowing sand drove through the unquiet night and sifted into the fort's buildings, coating floors and furnishings, grit grinding into the wool blankets of fretful soldiers, making them toss and turn and groan in hot, troubled sleep.

Attracted by the rectangles of amber light that spilled onto the ground from the hospital windows, a thin, stunted calico cat blinked in the wind like an owl, then climbed onto a sill and looked through a dusty, fly-specked pane.

The cat saw, but could not comprehend, the scene inside. She would never know it, but that night her ignorance of humans and their ways was a rare stroke of good fortune in her hard, desperate life.

There were four people in a room curtained off from the rest of the empty hospital ward. The single guttering oil lamp that hung from a ceiling beam touched three of them with halos of light and shadow, darkness pooling in the hollows of their cheeks and eyes, giving them the austere look of painted medieval saints.

The man sitting up in the bed, the object of their interest, had no face.

His head was wrapped around and around in white cotton, like a museum mummy. Only his eyes, sky blue, frightened, were visible. Those and the gash of his mouth, the bandages above and below stained by the food he'd eaten that day.

His hand, once strong and tanned mahogany brown, but now thin, white and veined with blue, was clasped in both those of the beautiful girl sitting on the man's bed. Her brown eyes sought his, penetrating the fearful mummy mask, concerned . . . adoring.

"It will be all right, Steve," she whispered, smiling. "Dr. Decker says you're as good as new."

Colonel Abel Lawson beamed at his daughter. "Of course he is, Millie." He took a step toward the bed and looked down at the bandaged man, grinning from under the sweep of his great dragoon mustache. "It's been two months, Steve. I've never known Surgeon Major Decker to stay sober that long."

"Indeed, sir, but it's a state of affairs I intend to remedy as soon as Lieutenant Stryker's bandages come off," Decker said. He was a small, gray-haired man, buttoned into a white coat worn over a careless, shabby uniform.

Decker's eyes moved from the colonel to his daughter and back again. Like a man who can't swim and stands on the bank of a turbulent river, asking how deep the water is, the doctor's voice held a note of uncertainty.

"It's been this long," he said. He looked at Stryker, as if seeking his support. "It could keep until morning."

"Nonsense, Major," Colonel Lawson blustered. "The sooner the lieutenant is back on his feet"—he knew this next would bring smiles, and it did—"and safely wed to my daughter, the better."

He looked at Stryker. "I need you at my side in Washington, Steve. A few more days for your cuts and bruises to heal, and then a captaincy and the capital, as my aide. It will make your career, especially with my lovely daughter on your arm to dazzle the men and turn the women green with envy."

"Father, I fear I may have to fend the women off." Millie smiled as she squeezed Stryker's hand. "Steve will be quite the handsomest man in Washington, you know."

"Indeed," Lawson agreed. "Now, you haven't changed your mind, Lieutenant—or should I say Captain? Are you still willing to leave this Arizona hellhole for the shady boulevards of the capital?" The colonel, eager to seal the deal, added a barb. "As for myself, I should think you would. It's not often a junior officer with no connections or social position is given such an opportunity. Your father is a clergyman, is he not?"

"Papa," Millie scolded, a frown gathering between

her eyebrows, "what a singularly unfortunate thing to say."

"I speak only the truth, my dear. Lieutenant Stryker is a soldier. He understands such things."

Stryker tried to smile, but his mouth felt stiff and unyielding under the bandages.

For a moment he felt a surge of panic that quickly passed. As far as he could tell, the bullet wound in his side had healed, thanks to Decker. When the man was sober he was a good doctor, and Stryker told himself that his smashed face was no doubt back to normal.

Time would tell . . . when the bandages were removed.

"I haven't changed my mind, Colonel," Stryker said. His voice was a harsh croak, far removed from the usual fine baritone that he had so often used to entertain his fellow officers with selections from Mr. Gilbert and Mr. Sullivan's latest operettas.

He had not lied to Lawson. He hated, with a passion, the silent, brooding desert, its infinite distances, the land and sky scorched to the color of chalk. And there was no honor to be gained fighting Apaches, no medals awarded for killing Stone Age savages.

Without the colonel, he could end up as so many others had done in the frontier army, an aging captain, if he was lucky, with nothing to look forward to but a retirement of genteel poverty eked out in some dusty western town, with stories to tell but no one to listen to them.

As though he'd read the lieutenant's thoughts,

Lawson slapped his hands together and said heartily, "Come now, Major Decker, shall we proceed with the"—he smiled—"unveiling?"

"The Man in the Iron Mask," Millie whispered. She put a hand to her mouth. "Why did I say that?"

"Understandable, my dear," Lawson said smoothly. "After all, the only person who has seen Lieutenant Stryker's handsome features this past two months is Major Decker. A mask indeed, but of cotton, not iron."

The doctor, a stricken look on his face, leaned over Stryker and whispered into his ear, low enough that only he could hear. "Steve, God help me, I tried my best."

Stryker swallowed hard, a growing apprehension in him that was but a step away from fear. As Decker began to unroll the bandages, the lieutenant listened into the wind-lashed night, a man afraid of what was to come.

He winced as the cotton gauze ripped away from dried blood, and Decker whispered, "Sorry."

Stryker stared at the dusty ceiling, which was cobwebbed in the dark corners where the spiders lived. He again felt the spike of panic.

Two months, and in all that time Decker had not let him look into a mirror!

For God's sake, why not?

Millie's hands were hot in his own and he felt sweat on her palms. She was breathing unevenly, quiet little gasps that were now coming quicker as the layers of bandages were peeled away.

Outside, in the darkness, the coyotes were talking, and Stryker heard sentries call out to one another. The wind pounded around the eaves of the hospital, as though eager to be let inside and witness what was happening.

Made uneasy by the hunting coyotes and bored with the human activity, the little calico jumped down from the sill and found a sheltered spot behind the wheel of a parked freight wagon. She curled into a ball, nose to tail, but did not sleep.

When she heard the woman's scream, she jumped to her feet, head lifted, eyes aglow with emerald fire.

"I'm sorry, Steve!" Millie Lawson jumped to her feet. She didn't look at him again. "I'm so sorry! I can't. . . . I just can't—"

She turned and ran to the door, ignoring her father's call to stop. The girl threw the door open wide, then dashed blindly into the darkness, her sobs drifting behind her like leaves in a wind.

Shocked, his face drained of color, Colonel Abel Lawson pointed an accusing finger at Decker. "Damn you, Major!" he yelled. "Damn you to hell!"

The doctor looked like a man who had just been punched in the gut. "I did my best to piece him together," he said. There was no defiance in his voice, only weary resignation.

"Then your best wasn't good enough, was it?" Lawson snapped. "The damned mule doctor could have done better."

Stryker looked at the two men, then traced his fingertips over his face from forehead to chin. Battling to keep his voice steady, he said quietly, "Major Decker, please bring me a mirror."

He didn't look at his reflection or scream until he was alone.

By then, Surgeon Major Decker was already stinking drunk.

Chapter 2

Lieutenant Steve Stryker watched Joe Hogg ride toward him at a slow canter. The scout's head was on a swivel, his eyes constantly scanning the chaparral-covered hills around him.

Hogg was by nature a careful-riding man, but his vigilance put Stryker on edge.

He turned to the soldier at his side, like himself stripped down to long johns, hat and boots against the merciless heat of the day. "Draw carbines and form a skirmish line, Sergeant Hooper."

Hooper swung his horse away and yelled at the eighteen troopers behind him. "You heard the officer. Draw carbines an' form a bloody skirmish line."

The cavalry troopers, tough, hard-bitten runts riding grade horses, drew their Springfields and shook out into a ragged line, leaving one man with the pack mules. Then, like Stryker, they sat their mounts silently and watched Hogg come.

The scout was a narrow wisp of a man who seemed to be formed only of height and width, like a figure on a playing card. He had the thin, hard-boned face of a desert rider and his shabby, trail-worn coat and pants had faded to the color of the desert itself. In a close-up fight, he was good with the heavy revolver that rode his hip, better with the Henry .44-40 booted under his left knee.

Stryker had been told that Hogg had killed eight white men in gunfights, and he believed it. The scout was sudden, dangerous beyond measure, and if there was any softness in him, Stryker hadn't found it yet.

The lieutenant waited, knowing that Hogg, a taciturn man who didn't like to be pushed, would speak in his own due time.

"Apaches—a mixed band by the sign," Hogg said finally. "I found Chiricahua and Mescalero arrows up there."

"Where are they?"

"Not where they are, Lieutenant, but where they was." Hogg turned in the saddle and pointed. "Beyond the ridge of the saddleback yonder. Norton and Stewart stage out of Globe. Five men dead and one woman." The scout's black eyes sought Stryker's, deciding not to rein in his tongue. "The woman was young and she was used, rode hard fore an' aft, afore they cut her throat."

"An officer's wife headed for the fort?"

"Could be. But now it don't matter a hill o' beans who she was, do it?"

"Damn it, Joe, I thought the Chiricahua were still holed up in the Madres, licking their wounds after the beating they took from the Mexicans in the Tres Castillas last year," said Stryker.

"I'd say the twenty young bucks who attacked the stage didn't learn that lesson." The scout shrugged. "They must have just broke out recent, lookin' to raise hob in general and avenge the deaths of ol' Victorio an' sixty warriors in partic'lar."

"They're succeeding."

The sun was very hot and gulping the still, dry air was like breathing inside a blast furnace. Buzzards were gliding lazily over the saddleback, patiently anticipating the feast spread out below them.

"Where are they headed, Joe?" Stryker asked.

"North, toward the Cabezas. They cut out the stage mules. I'm guessing they'll camp in the foothills tonight and fill their bellies with mule meat."

"Then we can catch them?"

"We can. Them bucks don't even know we're here. Looks like all of them headed north."

Stryker took time to roll a cigarette, aware that Hogg's eyes were still on his face.

He was the only man who looked at him straight. Stryker had grown used to people staring at the tunic buttons on his chest when they spoke to him, unwilling to raise their eyes and confront the horror of his disfigured features. But the scout looked and never flinched.

He'd recently asked Hogg why this was so, and the man had answered only, "Lieutenant, I seen the wounded at Gettysburg, Chickamauga and a dozen other places."

Stryker lit his smoke, then turned again to Sergeant Hooper, telling him he needed a smart soldier to carry a message to Fort Bowie.

"Beggin' the lieutenant's pardon, but I don't have one o' them," Hooper said.

A smile tugged at the corners of Stryker's mouth, doing nothing to soften the stiff, grotesque mask of his shattered and deeply scarred face.

"Then send me a stupid one," he said.

"Plenty of those, sir," the sergeant said. He turned to his left in the saddle and yelled, "Trooper Sullivan. Come 'ere an' speak to the officer."

Sullivan, a small man with the look of a belligerent rodent, rode out of line and drew rein in front of Stryker.

"Now mind your manners, Sullivan, or I'll be 'avin you," Hooper warned. He wore a ferocious scowl on a countenance as round and red as a penny. The sergeant had been a desert soldier for nearly fifteen years, but, unlike most men, his skin still burned scarlet in the sun and never tanned.

Stryker returned Sullivan's salute and said, "Ride to Fort Bowie and tell them the Norton and Stewart stage has been attacked. Six dead. No survivors. Ask them to detail a burial party, then lead them here to the saddleback yonder. Tell them I am headed north toward the Cabezas in close pursuit of the hostiles."

The lieutenant studied the trooper's face. "Can you remember that?"

Sullivan repeated the message word for word, and Stryker decided the man was not as dumb as Hooper alleged.

"Then get going," he said. "And good luck."

After the trooper rode away, cantering to the west

in a cloud of yellow dust, Stryker spoke to Hooper again. "Sergeant, Mr. Hogg and I will ride ahead. Follow on with the rest of the patrol and the pack mules."

Lieutenant Stryker sat his horse and studied the scene before him, his mouth working. He'd prepared himself for the worst during his ride to the saddleback, but this was beyond the stretch of his imagination.

His eyes met those of Hogg, and the scout grimaced. "Damned Apaches never clean up after themselves, Lieutenant."

Perhaps it was an attempt at humor. More likely Hogg was reaching out to him in clumsy reassurance, telling him that any normal man would be appalled by what he saw.

One thing Stryker did not need was sympathy. He'd read too much of that in the faces of others over the course of the past few months, not only for his broken face, but for losing his beautiful wife-to-be and promising Army career.

Without a word he swung out of the saddle and stood with the reins in his hands, looking around, forcing himself to swallow every bitter drop of this vile medicine.

The woman, a girl really, was the most noticeable, her body being the only one that had been stripped naked. She was lying spread-eagled on her back, her open blue eyes fixed on the indifferent sky, as though horrified that it thought nothing of how she'd been outraged.

Hogg had said the girl had been used hard, and she had, probably by all twenty of the Apaches. They had not been gentle.

And she'd been pregnant.

Her belly had been cut open, and her unborn son, a small, white, curled thing about six inches long, had been placed at her left breast as though suckling.

An Apache joke.

The scout was at Stryker's side. His eyes went to the girl, then back to the officer. "Lieutenant, you ever been in Kansas?" he asked.

Stryker shook his head, saying nothing, his eyes still on the woman's ravaged, bloodstained body.

"Some flat, long-riding country up there. A man on a tall horse can stand in the stirrups an' pretty much see forever. Into tomorrow, if a feller's farsighted enough."

"You say."

"Uh-huh, I do say. I was only there oncet, back in 'seventy-eight when ol' Dull Knife an' his Cheyenne was playing hob from one end o' the state to t'other. Right pretty country though, Kansas, even in winter."

"We'll find something to cover her, Joe," Stryker said. "Then lay her out alongside the others."

Hogg looked over at the stagecoach. "The driver and guard are still up on the box—must have been killed in the first volley. The two passengers tried to protect the gal though. See that tall feller lying by the door?"

"I see him."

"That there is 'Five-Ace' Poke Fisher, a gambler out of El Paso, Texas. Ol' Poke was a fair gunhand,

and in his day he killed more'n his share. If you look at him, he was shot maybe four, five times, an' all his wounds are in the front."

Hogg shook his head admiringly. "He died hard, did Poke, while a-trying to save the little lady. Who would have figgered ol' Five-Ace for a hero?"

Stryker turned to Hogg. His eyes in their crushed sockets were as hard as blue steel and his voice was as level as Hogg's Kansas plains. "Joe, when we catch up with the savages, I want them all dead. I don't want prisoners that the Army will only slap on the ass and send to San Carlos. If there are women and children with them, I want them dead too, every damned one of them. If I should fall, will you make sure my orders are carried out?"

Suddenly the scout's eyes were distant, as though he'd mentally put space between himself and his young officer. "Lieutenant, the Apache is a benighted heathen who only knows one way of making war—the way he was taught. He kills his enemies any how he can, then amuses himself by using their wives and daughters. He wasn't always like that—I mean, way back. The Spanish taught him their way of war, and then the Mexicans and now the white man. Every cruel, senseless thing he does, he's seen done to his own people many times over, and ten times worse."

Hogg shook his head. "Lieutenant, hating the Apache is like hating the cougar because of the way he kills a deer." He waited, then said, "Or you fer your face. Neither way of thinking makes much sense."

Stryker stood stiff and silent for what seemed an

eternity, then said, "I asked you a question, Mr. Hogg. If I fall in the engagement, will you see that my orders concerning the treatment of the Apache hostiles are carried out?"

The scout touched the brim of his hat. "I'll see that Sergeant Hooper follows your orders, Lieutenant."

"And you?"

"I hired on as a scout. Nobody said nothing about killing women and children."

Without another word, Hogg turned on his heel and greeted Hooper, who was leading the troop over the crest of the saddleback. "The lieutenant wants the bodies laid out and covered, Sergeant," he said. "See what you can find in the luggage to use as shrouds."

The cavalrymen were all young; one of them, Trooper Muldoon, was just sixteen. They had never been this close to dead people before and it showed in their strained faces as they laid out the already-smelling dead.

After the bodies were arranged in a row, covered by whatever items of clothing the soldiers had found in the luggage, Stryker stood in silence, looking down at the now-faceless dead. He lifted his head and yelled. "Sergeant Hooper, form the troop in line behind me."

Hooper did as he was ordered, and then the lieutenant said, "Now remove the coverings from the bodies."

When that was done, Stryker moved to the side of the line and addressed the men in a loud, harsh voice. "Look well, all of you, and know your enemy.

The Apache is not a warrior, not a soldier, but a killing animal. The only way to deal with such a savage beast is to kill him before he kills you."

Stryker walked down the line, looking into the young faces of undersized boys recruited from city slums. To favor its horses, the United States Cavalry preferred troopers to be small and light, and their rations of hardtack and greasy salt pork—and not much of it—were designed to keep them that way.

"Men," Stryker said, "we will meet up with the Apache later today. When we find them, what do we do?" He glanced down the line. "You, Trooper Muldoon, what do we do?"

The young man's face was flushed from being singled out for attention. He swallowed hard. "Kill them, sir."

"And their women?"

"Kill them, sir."

"And their children?"

"Kill them, sir."

"God curse the savages to hell! That's the spirit, Trooper Muldoon," Stryker yelled.

Another voice, from the end of the line, said, "I wish we had our sabers, sir."

Stryker strode in the direction of the voice. "Damn his eyes, who said that?"

"I did, sir. Trooper Murphy."

The lieutenant stopped in front of the man, a slight, stooped towhead with eyes the color of rain. "True blue, Murphy. And so do I wish I had my saber. But if we can't give them the steel, we'll give them good old American lead."

A ragged cheer went up from the soldiers, and even the normally staid Hooper joined in the clamor.

Hogg stepped to Stryker. "You fight Apaches afore, Lieutenant?"

"No, this will be my first action."

"You're learning fast."

Stryker smiled his crooked smile. "Look at my face, Mr. Hogg. It's because I've got hell on my side."

Chapter 3

Lieutenant Stryker rode beside the guidon, Hogg taking the point somewhere ahead of the patrol. The sun was now full in the sky, and the brush-covered hills around them were free of shadow. Scattered stands of mesquite and juniper grew in the valleys, and once Stryker saw an isolated cottonwood standing as a lonely sentinel near a dusty dry wash, close to the burned-out skeleton of an old freight wagon.

Four miles due east lay Apache Pass. To the west arced the worn track of the old Butterfield Stage route. Ahead of Stryker the rocky southern peaks of the Dos Cabezas Mountains shimmered in the heat haze.

Stryker dismounted the patrol to rest the horses, and led his men forward at a slow, shuffling walk. The only sounds were the creak of leather and the rattle of horse harnesses, the click of hooves and boots on rock.

The lieutenant's long johns stuck to his upper body and legs, and sweat trickled through the gray alkali dust on his cheeks. Behind him, covered in that same dust, the soldiers plodded forward like a column of ghosts. Trooper Kramer, who had a weak chest, wheezed with every step, and his mouth was wide-open, battling for each tortured breath of bone-dry hot air.

Nothing moved in the vast land, but somewhere up ahead were the Apaches, unseen, yet a palpable presence all the same.

Ahead of Stryker the figure of a mounted man undulated in the heat waves, his horse's legs impossibly long as it picked its way forward like a distorted giraffe.

Gradually the image settled and re-formed into its usual shape, the buckskin-clad figure of Joe Hogg astride his mustang.

Stryker halted the column and waited for the scout to come.

"Water ahead, Lieutenant," Hogg said, drawing rein. "And dead people."

The lieutenant said nothing, waiting.

"Ashes of the ranch house are still warm," the scout continued. "I'd say it happened no more'n two hours ago."

"The dead?"

"Man, woman, three children."

"Where are the Apaches?"

"I don't know. But they're around, lay to that."

Stryker turned. "Mount up," he yelled.

But before he could swing into the saddle himself, Hogg stopped him. He dug into the pocket of his coat, leaned from the saddle, then dropped a handful of spent shells into the officer's palm.

"I found some of these at the stage and more at the ranch. Shiny brass, .44-40 caliber. This was brand-new ammunition fired from repeating rifles."

"What do you think, Joe?" Stryker asked, looking into Hogg's eyes.

"I think at least half of them bucks have repeaters, Henrys or Winchesters. Judging by the firing pin strikes, I'd say, like the ammunition, the rifles are new."

Stryker's voice was tense, tight. "Somebody running guns to them?"

"That would be my guess."

"Tell me it's Rake Pierce, Joe. Damn you, tell me it's him."

Hogg was quiet for a while. A horse shook its head, the bit chiming. Trooper Kramer was agonizingly coughing up phlegm and dust, and somebody laughed and slapped the man's back.

Finally Hogg sat back in the leather and said, "Well, before we left Fort Merit, Colonel Devore told me that Pierce was running guns to the Apaches. But he said he was in the Madres."

"Why didn't you tell me, Joe? Why didn't Colonel Devore tell me?"

"We didn't want to get you worked up over nothing, Lieutenant. The Madres are a far piece away and it's a heap of country to cover, even if the Mexicans would allow it, which they wouldn't."

"But Pierce could be here, in the Arizona Territory."

"Anything is possible, Lieutenant. For sure, Sergeant Pierce was always a man who didn't cotton to being penned up in one place for too long."

Stryker swung into the saddle and gathered up the reins. "I want him, Joe. I want that bastard at the end of my gun."

"If he's in the territory, I'll do my best to find him for you, Lieutenant."

"Yes, find him. And when you do, let me be the first to know," Stryker said. "I'd sell my soul to kill that man."

Hogg was silent, obviously thinking about what he had to say. Then he said it, a plainspoken man with harsh words wrenching out of him like whetted iron.

"Lieutenant Stryker, from what I've seen an' heard on this patrol, you no longer have a soul to sell."

It was difficult to read Stryker's face, a stiff, misshapen mask that could no longer reveal emotion. Only the eyes were alive, now clouded like a sky before rain.

"Then I'll drag Rake Pierce down into hell with me, and consider my eternal damnation well worth the price."

Under his gray beard, a smile found its way to Hogg's lips. "Lieutenant, if I was a preaching man, about now I'd say, God forgive you."

Stryker nodded. "Mr. Hogg, I assure you, if you were a preaching man you would not be with this column."

Once again Stryker took his place beside the guidon. "Ride ahead," he told Hogg. "Find me those savages."

"There's water at the ranch, Lieutenant."

"The men and horses have water enough. We can always swing by there and replenish our canteens on our way back to Fort Merit."

"There's also six Christian people who need buryin'."

Suddenly Stryker was irritated. "Mr. Hogg, we're not a damned burial detail. The dead are beyond hurt. They can fend for themselves."

Hogg shook his head. "It just don't seem right, Lieutenant."

"Mr. Hogg, as long as I'm in command, I'll decide what's right. If you have any reservations on that point, you may return immediately to Fort Merit."

The scout was silent for a few moments, as though he was turning over that option in his mind. Finally he said, "I reckon I'll stick, Lieutenant. We can all go to hell together."

He swung his horse away and once again cantered into the shimmering heat of the afternoon.

Stryker waved the detail forward, and they headed due north for the next hour.

Directly ahead of the lieutenant, beyond the foothills, soared the domed peak of Government Mountain, where in ancient times mysterious peoples from farther south had once mined obsidian. Juniper and mesquite grew at the base of its slopes, giving way to brush as the mountain climbed to its full height of almost eight thousand feet. The peak's shadowed foothills spread away in all directions, like the knotted roots of a gigantic oak.

Somewhere in that tangle of arroyos, trees and hills were the Apaches.

Stryker took off his battered campaign hat and wiped sweat from the leather band. Were the savages watching them even now, waiting until they came into rifle range? And where the hell was Joe Hogg?

It was very hot. Dust drifted in thick veils around the column, and the men riding at the rear were suffering. The stale smell of horse and man sweat hung in the air and the red and white guidon drooped listlessly in the stillness. From somewhere close by a rattlesnake made its presence known, an angry buzzing that almost immediately lapsed into silence as the snake sought protection under a mesquite bush. The sun was the color of white-hot iron, branding the suffering sky, and in all the vast, naked land nothing moved and there was no sound.

Now the foothills of the Cabezas were drawing close and Stryker halted the column. He called Sergeant Hooper forward.

"Rest the men, Sergeant. No fires. We'll wait here for Mr. Hogg's report."

"Yes, sir," Hooper said. He snapped off a smart salute as though he were still on parade at Aldershot with the Queen's Own Rifles.

Stryker watched the man leave. Hooper was a good soldier, steady, but he had a fatal weakness for women. According to his record, it had been the rape of a fellow sergeant's sixteen-year-old daughter that had forced him to desert and flee England ahead of a rope.

Desperate for experienced soldiers, the United States Army had weighed Hooper in the balance, decided that he had value as an Apache killer, and had posted him to the Southwest. As far as Stryker knew, the Army had never regretted that decision.

As for himself, he had never liked the man. Hooper was a good soldier, but he was an overbearing bully and Stryker read something in his eyes that he did not like, something that crawled. . . .

Grateful to get out of the saddle, the troopers sprawled in whatever thin shade they could find. They could not boil coffee, but pipes were lit and a few of them chewed on evil-smelling jerky.

Hooper had pickets out, and the horses, used to making do or doing without, grazed on scattered clumps of bunch grass and mesquite beans.

Stryker eased the girth of the bay's saddle, then took his canteen from the horn. The water was brackish and warm, but it cut the dust in his throat, settled his burning thirst a little, and for that he was grateful. He watched his horse wander off in search of graze, then settled his back against a rock and waited.

Where was Joe Hogg? And where were the Apaches?

The lieutenant's sweat-stained long johns smelled stale and old, tinged with the odors of tobacco, horse and greasewood smoke. His canvas cartridge belt with its holstered, heavy Colt was digging into his waist, chafing the skin. He thought about pulling off his boots for comfort's sake, but decided against it. Just too much of a chore to drag them on again over his swollen feet.

A fly buzzed around his head and he waved it

away, but it persisted, attracted by the salty sweat on his skin. Stryker grabbed at the fly, missed, grabbed again. This time he caught it. He leaned over, rubbed the fly into a smeared mess between his palm and a rock, then wiped his hand clean on the sand.

He closed his eyes. Trooper Kramer was wheezing like a pipe organ as Hooper berated him at length for gasping on sentry duty like a two-dollar whore.

Stryker grimaced. Shut the hell up, Hooper.

Slow hours dragged past and shadows lengthened as the sun dropped lower in the sky. Soon the evening light would drift across the desert like gray smoke and add its more profound hush to the silence.

Where the hell was Hogg?

Rising wearily to his feet, the lieutenant looked toward the Cabezas foothills. He stepped to his horse, removed his field glasses from the saddlebags, and scanned the hills again.

Nothing moved and even the heat had ceased to shimmer.

Stryker lowered the glasses. All right, if Hogg wouldn't come to him, he'd go to Hogg.

"Sergeant Hooper!" he yelled.

Chapter 4

Two mounted troopers behind him, Stryker rode at a walk toward the hills.

The day was shading into night and the air had grown cooler. Like his men, the lieutenant was once again wearing his riding breeches, the wide canvas suspenders slung over a sun-faded blue blouse with its officer's shoulder straps.

The brush-covered hills gradually gave way to more level ground, but the going was made difficult by thickets of juniper, mesquite and unexpected parapets of white and tan rock.

Warily, Stryker rode west along the foothills, his eyes searching the shadowing country. Once a rustling in the brush sent his hand streaking for his gun. But he felt foolish when he saw that it was only a Gila monster seeking its burrow, a shy animal that spends only three or four minutes a year above ground.

Behind him, one of his men sniggered. It sounded like Trooper Rogers, a name Stryker mentally filed away for future reference.

For several minutes, he led his men northwest, following the gentle curve of the mountain range.

Apaches claimed they could smell white people, and the lieutenant figured that by now he must be within sniffing distance.

Ahead of him, the gathering darkness suddenly parted, and Joe Hogg, his Henry across the saddle horn, emerged from the gloom like a gray ghost.

When the scout rode closer he pointed over Stryker's shoulder, wordlessly indicating that he should go back the way he'd come.

Hogg rode on and the lieutenant and his men followed. After a hundred yards, the scout swung into the lee side of a rock and drew rein.

He got right to the point. "Lieutenant, the Apaches are holed up back yonder, maybe half a mile, in an arroyo that opens into a small hanging meadow. They got mule meat cooking on sticks, and—this is where it gets mighty interesting—they're passing around jugs. I reckon the rancher they killed must have been a whiskey-drinking man, because them bucks are well supplied and half of them are drunk already."

He paused. "Got a white woman with them. Red-haired gal, seems young."

"How many Apaches?"

"Pretty much as I guessed. Twenty young bucks, give or take a couple."

"No women or children with them?"

"Only the redheaded gal."

Stryker nodded. "She doesn't count."

He called over Trooper Rogers. "Head back to the

camp and tell Sergeant Hooper I said to bring on the rest of the detail. Tell him to come at a walk, no talking and no noise."

Rogers, a young man with freckles across his nose and a wisp of downy mustache on his lip, looked warily around him. "It's getting dark, sir."

Irritated, Stryker snapped. "What about it?"

"Well, sir, I mean . . . there are Apaches about, sir."

Hogg's teeth gleamed in the gloom. "Don't you worry about it, sonny. If the Apaches decide to git you, your hair will be gone an' your throat cut afore you even know it. You won't feel a thing."

Rogers swallowed hard, tried to talk and decided not to trust his voice, especially since his fellow trooper was sitting his horse, grinning at him.

"Carry out your orders, Trooper Rogers," Stryker said.

The man swallowed again, saluted and rode away.

"There goes a scared young man," Hogg smiled. "An' I can't say as I blame him. Apaches are nobody to mess with." He looked at Stryker. "Now we wait, huh?"

"Yes, for Hooper." The lieutenant found the makings and motioned toward Hogg. "Will they smell this?"

There was a smile in the scout's voice. "Lieutenant, if them drunken bucks are out on the prod, they already know we're here, so smoke away if it pleases you."

Stryker smoked his cigarette and then another.

The night air grew cool and a horned moon rose in the sky. Close by, among the shadowed arroyos, a pair of hunting coyotes called out to each other, and prowling critters made their small sound in the underbrush.

Leather creaked as Hogg shifted in the saddle, his eyes restlessly searching into the darkness. He looked at Stryker. "Hooper's close."

After years of Indian fighting, the scout's senses were honed as sharp as those of any Apache. If he said Hooper was close, then he was.

Stryker loosed the flap of his holster, thumbed a sixth cartridge into his Colt and replaced the weapon. He waited.

Sergeant Hooper led his men forward in an untidy column, riding over broken ground. He saluted the lieutenant and said, "Detail all present and accounted for, sir."

Stryker nodded, then glanced at Hogg. The scout read the question in his eyes and said, "Maybe another thirty minutes. Let them bucks get good an' drunk."

"Sergeant Hooper, we'll fight dismounted," the lieutenant said. He disliked the thought of weakening his command, but there was no alternative. "Leave Trooper Kramer and one other man with the horses."

Hooper saluted again. "Permission to picket the mounts, sir."

After nodding his approval, Stryker again turned to Hogg. "Will they be guarding the arroyo, Joe?"

A white moth fluttered past the scout's face. "Maybe, but I doubt it. The Apaches don't know we're here."

"You sure about that?"

"Sure I'm sure. If they were around, they would have smelled your tobacco smoke, Lieutenant. You'd be dead by now."

"Hell, Joe, you told me I could smoke."

"I said, 'If it pleases you.' I didn't say do it."

Stryker glared hard at Hogg. But the scout only shrugged and turned away, his talking on the subject done.

After Stryker judged that the thirty minutes had passed, he swung out of the saddle and Hogg did the same.

"Sergeant Hooper, we're moving out," Stryker said. "Carbines, but leave the canteens behind and, like I did with Trooper Kramer, anything else that makes a damned racket." He gave Hogg a sideways glance. "And no smoking."

If the scout felt the slightest pang of guilt, he hid it well. He stepped to his horse, reached into the beaded possibles bag that always hung behind his saddle and took out a tally book. He tore out a page, folded it lengthwise and stuck it in the front of his hat.

He stepped closer to Hooper. "I'll scout the arroyo again. When I come out o' there, tell them alley rats of yours to look for the white paper in my hat. I don't want them boys gettin' scared, taking me fer an Apache, an' cuttin' loose."

Hooper nodded and looked around him at the

troopers. "You heard Mr. Hogg. Look for the white paper in his hat. Got that?"

There were a few scattered nods; then Stryker stepped forward as the scout mounted his pony and drifted into the gloom.

"Men," he said, pitching his harsh voice low, "in a few minutes you will be fighting the tigers of the human species, an enemy cruel, crafty and quick to scent danger. The Apache is a treacherous animal, patient in defeat, merciless in victory. All you can do is kill him. And that's what I expect of every one of you—kill . . . kill . . . kill again."

Stryker's voice stilled the troopers' quiet cheers. "And here's good news. Any man who falls in the engagement will be posthumously promoted to corporal."

This time the only huzzah came from Hooper. He looked around at his men and said, "Now there's generosity from the officer for you, lads. It's not every day a dead man is promoted to full corporal." He saluted Stryker. "You can depend on us to do our bit, sir."

"Excellent," Stryker said. God, he disliked Hooper intensely. "Move out the men, Sergeant, and from now on keep it quiet."

The lieutenant in the lead, the detail moved into the gathering darkness. Above them, shedding a bladed light, the sickle moon silently reaped the stars. Stryker saw one fall to earth and he imagined that it thumped onto the desert sand and was now laying somewhere close, glowing red and smoking like a cinder.

He walked on across broken country, skirting the foothills. Behind him his troopers, cavalrymen who had an intense dislike of walking, stumbled and cursed softly, drawing muttered threats from Hooper.

Suddenly Hogg emerged from the gloom, leading his horse at a jog, the white paper in his hat bobbing.

"Hold your fire, it's Hogg," Stryker whispered, words repeated down the line.

The scout pulled up in front of his officer. "No guards at the arroyo. They're drunk, Lieutenant, all of them."

Stryker smiled. "Then we'll go at once and kill every man jack of them."

"The girl will be in the line of fire."

"I'm afraid she must shift for herself, Mr. Hogg."

Stryker had no way of knowing, but right then the scout was wondering about him.

Had the shackle chain that destroyed his features also destroyed everything inside him that was once good and decent? Did his face now reflect the true nature of the man?

Joe Hogg was a traveled man, and Stryker's face in the pallid moonlight stirred a memory. A mask, Chinese or Nipponese, he couldn't recall. He'd seen it at a theater in Denver—or was it San Francisco?—a grotesque, twisted, furious thing worn by a dancer. Later, the dancer had removed the mask, revealing the face of a pretty, oriental girl. But if the lieutenant removed his mask, would the face underneath be the same . . . unchanged . . . a mask within a mask?

Hogg, who was afraid of no man or of anything that walked, crawled or flew, shuddered. A night breeze probed the skin of his face, reminding him that each one of us wears a mask.

But not like Stryker's, he told himself. Never like that.

"Move out," the lieutenant whispered. "The thoughtful Mr. Hogg will lead the way."

Chapter 5

The entrance to the arroyo was a rectangle of blackness that stood out against the greater gloom of the night. The land was silent, except for the coyotes talking among the hills and the rustling rush of the breeze.

Rising almost perpendicular to a height of ten feet, the walls of the arroyo were crested by stunted juniper and mesquite, a perfect hiding place for an ambushing Apache. The defile itself was narrow, choked with brush and stands of prickly pear, allowing the passage of only one soldier at a time.

Stryker held up a hand, halting Hooper and his men where they were; then he and Hogg advanced deeper into the arroyo.

After thirty yards the walls spread farther apart, then opened up into a grassy area about two acres in extent. A small fire burned in the middle of the clearing, close to a single cottonwood and willow. Apaches were sprawled around the fire, one of them lying on his back, snoring loudly.

Stryker and the scout lost themselves in the shadows at the base of the twenty-foot wall of ridged, yellow rock that formed an amphitheater around the entire area. The moon was still visible, riding high, ringed by a halo of pale red and blue.

Beside Stryker, Hogg broke off a stem of bunch grass and stuck it between his teeth. The scout had his revolver in his right hand, thumb on the hammer.

An Apache, wearing a breechcloth, moccasins to his knees and a fancy Mexican vest, struggled to his feet and walked closer to the fire. He had a dark, cruel face, flat-lipped, his eyes deep in shadow.

The man staggered to a jug, picked it up, shook it, then threw it aside. He stepped to a woman, her red hair cascading over her shoulders in dusty waves. Naked, she sat with her legs drawn up, forehead resting on her knees.

The Apache dug his hand into the woman's luxuriant hair, yanked back her head and stared into her face. He looked at the redhead for a few moments, grunted, then forced her head back on her knees.

Hogg's black eyes were glittering in the firelight, aware of the woman, watching the Apache, teeth bared around the grass stem. He raised his gun, but Stryker tapped him on the shoulder and shook his head. He motioned to the arroyo and, crouching low, began to back away in that direction.

For a few seconds Hogg remained motionless.

The Apache walked away from the woman, staggered and fell flat on his face. He didn't get up again.

Silently, the scout followed Stryker into the arroyo and rejoined the lieutenant who was talking with Hooper.

"They're dead drunk and snoring," Stryker was saying. "Sergeant Hooper, you will form two ranks on me and shoot into the savages at my command." He turned. "Mr. Hogg, you will fire independently at targets of opportunity. Use your Henry to good effect."

The scout said nothing, but Hooper snapped off a salute and said, "We're ready, sir."

"Then let's proceed with the attack," Stryker said.

Quietly, Hogg again reminded the lieutenant about the woman.

"Ah, yes," Stryker said. He looked at Hooper. "There's a white woman back there. Try to avoid shooting her if you can."

Hooper and the men followed Stryker into the clearing and shook into two lines on the officer's left. "Front rank, kneel," Stryker whispered. "Now pick your targets." Then, "Front rank, *fire*!"

Bullets crashed into the sleeping Apaches. Indians rose, groggily fumbling for their weapons.

"Rear rank, *fire*!"

Apaches staggered under the impact of the powerful .45-70 rounds and went down hard. At Stryker's side, Hogg was working his Henry.

"Front rank, *fire*!"

At least half the warriors were hit. The others tried to regroup and a couple were ineffectually firing their rifles.

"Rear rank, *fire*!"

The Springfields crashed and more Indians went down.

"*Independent fire!*" Stryker roared.

As a ragged volley swept the clearing, an Apache charged directly at Stryker through a hanging pall of gray gun smoke, a knife in his upraised hand. At a distance of eight feet, the lieutenant shot into the man's stocky body, then fired his Colt again. The Indian screamed and went down.

"Advance five paces!" Stryker yelled. "Get the hell out of the smoke."

All the troopers but one obeyed the command. Stryker didn't wait to see who had fallen, but stepped forward into cleaner air.

The clearing looked like a charnel house. Apache bodies, stained scarlet, lay in heaps and a few wounded groaned and tried to crawl away from the terrible firepower of the Springfields. The indifferent moon braided silver light over the scene and smoke drifted everywhere, like spirits rising from the dead warriors.

"No prisoners," Stryker yelled. "Sergeant Hooper, see that it's done."

Hooper was invisible somewhere in the crashing darkness, but his loud, "Yes, sir," carried in the breeze moaning through the stillness.

Joe Hogg appeared from the gloom, a Winchester in his hands. "Brand-new, like I figgered, Lieutenant."

"It's got to be one of Rake Pierce's guns," Stryker said. He looked around him as though searching the arroyo walls for the man. "Where the hell is he?"

"My guess would be the Madres, Lieutenant," Hogg said mildly.

Stryker swore. "Damn him, damn him to hell."

Shots echoed around the clearing, the sound hitting the hard rock walls like a hammer on an anvil.

"I took this rifle off'n a wounded buck," Hogg said. He inclined his head. "Over there by the base of the wall. Maybe we should talk to him afore Hooper does for him."

"Will he tell us anything?"

"No. But I'll talk to him anyhow."

The Apache was young, gut shot and dying tough. There was defiance in his black eyes and a bottomless well of hatred.

Stryker looked down at the man, no pity in him. "Ask him where he last saw Rake Pierce."

The scout jabbered words that Stryker did not understand; then the Indian raised his eyes to Stryker. He spat in the lieutenant's direction, a feeble effort, his spit full of black blood.

Hogg smiled. "He just told you to go to hell, Lieutenant."

"I gathered that."

But to Stryker's surprise, the Apache began to talk and Hogg cocked his head and listened intently.

When the Indian stopped speaking, the scout turned to Stryker. "He says the white man will soon be driven from all the Apache lands. Old Nana broke out of the San Carlos four days ago and he's joined up with Geronimo. Between them, they plan to raise hob by killing as many settlers, soldiers and Mexicans as they can find."

"Do you think Colonel Devore knows this?"

Hogg again smiled his slight smile. "By now? Depend on it."

Stryker glanced at the dying Apache. "Ask him again where I can find Rake Pierce."

"He won't tell us, Lieutenant."

"Joe, ask him, damn it."

Hogg spoke to the Indian. The dying man closed his eyes and a thin, wavering chant escaped his lips like a mist.

"That's his death song, Lieutenant. He's all done talking."

"So am I."

Stryker drew his revolver and shot the Apache in the head. He turned away immediately. "Sergeant Hooper!"

The man came at a trot. "Pile the dead against the wall over there. They won't stink until tomorrow, so we'll camp here tonight. And bring the horses inside." He glanced over at the Indian ponies. "Any worth saving?"

Hooper nodded. "Five mules, three cavalry mounts and a good-looking Morgan mare."

"We'll take those back to Fort Merit. Shoot the other ponies before we pull out in the morning." He looked at Hooper. "How many did we kill?"

"Twenty-one, sir. All of them prime young bucks."

"And the butcher's bill?"

"Trooper Murphy dead. Trooper Rogers slightly wounded."

"Lay out Corporal Murphy well away from the other dead. I will not have a brave Christian man lying among savages. We'll take him back to the fort for burial."

"Yes, sir." Hooper waited.

"The soldiers can cook their supper and boil their coffee when you are ready, Sergeant. Don't let them eat mule meat, it's poisonous to white men."

"Yes, sir."

Stryker nodded. "Very good. Dismissed."

After Hooper left, Stryker turned to Hogg. "If Nana is out and raiding with Geronimo, I'd bet the farm that Rake Pierce is here. For a while at least, the Arizona Territory is where the gun business will be."

"Like I told you afore, Lieutenant, if he's around I'll find him for you."

Stryker's fingertips strayed to his broken face, a gesture he was not aware of making. "I'll cut him, Joe. I'll rip his damned guts out and knot them to a pine tree while he's still breathing."

Aloud the scout said, "Yes, Lieutenant, I believe you will."

To himself, he wondered who the real savage in this mad slaughterhouse was.

Chapter 6

"Lieutenant, you better come see this."

Joe Hogg stepped into the circle of firelight where Stryker was sitting, drinking coffee. "What's all the hooting and hollering about, Joe?"

"That's what you better come see."

Carefully, Stryker laid his cup beside him and wearily rose to his feet. The shouting was coming from the cottonwood beside the narrow creek that ran from somewhere inside one of the surrounding mountains.

As he walked closer, he heard Sergeant Hooper yell, "Hell, lads, once she's washed herself out real well, she'll be as good as new."

"Sarge," a trooper said, "I don't think I want a white woman that's been done by Apaches."

"Hell, Henderson, you idiot," Hooper snapped. "You're going to screw her, not take her home to meet ma."

The other men who were gawking at the naked redhead frantically washing herself in the creek laughed, and Hooper said, "Look at the tits an' ass she's got on her, an' her not more than sixteen or seventeen I'd say. Damned little whore has been done by more than Apaches—lay to that, my lads."

More laughter until it was instantly stifled by Stryker's voice. "Sergeant Hooper, that will be enough." He turned to Hogg at his side. "Joe, get her out of there and find a blanket to cover her. Her clothes must be around here somewhere."

The scout stepped to the creek, but Hooper yelled, "Hogg, you leave that woman be."

"Sergeant Hooper," Stryker said sharply. "Do not ever again countermand my orders."

"He's a civilian," Hooper snapped. "And I'm telling him to leave the woman be. I'm laying claim to the bitch."

"Or what, Sergeant?" Hogg said, his voice low, quiet, significant.

The scout stood as still as death, his right hand close to his holstered Colt.

Hooper was reading something cold in the other man, something he had not seen before and did not like. Suddenly his voice wavered with uncertainty. "I said leave the woman be. She's crazy, out of her bleedin' mind." He took on a wheedling tone. "Me an' the lads only want to have a little fun, some quick in an' out, you understand."

Hogg's smile was as dangerous as a flash of mountain lightning. "I said, 'Or what, Sergeant?'"

Now Hooper was desperately seeking a way out. He glanced at Stryker, his eyes begging. Miles Hooper was not a coward and his army career had never been easy, but the old scout who had prodded him into a corner was a named revolver fighter and Hooper had never braced his like before.

The girl in the creek was still washing, but now she was singing in a high, reedy voice, a song without words or meaning.

It was in Stryker's mind to let the scene play out and let Hogg settle it, but the habit of command overcame his dislike of Hooper. "Mr. Hogg, please do as I asked. Sergeant, we will take up this matter again when we return to Fort Merit."

But to the lieutenant's surprise, Hooper was not prepared to let it go.

"Damn you, Lieutenant, to the conqueror belong the spoils. The woman is mine by right of conquest and I want her," he yelled. "Me and the other lads, we won the battle for you fair an' square."

"Battle? Is that what you call it?" Stryker said. "I would call it something else."

Now it was Hogg's turn to be surprised. He stared through the darkness at Stryker, again wondering at this strange, tormented man.

Then Hooper took a step too far, right into a hangman's noose. "Stryker," he said, "I want the woman. She's nothing to you and you know a white man will never touch her now. But I will. Damn it, I can smell her from here and it's driving me mad." He looked over at the troopers who'd been watching him in amazement, their unshaven jaws hanging slack. "Bear me up in this, lads," he yelled. "Is the woman mine by right?"

One man, Trooper Louis Ruxton, a hard-faced product of New York's Five Points slums, said, "Aye, she's yours right enough." He looked across at Stryker, then at the men around him. "Hell, Lieutenant, after nearly two dozen Apaches that redheaded gal will be so stretched, she won't even feel horny ol' Miley slide in."

If Ruxton expected laughter, he was disappointed. The soldiers stood silent, their faces grim. They were young and green, and although they feared their sergeant, they feared the lieutenant more. To the troopers his shoulder straps represented the awesome authority of the United States Army and its government, a terrifying power they had no desire to cross. But if any had lingering doubts, Stryker now spelled out the consequences of Hooper's action.

His tight voice revealing a barely suppressed anger, he said, "Sergeant Miles Hooper, this day of July seventeen, 1881, under Article 94 of the United States' Uniform Code of Military Justice, you are charged with an intent to usurp or override lawful military authority, refusing, in concert with one other person, to obey orders or otherwise do your duty, creating violence and disturbance. The crime is mutiny and if you are found guilty you shall be punished by death or such other punishment as a court-martial shall direct."

Stryker looked past Hooper. "Trooper Louis Ruxton, you are under arrest for inciting mutiny. You men, disarm him."

Without waiting to see if his order was carried out, the lieutenant again directed his attention to Hooper. He held out his hand. "Your sidearm, Sergeant."

Hooper, his face black with anger, took a step back, his hand going for the holstered revolver at his right side. "You go to hell, you goddamned scar-faced freak!"

Stryker, angry, was going for his gun, but Joe Hogg stopped it.

His voice like ice crystals in the breeze, he said quietly, "Hooper, surrender your gun or I'll drop you right where you stand."

For an instant the sergeant thought about it, backed off, and slowed his hand above his Colt.

"Use your left, Hooper," the scout said. He had made no attempt to draw his gun. "You're making me nervous and when I get nervous bad things happen."

Hooper lifted the revolver with his fingertips and passed it to Stryker.

"If Mr. Hogg hadn't killed you, I would have," the lieutenant said slowly, taking his time. He called over a couple of men by name. "Take Sergeant Hooper into custody with Trooper Ruxton. Hold them in the arroyo and guard them well."

The soldiers leveled their carbines and motioned to Hooper to move. The sergeant cast one look of burning hatred at Stryker, then walked into the darkness, his captors stepping warily at his heels.

Hogg came closer and smiled. "Don't have much luck with sergeants, do you, Lieutenant?"

"Seems like." He nodded toward the creek. "Get the woman and cover her with something. She can sit by the fire with me where I can keep an eye on her."

A few minutes later, the scout returned, cradling the woman in his arms. She was young, pretty and silent.

"How is she?" Stryker asked as Hogg settled her beside him.

The scout shrugged, saying nothing.

"Did she give her name?"

"She doesn't talk."

"The women at the fort will help her."

"No one can help her, Lieutenant. Not now. Somewhere in what's left of her mind she's following the buffalo and she's never coming back."

Stryker looked at the woman, at the mane of red hair hanging over her shoulders in damp ringlets. "Were those her folks at the ranch?" he asked.

"Maybe. Or she was just visiting."

"Joe, keep an eye on the arroyo. I want those two to face a court-martial."

The scout nodded. "I'll drift by there now and again." He smiled. "I'd like nothing better than to put a bullet into Sergeant Hooper. Hell, I never did cotton to Englishmen anyhow."

After Hogg walked silently away, Stryker picked up his coffee. It was cold. He shoved the tin cup into the coals of the fire, then looked at the girl again. She had assumed her old position, legs drawn up, forehead on her knees. He could hear her breathe.

The troopers had built a second fire a safe distance away from their mercurial officer and were frying bacon. The coyotes were yipping and somewhere, higher up the mountain, an owl asked its question of the night.

Stryker lifted his head, testing the air. He smelled desert bluebells in the breeze. . . . Were they real? Or was it only a remembrance of a time past . . . ? The fragrance of Millie's hair . . . ?

She was sitting close to him. So close he could smell the musky, womanly scent of her.

Colonel Abel Lawson had graciously allowed his daughter to use his office for her farewells. But, since she was no longer betrothed to First Lieutenant Stryker, the proprieties had to be observed. There were two officers present, shuffling, grinning, embarrassed to be there.

"Yes, Steve," Millie was saying, "Papa and I leave on the morning stage tomorrow." She smiled brightly. "Then it's on to Washington."

"Washington," Stryker repeated. "Yes, on to there."

Millie's beautiful brown eyes lifted to his, then, quickly, as though burned, slid away. "I came to say good-bye, but, oh dear, I'm making rather a mess of things, aren't I?"

"It's never easy, Millie, saying good-bye."

The two officers had moved to the window where they were apparently studying something of great interest in the deserted, dusty parade ground.

"I'm sorry, Steve, so sorry. My father has political ambitions and he has plans, great plans, and I am part of them. They involve a deal of socializing, meeting influential people . . ." her voice trailed away lamely. Then, "*Beaucoup* of that, I'm afraid."

Stryker nodded. "I understand."

But I don't understand, Millie. My face is ruined but

inside I haven't changed. I'm still me, the man you wanted to marry. Did you fall in love with handsome features and a dashing mustache you once told me made your female heart go all a-flutter? Are you that shallow?

"You must think me very shallow, Steve, but I must do what I think is best for Papa and my country. I am not a stalwart soldier like you; I am but a weak woman and I must go where the winds of family blow me. You will go on living, Steve, and make a fine career for yourself as a cavalry officer. I just know you will."

"Yes, you must do what is best for your family."

Just tell me how I go on living when everything inside me is dead.

From the window, young Second Lieutenant McIntyre prodded gently, "Steve, the colonel said no more than five minutes." He looked embarrassed but attempted a smile. "Tempus fugit and all that."

"I must be going," Millie said. Without looking at his face, she gave Stryker a brief, cool hug, then stood back from him. Her eyes misted. "I'm sorry," she said. "Sorry for everything."

Then she was gone in a rustling flurry of green silk and snowy petticoats and only her perfume lingered, the desert bluebell fragrance of her hair. . . .

"Hey, Lieutenant, your coffee is bilin' over."

Stryker looked up at Joe Hogg. "Huh?"

"Your coffee, on the fire."

Stryker saw his sizzling cup and grabbed the handle, dragging it from the coals. It was hot and he let it go quickly, shaking his scorched fingers.

Then he noticed that Hogg was holding a wincing Trooper Kramer by the ear.

"What are you doing with my soldier, Joe?" Stryker asked.

"Lieutenant, I've grown mighty tired of hearing this boy wheezing like an old steam engine. Me an' him is going to search the creek for a frog an' then I'll cure him of his misery." Hogg tugged the young man's ear. "Ain't that right, boy?"

Kramer, a towheaded youth of about twenty, did a little jig, his face screwed up against the pain in his tortured ear. "Mr. Hogg, I ain't eating no damned horny toad, an' you can take that to the bank."

The scout squeezed Kramer's ear harder. "You don't eat it, boy. I done tol' you that already." Hogg looked at Stryker. "Lieutenant, do I have your permission to take Julius Wheezer here on a frog hunt?"

"Did you check on Hooper and Ruxton?"

"Yeah, they're under guard and when I last looked Hooper was sleeping, or pretending to be."

Stryker smiled. "Then good hunting, Mr. Hogg."

The scout dragged away the protesting Kramer, the scout assuring him that a cure for his asthma was imminent, and Stryker tried his coffee again.

He was impossibly tired. Around him firelight touched the crouching shadows with dull crimson and the troopers were noisily horsing around, working off the tensions of the day. Soon he would order them to their blankets. The detail would ride out at first light.

A soldier brought him a plate, fat bacon and pounded up hardtack fried in the grease. The man offered some to the girl, but she did not change position or even lift her head.

Surprised at how hungry he was, Stryker wolfed down the meal and was chewing on the last of the hardtack when Hogg reappeared with the suffering Kramer.

"Sit by the fire, boy, an' do what I tell you," the scout ordered.

He waited until Kramer squatted, the young trooper tense and uneasy about being this close to his officer, then handed him a small, lime green frog.

"Now pry the critter's jaws open and breathe into its mouth," Hogg said.

The frog croaked and Kramer wheezed, staring at the creature in his hand.

"Do as I tell you, boy," the scout ordered. "Or I'll kick your ass all over this clearing."

Reluctantly, Kramer forced the amphibian's jaws open and wheezed into its open mouth.

"Get closer, boy, damn it," Hogg said. "A few good breaths."

Stryker smiled. "I don't think Trooper Kramer has a good breath, Joe."

"He does, Lieutenant. He only thinks he doesn't." Hogg stared down at the unhappy soldier. "Now get close, and give 'er a few good breaths." He glared at the young man. "Unless you want me to pull that ear right off'n your head."

This time Kramer did as he was told.

"Good," Hogg said. "Now that asthma misery of your'n has gone into the frog."

"What do I do with it, Mr. Hogg?" Kramer asked.

The freckles across his nose stood out like ink spots in the firelight.

"You keep an eye on that critter, an' if it dies afore sundown tomorrow, you're cured fer sure."

"Keep an eye on it? Keep an eye on it where, Mr. Hogg?"

The scout sighed. "Do I have to tell you every little thing, boy? Stick him in your pocket an' check on him every now an' then. But don't sit on him an' squash him. The critter has to die by its ownself."

Kramer rose and shoved the frog into the pocket of his breeches. "Thank you, Mr. Hogg," he said. "I feel better already."

"You won't be better unless the frog dies," the scout said. "Now, you keep an eye on him until sundown tomorrow."

After the young soldier left, Stryker stretched out by the fire and looked up at Hogg. "Do you really think the frog will cure him?"

The scout nodded. "If he thinks it will, Lieutenant, then it will."

"While Kramer is watching his frog, you watch Hooper, huh?"

"Depend on it, Lieutenant."

A few minutes later, the last thing Stryker saw before he drifted into sleep was the redheaded girl. She still had not moved.

Chapter 7

By Joe Hogg's watch, it was 2:12 in the morning when rifle shots heralded the escape of Sergeant Miles Hooper.

Trooper Lou Ruxton he threw to the dogs.

The racketing echoes of the rifle were still tying tangled knots around the clearing as Stryker jumped to his feet and ran for the arroyo, gun in hand.

Ruxton lay barely conscious and groaning in a stand of prickly pear and a trooper was dragging him out of the thorns by his boots.

"Where's Hooper?" Stryker snapped.

"He ran for it, Lieutenant," the man said. "Ruxton made a break with him, but then the sarge turned and dropped him with a punch."

That made sense. Hooper knew one of his guards would stay behind to secure Ruxton, leaving him with only one rifle to deal with.

"If Ruxton tries to run, kill him," Stryker told the trooper, who had succeeded in pulling the man free of the cactus. "Got that?"

Without waiting to hear a reply, the lieutenant

made his way to the mouth of the arroyo and his eyes searched into darkness.

He turned south, stepping warily, his gun up and ready, letting his vision adjust to the gloom.

There was no sound but the soft sigh of the wind and the rustle of junipers and mesquite. The moon had slid lower in the sky and the stars had reappeared, scattering a pale, opalescent light. Shadows hunched among the foothills and the mountains soared in stark outline, like black, impossibly ancient pyramids.

Stryker found the trooper's body in a narrow dry wash. The young soldier had a round, pleasant face, now composed in death. His neck had been broken and his carbine and gun belt were missing.

Hooper, who knew the ways of the desert as well as any Apache, had crouched in the wash and waited. In comparison to the small, slight troopers, cavalry sergeants and officers tended to be taller and stronger. Hooper was a big, heavy-muscled man and the soldier had not stood a chance.

Stryker rose to his feet, his eyes probing the darkness. The shadows were still, unmoving. The night was so quiet he heard the beat of his heart.

"Hey, Stryker!" Hooper's voice called out from somewhere among the foothills to his left.

"I know you can hear me, Stryker, lad. Or have you gone deaf since you ain't humping the colonel's daughter no more?" A pause, then, "How was she, Stryker? Did she buck like an unbroke pony or just bend over, bare her ass and think of daddy?"

The lieutenant moved to his left. A mistake. Hooper saw the flicker of movement and fired. Stryker felt the bullet burn across the meat of his right shoulder and he dived for the cover of the sandy wash bank. Here a huge boulder cast its shadow over Stryker and he could not be seen unless he moved again.

"Hey, Stryker?" Hooper assumed a Southwestern accent. "Dang it all, boy, did I get ye?"

The lieutenant raised his head over the bank and pushed his cocked revolver out in front of him.

Move, Hooper, just move. . . .

"Hey, Stryker, know what the two-dollar whores say at the hog ranch back at the fort? No, you haven't heard? They say they won't even let you pay to screw 'm because you're too damned ugly."

Stryker's mouth was dry, his eyes burning. He wiped a sweaty right palm on his breeches and took up his Colt again.

Move, you bastard, move. . . .

A chuckle from the shadows, then, "Know what sweet little Millie is doing right now up in Washington, Stryker? She's got some general's head between her thighs and she's saying"—now he affected a high, girlish voice—"'Oh, General Beauregard, dear, that horrible Lieutenant Stryker, he was so damned ugly he couldn't have paid me to open my legs for him.'"

Hooper laughed again, a harsh bellow devoid of humor.

Seeing the dead at the stage and the ranch had stressed Stryker, and the battle with the Apaches that had turned into a turkey shoot with no honor on either side had made matters worse.

Something inside him snapped and his muscles bunched as he prepared to jump to his feet.

He never made it. A strong hand pushed him back down and Hogg's voice whispered in his ear, "He's trying to draw you out, Lieutenant. Once you're in the open he'll set his sights right between them yellow shoulder straps and you'll be a dead man."

Stryker opened his mouth to protest, but Hogg's shout stopped him. "Hooper, this here is Joe Hogg. You stay right where you're at. I'm a-comin' for you."

A startled rustle of juniper branches in the distance . . . then silence.

The scout looked at Stryker and smiled. "I guess ol' Hooper didn't like his choice of partner to open the ball." He rose to his feet. "I came across a dead trooper back there."

Stryker nodded. "Hooper killed him." He glanced at the sky. "Come first light we'll go after him."

"Lieutenant, Hooper has been in the territory a long time," Hogg said. "He'll be like an Apache in those hills. Sure, I can track him but it will take days, maybe weeks, and you'll lose a bunch more men. With Nana out, you should return to the fort."

"Just let Hooper go?"

"No, Lieutenant. We'll catch up with him again, that is if the Apaches don't get him first." Hogg's eyes gleamed in the starlight. "Something you should know: When they were both sergeants, Hooper and Rake Pierce were drinking and whoring buddies. If Hooper survives, he could lead us right to Pierce."

"That's damned thin, Joe."

"I reckon it is. But it's a chance. Maybe the only chance we got."

Stryker bent his head and lost himself in thought. After a couple of minutes he looked at Hogg and said, "All right, we'll take our dead back to Fort Merit. I'll show Colonel Devore the new Winchesters and tell him that there's one sure way to slow Nana and Geronimo—stop Rake Pierce selling them rifles. And I'll tell him I want the job."

"Sounds like an excellent plan, Lieutenant," Hogg said. "But don't think of going after Pierce with anything less than a full cavalry troop."

"There are two troops of the Second at Fort Merit. I'm sure the colonel will be willing to spare one of them."

The soft, desert starlight did nothing to improve the appearance of the horrifically mutilated face Stryker turned to his scout. "Of course, I could be calling this all wrong. I'm bringing back dead, a crazy woman and now I've lost a murdering deserter. Maybe Colonel Devore will throw me in the guardhouse."

Hogg's teeth glinted as he smiled. "Lieutenant, the whole time General Crook was here, he never killed twenty-one bronco Apaches in a single battle. Hell, you could be a hero an' get a gold medal."

Aware that he was treading along the slippery edge of self-pity, Stryker said, "Look at me, Joe. Do feathered generals pin medals on officers who look like me?"

Hogg was a man born and raised to the habit of honesty. "No, Lieutenant Stryker, quite frankly they don't." Then, an unlikely gesture for him, he placed a hand on the lieutenant's shoulder. "But there's a first time for everything."

Chapter 8

Fort Merit was one of seventy military posts scattered throughout the Arizona Territory, though most were destined to last only a few years before their adobe buildings crumbled away and were reclaimed by the desert.

Like Fort Bowie to the south, built to protect Apache Pass and its springs, a small settlement had grown up around Fort Merit, a sprawling maze of adobes, jacals and ramshackle outbuildings.

The parade square was enclosed on three sides by barracks, the hospital, the quartermaster's warehouse, a bakery, a blacksmith's shop, stables and the headquarters building. To the west of these, wandering into the desert, was a creek lined by willows and cottonwoods. Near the creek a hog ranch had sprung up and a couple of other dives, optimistically called saloons, offered forty-rod whiskey, gambling and whores.

There was no sutler, but a general store owned by a gloomy Scotsman named Cameron offered the soldiers everything from bone-handled penknives to caviar and champagne. He also offered his wife, a bony, hard-faced Swede, but, by Cameron's own account, got few takers.

Stryker led his detail through the usual noisy throng of children and dogs around the jacals, then rode into the parade ground. In the noon heat, the Stars and Stripes hung from the flagpole like a damp rag, and the brass barrels of the post's two six-pounder cannons—they had never fired a shot in anger at Apaches—were being polished to a marvelous sheen by a wretched trooper who had managed to irritate somebody in authority.

Fort Merit was no spit-and-polish post to gladden the eye of a fuss-and-feathers general. It was mean, shabby, dirty and run-down, but to Stryker it was home, a haven of safety and rest in a hard and dangerous land.

He turned the redheaded woman over to the enlisted men's wives of suds row, who bustled and fluttered around her and led her into one of their tiny quarters.

"She was captured by Apaches and she won't talk," Stryker told a large, busty woman with a fierce mustache that must have rivaled her husband's. "I think her mind is gone."

"We'll take care of her, poor little thing," the woman said. "Did the Apaches . . . ?"

"Yes, they did, ma'am," Stryker said quickly.

The woman nodded. "Then she'll need all the attention and love we can give her."

The lieutenant felt awkward and clumsy. "Well, please carry on, ma'am."

He turned on his heel and walked away, glad to be gone from there and the concerns of womenfolk.

After he'd seen his wounded and dead carried into the hospital, Stryker had Trooper Ruxton taken to the guardhouse and then dismissed the detail. Before entering the headquarters building, he untied a new Winchester from the saddle horn, then gave his horse over to the care of Trooper Kramer. He heard the young soldier tell Hogg that the frog in his pocket was still alive, though it was exhibiting definite signs of being down in the mouth and he confidently expected the creature would bite the dust before nightfall.

"Keep checking on it until dark, boy," the scout said. "As any doctor will tell you, the frog cure is the sovereign remedy for asthma and it has never been known to fail."

Stryker watched Trooper Kramer leave. Was it only his imagination or had the boy's breathing sounded easier? Then another thought hit him hard: Why the hell did he care?

But he did. And that gave him pause. It was something to think about . . . later.

A couple of loungers propped up the timber poles that supported the headquarters' porch. The younger man was a drover in from one of the surrounding ranches with a supply of beef. The other was a scout Stryker had seen hanging around the fort. Long John Wills was nearly seven feet tall in his moccasins and sported a magnificent red beard that hung all the way to the crotch of his greasy buckskins. He had a vague reputation as an Indian fighter and a more definite one as a ladies' man.

"Seen you ride in, Lieutenant," he said, "bringing in dead and wounded, an' all. Run into Apaches?"

Stryker nodded. "West of here."

"Ol' Nana's out."

"Yes, so I heard."

Wills inclined his head. "See the tents over yonder?"

"I saw them as I rode in."

"Two companies of the Twenty-third Infantry. Them boys are green as can be and their major is a little feller who looks like he's about twelve years old. All the cavalry, including the Second, is being sent to Fort Bowie."

"Then the Twenty-third has been ordered here to guard the fort?"

Wills smiled. "Never was a truer word spoke, Lieutenant." He looked over at the tents, then threw up his hands. "God help us all."

"Colonel Devore inside?"

"He is, with that major I told you about. I think his name is Hayes . . . Haynes . . . something like that."

Stryker put his hand on the door, but Wills' voice stopped him. "Lieutenant, Colonel Devore is right testy today. He's sore about losing his cavalry."

"Thanks for the warning."

After the oppressive, dusty heat of the day, the inside of the adobe felt cool, its windows shuttered against the blaze of the sun. An elderly corporal sat at a desk to one side of the door to the colonel's office.

The man rose to his feet and saluted when Stryker

entered, his eyes darting everywhere, unwilling to settle on the contorted mask of the lieutenant's face.

"First Lieutenant Stryker's compliments to the colonel, and ask him if now is convenient to make my report."

The corporal seemed relieved that he no longer had to meet the lieutenant's eyes. He knocked on the colonel's door, stuck his head inside and repeated Stryker's words.

"Send him in," Devore said.

Stryker stepped inside, the Winchester hanging loose at his side.

Colonel Michael Devore sat behind his desk, a grizzled, medium-sized man of forty-five who had begun his career as a cavalry private at the outbreak of the War Between the States and had risen through the ranks to brevet brigadier general.

Devore was no spit-and-polish soldier, but a fighting man who understood the limitations of light cavalry in Indian warfare but used its flexibility and speed of movement to full advantage. He knew his men, loved the desert and admired the Apache as a skilled guerilla fighter.

He also looked another man directly in the eye, as he did now to Stryker.

"You've been through it, Lieutenant."

Stryker nodded. "Yes sir, some."

Devore waved a hand. "Meet Major Hanson; he commands the infantry you must have noticed when you rode in."

Hanson was blond, boyish and small, wearing a neat tunic that somehow had not gathered a coating of gray desert dust. Stryker suspected the major had carefully brushed his uniform before meeting with his formidable superior officer.

After registering the initial shock that Stryker's appearance always caused, Hanson stood and gave the lieutenant a surprisingly firm handshake and a friendly grin. Like Devore, he sought eye contact.

Stryker and Hanson made the usual polite exchanges expected of officers, "Welcome to Fort Merit, sir," and "Delighted to be here, Lieutenant," but Devore cut it short. "Since he's going to be directly involved in the defense of this post, Major Hanson should listen to your report, Lieutenant."

Using as few words as possible, Stryker told of the attack on the Norton and Stewart stage and the massacre at the ranch. He then described the action in the arroyo and the murder committed by the mutinous deserter Sergeant Miles Hooper.

"And this man, Trooper Louis Ruxton?"

"In the guardhouse, sir. He's charged with inciting a mutiny."

"I have a short way with mutineers, Lieutenant, especially in wartime." Devore's face hardened. "I'll convene a court-martial for later this afternoon, to be followed immediately by the firing squad."

He rose and took the Winchester from Stryker's hand. "You've done well, Lieutenant. This is from the arroyo battle?"

"Yes, sir, one of six we took off the Apache dead."

"And you suspect Sergeant Rake Pierce supplied these?"

"Yes, sir, I do. New guns and new ammunition."

"Well, it's possible. But last I heard he was in the Madres."

"I think he may be closer," Stryker said. "With Nana out and joined up with Geronimo, this is where the market is for his guns."

"The consensus of opinion is that Nana will leave the territory and raid deep into Mexico, Lieutenant. That's why the cavalry, myself included, is being recalled to Fort Bowie. We will pursue Nana and Geronimo and make sure they remain south of the Rio Grande."

"Nevertheless, sir, I believe that Pierce is somewhere in the Cabezas Mountains. If he is out of the picture and the Apaches can't get guns and ammunition, Nana will be forced to return to the San Carlos."

Devore's smile was barely a twitch of his lips under his mustache. "There's nothing personal in your request, of course?"

"You know it's personal, sir. I make no secret of it."

Seeing the confused look on Major Hanson's face, the colonel said, "Mr. Stryker and Rake Pierce have a history. The lieutenant's last detail before he was to be transferred to Washington was to bring Sergeant Pierce from Fort Bowie to here to be court-martialed for desertion."

"Sir, with all due respect, do you feel this is necessary?" Stryker asked. He suddenly felt vulnerable, like a man, naked from the bathtub, who walks into a surprise party.

"Lieutenant, your face speaks volumes, and I think

Major Hanson should be aware of the reason," Devore said. "He's too much of a gentleman to ask, but he will soon be in command of this post and he has a right to know what kind of man Pierce is, and indeed, what kind of man you are."

Then, damn you, let me tell it, Colonel.

"Major, it was drawing on to dark when I left Fort Bowie, so we camped for the night close to Silver Strike Spring. Somehow Pierce got out of his shackles—maybe one of his friends at Bowie had passed him a duplicate key—I don't know. Anyway, he grabbed the gun of the other escort and shot him dead. He also wounded me. Then he took the shackle chain and swung it back and forth across my face, screaming that I'd never put those irons on him again.

"Pierce left me for dead, but I was picked up by a passing stage and returned here." Stryker managed a smile. "The post surgeon did his best, but Pierce is a big man and strong, and the damage was too great. The handsome specimen you see before you is the result."

Hanson, obviously embarrassed, tried to say the right words, but finally gave up, his mouth working.

"Major, I've grown used to children running from me in fear and women shrinking away when I turn and they see my face. The Mexicans call me *la Fea Una*, the Ugly One. I don't know what my own men or the Apaches call me."

"Let me just add that Lieutenant Stryker is a fine officer, and I'm glad he's here and not playing drawing room soldier in Washington," Devore said quickly. He looked at Stryker. "I plan to recommend you for promotion to captain for your successful action against the Apaches, Lieutenant. I think I still have enough influence among the old Civil War generals to see that it's done."

Stryker nodded. "Thank you, sir, but I'd rather have your permission to go after Pierce."

Devore said nothing. But when he laid the Winchester on his desk, then opened a desk drawer and took out a bottle and three glasses, it seemed to Stryker a polite preface to a vehement no.

"A glass of whiskey with you, gentlemen," the colonel said. "To celebrate Lieutenant Stryker's success against the Apaches and his coming promotion." He filled the glasses and raised his own. "To the confusion and defeat of Nana and Geronimo, damn their dirty hides."

When the glasses were drained, Devore refilled them. He offered cigars. Hanson declined, but Stryker gladly accepted. It was said the colonel's cigars were the finest, sent to him regularly by General Grant, his old comrade-in-arms.

The colonel told Stryker to pull up a chair, and when he was settled he resumed his own seat behind his desk and studied the younger officer through a cloud of blue smoke.

"Lieutenant, as to your orders: Tomorrow at sunup you will take a full company of Major Hanson's infantry and march south, full packs, no mules or supply wagon."

Stryker was appalled, like he'd been hit by a sledgehammer.

Infantry! He'd never catch up to Pierce with a bunch of green web-feet weighed down by knapsack, haversack, blanket, overcoat, canteen, rations, cartridge box, waist belt, bayonet scabbard and the nine pound Springfield rifle.

But military protocol demanded that he remain silent and he did.

Devore was still talking. "You will march to where Big Bend Creek enters the Pedregosa Mountains, about two miles south of the Packsaddle, and take into custody the Apaches you find there."

The colonel relit his cigar, taking his time, his eyes on Stryker. The lieutenant's ruined face no longer reflected his emotions, but his stiff, upright posture in the chair eloquently betrayed how he felt.

"The rancheria is more or less ramrodded by an old chief who goes by the name Yanisin. He's always been friendly to whites and we want him to remain that way. You will move the old man's people to Fort Bowie, and, contingent on further orders, to the San Carlos."

Stryker said nothing, but Hanson's question filled in the silence. "How many Apaches are involved, Colonel?"

"According to Long John Wills, about a hundred and fifty, at least twenty-five of them warriors."

The major nodded. "I can see why you want to keep them away from Nana and Geronimo."

"Indeed, Major, if they joined Nana and his band, that would be a disaster," Devore said. "You can understand, Lieutenant, why speed of march is of the essence. I want those Apaches in Army custody as quickly as possible."

"Then give me a troop of cavalry, sir," Stryker said. "If memory serves me correct, Saddleback Mountain is about fifty miles due south of here. If I push the horses I can be at the rancheria in two days. Infantry weighed down by seventy pounds of rifle and backpack could take nearly twice that long."

"Lieutenant, I assure you that my men will still be marching when your cavalry mounts are lamed up and weak from lack of water," Hanson said edgily, revealing the foot soldier's hereditary antagonism toward the mounted warrior. "The Twenty-third can cover that distance as fast as horses and will still be capable of fighting when they get there."

Stryker studied Hanson more closely. It was true that the man looked like a baby-faced boy masquerading in an officer's uniform, but he wouldn't have gotten to be a major in the frontier army unless there was steel in his backbone, and he'd just proved that.

"There's no point in arguing about something that won't happen," Devore sighed. "Lieutenant, all the cavalry has been recalled to Fort Bowie, and I mean all. And the scouts have also been called in, but if you can make an arrangement with Joe Hogg, then I'm willing to turn a blind eye. At any rate, at dawn tomorrow you will begin your march to Chief Yanisin's rancheria with Company E of the Twenty-third Infantry as ordered. Do I make myself clear?"

"Yes, sir. But perhaps the colonel can tell me how I feed and water one hundred and fifty savages on the march back to Fort Bowie. I understand that Camp Rucker had been abandoned, so I can't look to supplies from there."

Devore's smile was good-natured, without a trace of malice. "There are plans to reoccupy Camp Rucker, but not in the immediate future. Lieutenant Stryker, one of the reasons you were commissioned into the United States Army from West Point is because you were judged to possess the initiative to solve problems as they arise, including the proper care and feeding of Apaches."

Now Stryker smiled, but he looked anything but good-natured. He was hard-eyed and cold. "I'd solve the problem by marching into the Apache village, killing Yanisin and his twenty-five young bucks, and leaving the women and children to shift for themselves."

"It's a way, Lieutenant," Devore said, almost wearily, "but it's not the right way. We're trying to pacify the Apaches, not wipe them from the face of the earth."

Before Stryker could say more, the colonel rose to his feet and glanced at his watch. "I'm sure you gentlemen are eager to get back to your duties," he said. He held out a hand. "Good luck, Lieutenant."

Then, to Hanson, "Major, I'll need you later for the court-martial of Trooper Ruxton, and bring another of your officers. I'll tell you when."

"I'm at your service, sir."

"And you will testify to this soldier's guilt, Lieutenant," the colonel said.

Before Stryker followed Hanson out the door,

Devore's voice stopped him. "By the way, Lieutenant, you have the right to dislike Apaches, even hate them if you must, but remember, they're still God's children."

Stryker nodded, but said nothing.

Chapter 9

At five minutes after seven that evening, as the day shaded into night and a cool, desert wind gusted the rising moon, Trooper Louis Ruxton, age twenty-seven, birthplace Cork, Ireland, was condemned to death by firing squad for the crimes of inciting mutiny, insubordination and the attempted escape from lawful military custody.

Sergeant Miles Hooper, age thirty-eight, birthplace Birmingham, England, was found guilty in absentia and sentenced to death.

At seven-forty-five, without benefit of the last rites, there being no Catholic chaplain present at the post, Trooper Ruxton was shot to death by firing squad, the coup de grace administered by Major Hanson.

Small mercies had been extended to the condemned. The firing squad was chosen from the Twenty-third Infantry, and not from among Ruxton's own comrades, and Colonel Devore ordered the condemned to be given as much brandy as he could drink.

That Ruxton puked all over himself as he was being taken to the place of execution became a topic of discussion among the post's enlisted men. A few said it was due to cowardice, but most agreed that a surfeit of brandy had been his undoing.

Stryker watched the proceedings impassively. There were many deaths. Trooper Ruxton had merely been one of them.

"I don't particularly like you, Lieutenant," Joe Hogg said, laying his glass on the rough pine counter of the Bull's Head saloon, a sod and canvas building a hundred yards from the fort. As was his habit, the scout looked Stryker in the eye. "You hate too much, and that could get us all killed."

"Liking or not liking doesn't come into it, Joe. Damn it, man, I need you to scout for me."

"The scouts have been called in. We're ordered to report to Fort Bowie with the cavalry tomorrow."

"I know—Colonel Devore told me. He said I could talk to you. I have to bring in a chief by the name of Yanisin and his people. Long John Wills says there's about twenty-five bucks of fighting age in the village."

"I hear you've got a company of the Twenty-third."

"Yes, if thirty-four men and a second lieutenant fresh out of the Point can be called a company."

Hogg picked up his glass. "Drink up; it's my call."

Stryker downed the raw whiskey in a gulp, then built a cigarette as the bartender poured for them.

"Did you ever hear of ol' Yanisin afore today?"

Stryker shook his head. "Can't say as I did."

"He's a tame Apache, maybe the only one. When you get to the rancheria, Lieutenant, he'll be there with the women, children and the old folks. But his young men will be long gone, jined up with Nana an' them."

"My orders are to return Yanisin and his people to Fort Bowie. If the bucks are not there, I'll hunt them down."

Hogg shook his head. "Not with thirty-four infantry you won't. Them twenty-five Apaches have you outnumbered, Lieutenant."

Stryker tried his whiskey and liked its harsh taste. "Then scout for me, Joe. Hell, you're worth an extra ten soldiers."

"Is that all?" Suddenly Hogg seemed distracted. "I thought I was worth a heap more'n that." He was looking over Stryker's shoulder, his eyes wary and puzzled. "Feller over yonder making noise," he said.

Stryker turned and met the belligerent stare of a tall, exceptionally thin man dressed in a stained black frock coat, checkered pants and a battered top hat.

"What the hell you looking at, soldier boy?" the man asked, smearing each word with insolence. "I don't like being looked at by the damned freak who murdered my friend Lou Ruxton tonight, as fine a man as ever lived."

The man had the look of the frontier gambler/gunman and some primitive instinct warned Stryker that he was best left alone. Beside him sat a younger man in dusty range clothes, but the gun on his hip was clean enough and his grin held a challenge.

But, despite himself, Stryker's anger flared. He stiffened, his hand dropping to his holstered Colt.

"Lieutenant, let it be," Hogg whispered.

The tall man heard. "That's right, pappy—let it be," he said. "For now at least. Jake Allen is in a killing mood tonight."

There were a dozen men in the room, and a hard-eyed saloon whore, in a shabby yellow dress, her cheeks and lips the same shade of crimson, her eyelids bright green. She grabbed a bottle from the bar and walked toward Allen's table. "Have a drink, Jake," she said, smiling. "This one's on me."

"Get away from me, you tramp," Allen said. "I'm hungry, and you wanna know what I like when I'm hungry? A dead man for supper, served up blue."

He glared around the bar, his eyebrows lowered. "All right, somebody speak up. Who wants to die tonight, or do I have to pick a volunteer?"

No one in the room made a sound, including three tense young cavalry troopers sitting at a table with a bottle of rotgut. All three were unarmed.

"You, Allen or whatever the hell you call yourself, sit down and behave or I'll place you under arrest," Stryker snapped.

Allen grinned, showing a few, blackened teeth. He looked elated, the unholy joy of a man whose finger had just found a trigger. "Is that so?" he said. He swept back the skirts of his frockcoat with an unnecessarily dramatic flourish, revealing a fancy two-gun rig. "Then why don't you arrest me, ugly soldier boy?"

Behind him, the younger man had also gotten to his feet. His eyes had an eager, reckless light, the acolyte prepared to sweep up the master's leavings.

Stryker knew it had come down to it, but he'd never faced a draw fighter before and his flapped and buttoned holster gave him pause. How many bullets could Allen get into him before he unlimbered his artillery? Could he take the hits standing and return fire?

As it happened, he had no need to answer those questions, because Joe Hogg stepped into it.

"Jake Allen, do you know me?" he asked.

Allen sneered. "Why the hell should I know you, grandpa?"

"Because I know you. You're Jake Allen, out of Waco, Texas, the famous back-shooter and woman killer."

Allen had wanted to kill before, but now he was in a homicidal rage. "Damn your eyes, give your name," he snarled. "Let me hear it before you die."

"Why, it's Joe Hogg, as ever was."

Allen didn't move an inch, but everybody in the saloon saw him mentally back up a step. "I have no quarrel with you," he said. His cheeks were suddenly chalk white. "My gripe is with the soldier boy."

The young man had quietly resumed his seat. Suddenly he wanted no part of what Joe Hogg had to offer.

"Lieutenant Stryker is my friend, Jake. If you have a gripe with him, you got one with me." He smiled. "You're wearing double irons, Jake, let's see how fast you shuck 'em and get to your work."

Allen swallowed hard. Eating crow never comes easy, but he had to force this down. "No harm done, Joe. I was somewhat in depressed spirits this evening, is all. Now, if you'll give me the road, I'll be on my way."

The scout made a bow and a sweeping gesture with his arm. "Just make it a long way, Jake."

Allen hesitated. "Hell, man, the Apaches are out."

Hogg smiled. "I know."

Allen, aware that every eye in the saloon was on him and of the triumphant smile on the carmine lips of the whore, knew he had it to do. He could walk out with his tail between his legs or trust to his gun.

How many men had Joe Hogg killed? He couldn't remember. He didn't want to remember. All that mattered was that a man who had plans to go on living didn't draw down on him.

Stryker gave him an out.

"Get on your horse and ride, Allen," he said. "If you are not off the post in ten minutes I'll toss you in the guardhouse and throw away the key."

Allen grabbed at it like a drowning man clutching a straw.

"I'll go, soldier boy," he said, "but we'll meet again when you ain't got a gunfighter to hide behind."

"The pleasure will be all yours, I assure you."

Allen turned to the young man who was sitting at the table, his hands in view and very still. "Let's go, Sam," he said.

The man called Sam shook his head. "Reckon I'll stick right here, Jake."

Allen had run out his string. He turned on his heel and walked out of the saloon, the mocking laugh of the whore scorching his ears.

Hogg turned to Stryker. "Like to live dangerously, don't you, Lieutenant?"

"He's that fast, huh?"

"Faster than you can ever imagine. By the time you got your holster flap unbuttoned, Jake Allen would have emptied his Colt into you."

"But you seemed mighty sure you could take him."

"No, I wasn't sure, not sure a-tall. And, Lieutenant, what I said about you being my friend, don't go. That was just for ol' Jake's benefit."

"And mine?" Stryker smiled.

"Take it how you want."

The whore moved to the bar, her hips taking their time to catch up with the rest of her. "Can I buy you boys a drink?" she asked. "I've known Jake Allen since I was working the line in Deadwood a few years back, and I ain't never seen anybody put the crawl on him before."

Without waiting for Stryker or Hogg to answer, she said to the bartender, "Tom, let's have the Hennessy from under the bar."

The man looked surprised. "That's gonna cost you a dollar a shot, Lorraine."

"Yeah, well, it's worth it, ain't it?"

The bartender poured cognac for the two men, then filled the woman's glass. She raised it high. "Here's to you boys."

After they drank, Lorraine ordered the glasses filled again. Her eyes moved to Stryker's face. "What the hell happened to you?"

"A man rearranged my features with a shackle chain. Does it bother you?"

The woman shrugged her naked shoulders, the white skin scarred all over from bites. "Soldier, men have come at me all my life, saying different things, wearing different faces. I've seen them all, some handsome, most ugly, but lust turns any man ugly anyway, even the pretty ones. Makes them look like goats. Hell, after all that, if your face don't bother you none, it don't bother me."

Stryker drained his glass. "It bothers me." He touched his hat. "Thanks for the drinks."

He turned to leave, but Hogg stopped him. "I'll scout for you, Lieutenant. For sure, Jake Allen will come after you and I'll get a chance to put a bullet into him. I made him back down tonight and he'll never forgive me. I don't want to leave an enemy like him on my back trail."

"I appreciate it, Joe," Stryker said.

"And so you should." The scout's eyes were moving over the swell of Lorraine's breasts and hips. "Now, if you'll excuse me, I've got more important things to attend to."

Chapter 10

By noon, Stryker's command had cleared Picket Canyon, the columned ramparts of the Chiricahua Mountains soaring to the east, their slopes and hanging valleys green with silver oak, apache pine and carpets of wildflowers.

The day was hot, the sun a brazen disk in the sky, and the infantrymen were beginning to suffer under the weight of their packs. To the west, the Sulphur Springs Valley, a vast wilderness of sand, scrub and mesquite, drowsed in hard, white sunlight and made no sound.

Behind Stryker, the brogans of the infantry thudded on the hard-packed earth, and now and then a man muttered a curse as something with thorns clawed viciously at his passing legs.

Beside Stryker rode Second Lieutenant Dale N. Birchwood, the scion of a blue-blooded Boston family who looked as though he was already rethinking his Army career.

Birchwood was hot, sticky and uncomfortable in a

uniform that seemed a size too small for him, and his young face was bright red, rivulets of sweat cutting through the dust on his cheeks. He rode a gray Thoroughbred that smelled strongly of sweat and seemed more suited to the green, foxhunting pastures of Massachusetts than the desert country of the Arizona Territory.

To his credit, Birchwood had not uttered a single word of complaint since leaving Fort Merit, and his eyes sweeping the shimmering terrain ahead were alert and searching.

Now he turned and looked at Stryker. If he was revolted by his fellow officer's smashed face, he had the good breeding not to let it show.

"Sir, Mr. Hogg has been gone for quite a while," he said. "Do you suppose he's contacted Apaches?"

Stryker shook his head. "His immediate concern is to find water, and that's not easy to do in the Chiricahuas. If he'd bumped into Apaches, trust me, he'd be back here by now, hell-for-leather."

"Major Hanson told me you had quite a battle with the Indians yourself, sir."

Stryker smiled. "I bushwhacked a bunch of drunken Apaches in a box canyon." He shrugged. "Still, you kill them any way you can, don't you?"

Birchwood nodded. "I believe that's the way of it, sir."

"That's the way of it, Lieutenant." Then, as though talking to himself, he said, "Yup, that's the way of it, all right."

Fifteen minutes later, Joe Hogg rode out of the

blazing day, his Henry across the saddle horn. The scout rode tall and tense in the saddle, looking around him, not liking what the land was telling him.

Stryker halted the column and waited.

Hogg kneed his mustang close to Stryker, then took off his hat and wiped sweat from the band. "Hot," he said.

The lieutenant waited. Beside him, Birchwood's gray tossed its head, champing at the bit. One of the infantrymen hawked and spit dust.

Finally he said, "What's up ahead, Joe?"

"Apache sign, Lieutenant, a heap of it. And a dead white man."

Stryker stood in the stirrups, easing himself in the saddle. The dead man could wait. "Where are the savages headed?"

"I'd say right now they're in the Chiricahuas due east of the Sulphur Hills, trying to discover where the white man was headed. The man wouldn't have been riding alone if he didn't have a place to go and a mighty important reason for getting there. The Apaches must figure there's a ranch or a farm around there someplace."

"But eventually they'll turn south, huh?"

"I can't say that, Lieutenant. Geronimo is trying to make a name for himself as a war chief, and old Nana will go along with whatever he says." Hogg looked beyond Stryker, his gaze shifting to their back trail. "They could head north."

The implication of that hit Stryker immediately. "You mean attack Fort Bowie?"

The scout shook his head. "No, Geronimo is not

strong enough to tackle a post of that size. But by this time he's sure been told that there's only a single infantry company guarding Fort Merit."

"How many warriors does this Geronimo savage have?"

"Hard to say, but he might have fifty or more, and, judging by the tracks I saw earlier, more young men are joining him." Hogg shrugged. "He's got enough, especially if Yanisin's band throws in with him."

"Colonel Devore told me the Apaches would head for Mexico."

"Colonel Devore ain't here, Lieutenant."

For a few moments Stryker sat his saddle, thinking it through. Finally he looked at Hogg, his mind made up. "Joe, I want to see those tracks for myself. Lieutenant Birchwood, bring up the column at your best speed."

The young lieutenant saluted, and Stryker turned to his scout again. "Let's go." He set spurs to his horse and headed south, into the glowering heat of the dancing day.

The dead man lay where he'd fallen. He was on his back, his eyes burning out in the sun. He'd been struck by a volley of shots and was probably dead when he hit the ground.

"What do you make of him, Joe?" Stryker asked.

"Looks like a sodbuster to me, but he hasn't done none o' that lately. Look at his hands, they ain't guided a plow in some time." He glanced at Stryker. "It's getting hard to tell now the sun's got to him,

Lieutenant, but when I first saw him, when he was fresher, he had the look of a drinker."

Stryker looked around him. "Unshod ponies. How many would you say?"

"Six, maybe seven. They either broke off from Geronimo's main bunch or they were riding to join him when they stumbled on this man."

"What the hell was he doing out here by himself?"

"Like I said, he was goin' someplace."

"Someplace . . . in this damned, godforsaken wilderness?"

Hogg pointed. "The pony tracks head that way, toward the hogback yonder. My guess is the sodbuster's farm is back there." Stryker said nothing, and the scout prompted. "And maybe his woman and his kids."

"We'll wait for the company to come up," the lieutenant said.

Suddenly the crash of a rifle shot echoed through the foothills, and then another.

"Might be too late by then," Hogg said quietly.

Stryker shook his head. "Damn you, Joe. You do love to pick at a man's conscience." He turned and looked behind him. But Birchwood and his infantry were not yet in sight.

"Oh, hell." He drew his revolver. "Let's rescue the farmer's wife, even if it kills us, which it surely might."

A narrow game trail led between a series of low hills covered with mesquite and juniper. There was no relief from the pitiless sun that hammered at both men and their horses. Stryker smelled the rankness of his own sweat rise from the dark arcs under the arms of his faded blue shirt. The light was a hard glare that hurt the eyes and turned the sand into a lake of molten steel. The heat was a malevolent, living entity and in all the vast land only the slopes of the mountains, green with pines, looked cool.

"You're doing the right thing, Lieutenant," Hogg said, turning in the saddle.

"Joe, you can write that on my gravestone: He Done the Right Thing."

More shots, coming from beyond the hogback. The scout read them. "Five, six Apaches firing, but only one answering shot. From a Sharps .50, I'd say."

"The farmer's wife is fighting back."

"Seems like."

Stryker studied the land ahead of him. Nothing moved but a lone buzzard quartering the sky. There was no breeze here in the foothills and the air hung still, as thick and hard to breathe as warm cotton.

The game trail petered out as the hills gave way to a wide meadow, cratered with hollows. The ground was thick with cactus, mostly cholla and prickly pear, here and there vivid swathes of desert bluebells and marigolds.

The riders crossed the meadow, then hit the slope of the hogback at a canter, dislodging loose gravel that clattered behind them. Before they reached the ridge they dismounted. Stryker retrieved his field glasses from his saddlebags, and with Hogg at a crouching run beside him, covered the rest of the distance on foot.

Lying on his belly, he scanned the basin below.

The slope of the hogback dropped gradually into an open area of grass and broken land that looked as though it had once been plowed. There was a small cabin overhung by a huge cottonwood, a pole corral and sizeable barn. Among the outbuildings were a smokehouse, an open-fronted shed for a blacksmith's forge and a smaller cabin that seemed to serve no ascertainable purpose.

The place had once been a fine-looking farm, but now looked shabby and rundown, held together by baling wire and twine.

Hogg's elbow dug into Stryker's ribs. He held up two fingers, then pointed to a jumble of boulders about thirty yards from the cabin that looked like they'd been cleared from a field. Now the scout held up one finger and pointed to the pole corral.

Stryker scanned both areas with his glasses, but saw nothing.

Then an Apache moved. The warrior at the corral stepped from behind a fencepost and fired at the cabin. There was no answering shot.

Stryker indicated to Hogg that they should back away from the crest of the hill. Once he could stand on his feet again, he asked, "You saw three Apaches. Where are the others?"

Hogg shook his head. "Dunno. But I reckon there's two or three more. When an Apache don't want to be seen, you don't see him."

Stryker nodded. "Joe, position yourself at the top of the hill again and when the Apaches show, drop them with your Henry."

"Where are you going to be, Lieutenant."

"I'll mount up and head directly for the cabin. The savages are tightening the noose, and whoever is inside there could be hurt and needs help."

"Sounds like a mighty good way to cut a promising army career short," Hogg said, without a trace of humor.

The lieutenant smiled. "Then be sure to tell Colonel Devore about Stryker's gallant ride."

"I will, but he'll be sorely disappointed in you, Lieutenant. He had his heart set on making you a captain."

Stryker waited until Hogg was in position, then swung into the saddle. He wiped the fear sweat from his gun hand on his breeches, then fisted the Colt again.

He saw Hogg glance back at him, swallowed hard, and kicked the bay into motion. The big horse crested the hill at a gallop and plunged down the other side, the bit in its teeth, mane flying.

Now there was no turning back.

Chapter 11

Stryker saw a startled Apache rise up from the pile of boulders. He snapped off a shot. Missed. The Indian fired and Stryker felt the bullet burn across his canvas suspender where it crossed his shoulder. A rifle crashed from the rise and the Apache looked even more startled as a blood red rose appeared on the chest of his white shirt. He went down hard.

The cabin was closer now.

Bullets from all sides of the basin stung the air around Stryker. He thumbed off a fast shot at the Apache by the corral post. Another miss. Behind him Hogg was firing steadily but didn't seem to be scoring hits either.

The Apache stepped away from the corral and threw his Winchester to his shoulder. He and Stryker fired at the same time. The Indian's bullet crashed into the bay and Stryker cartwheeled from the saddle, landing hard on his back in a cloud of dust.

A man who is thrown by a galloping horse doesn't get up in a hurry. Stryker lay stunned as bullets kicked up startled exclamation points of sand around him. Finally he raised himself into a sitting position. Feet pounded to his right, coming fast. The Apache, grimacing in rage, had grabbed his rifle and was readying himself to swing a killing blow at the white officer's head.

A shot.

The Apache went down, screaming, half of his skull blown away. Stryker turned his reeling head and saw a woman standing at the cabin door, a smoking Sharps still to her shoulder. Gun in hand, he struggled to his feet and staggered toward the sanctuary of the open door. It seemed like it was an eternity away.

He almost made it.

Just as the woman stepped inside, pushing open the door for him, a bullet thudded into Stryker's right side, just above his cartridge belt. He felt like he'd been hit by a sledgehammer and slammed hard against the door jamb. Another bullet thudded into the rough pine of the door, driving splinters into his face.

Then he was through, stumbling into the darkness of the cabin on rubber legs.

A few splintered impressions quickly hurled themselves at Stryker. A woman slamming the wooden bolt shut behind him . . . a wide-eyed child cowering in a corner . . . empty shell casings scattered around the dirt floor . . . the woman's frightened face, showing him the Sharps, telling him she'd used her last bullet, the one she'd been saving for her daughter . . . blood, his own blood, dripping down his legs . . .

A heavy body threw itself against the door. Stryker

raised his Colt and fired twice through the timber. He heard a yelp of pain. Then the roar of volleyed rifle fire slammed across the basin. More shots, this time a ragged salvo, soldiers firing at will.

A few minutes passed, then, "Lieutenant Stryker!"

It was Joe Hogg's voice, calling from outside.

Stryker opened the door and stepped into daylight. Hogg was standing in front of the cabin, the Henry cradled in his arms. Behind him Birchwood's soldiers were checking the bodies of the dead Apaches.

"We killed two of them," the scout said. "And you winged another. The rest skedaddled when the troops arrived."

Stryker nodded, but said nothing.

Birchwood led his horse to the cabin. "Heard the firing, sir," he said. "Figured it had to be you."

"You did well, Lieutenant," Stryker said. He felt very weak and had trouble standing on his feet without swaying. He grimaced back a wave of pain. "I'll mention . . . mention that in my report."

Suddenly he was aware of the woman standing beside him. She glared at Hogg and Birchwood. "Can't you two see that this man is hurt?" she snapped. "Help me get him inside."

Hogg was shocked. "Did you take a bullet, Lieutenant?"

The woman answered for Stryker. "Yes, he took a bullet. Now are you going to help or not?"

Birchwood and the scout sprang to help. Stryker was a big man, and they half dragged, half carried him inside.

"Lay him down on the bed, over there," the woman said.

A brass bed was pushed against the far wall of the cabin, its patchwork quilt adding the only splash of color to the drab room.

"I'm fine," Stryker protested as he was pushed on his back and the woman lifted his dusty, booted feet onto the bed, ignoring the damage it might cause to her quilt. "I will proceed to the Apache village on Big Bend Creek as I was ordered."

Hogg clucked his tongue, his face troubled, looking at the spreading scarlet stain on Stryker's side. "Lieutenant, you ain't going anywhere for a spell. If you ain't gut-shot, then you've come mighty close."

The woman pushed the scout aside and began to unbutton Stryker's shirt. She slipped the suspenders off his shoulders and gently pulled the shirt over his head.

Stryker struggled to a sitting position and looked at the wound. It was ugly and red, raw meat around the edges of the bullet hole.

"How bad is it?" Stryker asked, seeking some reassurance that the injury wasn't as bad as he feared.

The woman met his eyes but said nothing.

Hogg was not so reticent. "It's bad, Lieutenant. As bad as I've seen, 'cept on a dead man."

"The bullet is still inside him," the woman said. "It's got to come out."

"Not if it's in his gut," Hogg said.

"Or close to the spine," Birchwood added.

Stryker let out a roar of exasperation. "Damn it, I'm still here, you know! And I can hear every word."

He looked at Hogg. "Joe, see if you can find the damned bullet."

"Leave it, I'll examine him," the woman said, pushing Hogg aside again.

Stryker noticed two things about his nurse. The first was the gentleness of her hands, the second, much more obvious, was the livid white scar that cut across her tanned cheek from her left ear to the corner of her mouth. The cut that caused it had been deep, meant to inflict the maximum damage.

Stryker looked at the scar and wondered. Who had done that to her?

An Apache maybe, but that seemed unlikely. A jealous lover? The woman was homely, made plainer by hard work and the hot desert sun, not the sort likely to attract such men. Her husband, if she had one?

Stryker had no answers and he did not speculate any further as she rolled him over on his belly.

After some gentle probing, the woman turned to Hogg. "The bullet is there," she said, pointing to a spot just under the ribs on Stryker's left side. "I can feel it."

"Let me take a look-see," the scout said.

Hogg's hands were no less gentle than the woman's. "I feel it," he said finally. "It has to be cut out of there."

"Can you do it?" the woman asked.

"I can do it," the scout said. "It's a mite deeper than I'd like, but I can do it. I've cut worse out of folks and critters alike, an' most of them lived."

Stryker felt panic rise in him. "Joe, can't the bullet sit there? Just bind me up real good and let it stay until we get back to Fort Merit."

Hogg nodded. "It can stay, Lieutenant, but then it will spread its poison and kill you quicker'n scat. You'll never reach Fort Merit."

Stryker let his head thud onto the pillow. "Then cut away, and be damned to you, Joe Hogg."

"Ma'am, I do not mean to imply in any way that ardent spirits hold any attraction for you," Hogg said, "but do you have whiskey in the house?"

The woman smiled. She looked strained, exhausted, the horrors of the Apache attack finally catching up with her. "We always have whiskey in this house," she said. "I'll bring the jug."

Hogg accepted the jug, pulled the cork and drank deeply. He wiped his mouth with the back of his hand and offered it to Birchwood, who declined.

After he'd helped Stryker into a sitting poison, he said, "Drink as much as you can, Lieutenant. That there busthead will dull the pain if it don't kill you first."

Stryker was irritated, piqued. "Seems to me the one with the bullet in him should have drank first."

Hogg shook his head. "No, first the surgeon, and then the second lieutenant, and then the patient. That's how it's done in medical circles." He smiled at Stryker like a benign uncle. "Now drink up—there's a good officer."

Stryker did as he was told; then Hogg said, "More."

"Damn it, Joe, this stuff is awful."

"So is havin' a bullet cut out of your back, Lieutenant. More."

For the next few minutes Stryker drank deeper and longer. When he lowered the jug, his head spun and the people in the room suddenly began to shift shape, as though they were walking out of a heat shimmer.

"Damn, but that's good whiskey," Stryker said, holding the jug at arm's length. His uncertain gaze fell on the woman, who had just lit a lantern and brought it closer to the bed. "Will you join me, ma'am?" He looked at Hogg. "What was it you called this, Joe?"

"Busthead."

Stryker nodded. "Damn right. That's what you called it. Will you join me, ma'am, and partake of some gen . . . geninin . . . genurine Arizona Territory busthead?"

"I'd love to, Lieutenant."

After he handed her the jug, the woman took a swig. "Thank you," she said. "I needed that."

"A pleasure, ma'am, a great pleasure." Stryker's broken face took on a surprised look. "I don't know your name, ma'am."

"It's Mary. My last name is McCabe."

"And mine is Steve. My last name is Stryker. I come from a long . . . oh, a long, long line of Strykers." He tried to focus on the woman. "Wait, I used to know a song about a woman called Mary. We sang it at the Point sometimes." He held up a hand in horror. "Oh, but I can't sing that, ma'am. Not in this polite company. See, it's about Dirty Mary who worked in a dairy and . . ."

"You're ready, Lieutenant," Hogg said.

"Another drink, Joe." Stryker took a pull on the jug. "Joe," he said, gasping from the raw fire of the whiskey, "you are a very intelligent man. You know all about busthead." He tapped the side of his flattened nose with a forefinger. "Only—only very intelligent men know what you know." He hiccupped. "About—about generinuine busthead, I mean."

Stryker held the jug to his chest, and gazed at Hogg like an owl. "Joe, I never—" he gulped a breath—"no, I didn't, I never, ever, asked you about Trooper Kramer's frog. Did you cure his asam-asth—"

"Hell, no," the scout said. "He took to liking the frog so much, he decided to keep it as a pet. Fed it mashed biscuit and flies and the damned thing never did die."

"So he still has his—"

"Gaspin' worse than ever," Hogg said. "Now roll over, Lieutenant."

Stryker saluted. "Yes, sir."

He rolled over—and immediately started to snore.

"Get the jug, ma'am," Hogg said.

He took a folding knife from his pocket, then said, "Pour the whiskey over the blade, ma'am." He saw the confused look on the woman's face and smiled. "I saw the young post doctor at Fort Bowie do that one time. I don't know why, but he must have had a good reason."

"When did you last use the knife, Mr. Hogg?"

"To gut an antelope, ma'am, a six-month ago."

"Maybe that's the reason."

"Could be, ma'am. But there's just no accounting for why Army doctors do things." He waved the woman closer. "Bring the lamp over here. I'm about to start the cuttin'."

Lieutenant Birchwood made his excuses and left, the opening and closing of the door allowing a blast of desert heat and dust inside.

"It's deep," Hogg said. His fingers and the knife were red with blood. Stryker groaned in restless sleep, the wound on his back like a scarlet, open mouth.

Sweat dripped from the scout's forehead and he cursed under his breath. "Damn it to hell, but it's deep. I'm cuttin' too much, ma'am. Way too much."

The woman called Mary's voice was level. "The bullet has to come out, Mr. Hogg."

"Get a rag, ma'am. Wipe away the blood so I can see what I'm doing."

Mary used a cloth to swab the blood from the wound, then held it for Hogg. "Wipe your hands and the knife."

The scout did as she said, and then his eyes met hers, his face a worried mask of orange light and shadow in the flickering glow of the oil lamp. "I could be killing him."

"Get the bullet, Mr. Hogg. If you don't, he'll die anyway."

Outside, Lieutenant Birchwood was yelling orders to his men, his voice distant and muffled. Stryker was breathing heavily, in short, tortured gasps. A random desert breeze rattled the shutters over the cabin windows and from the corner, a child's voice pleaded softly, "Ma . . . ma . . ."

"In a minute, Kelly," Mary said. "Just a little minute." The woman said to Hogg. "She's very afraid of men."

The scout was concentrating on his knife, his mouth set in a hard, tense line. "Bad for a little 'un to be that way, ma'am."

"Her father terrified her."

Hogg nodded. "I reckon that would do it, ma'am." His slippery knife skidded, scraped on bone. He let loose with a string of hair-raising curses, then muttered, "Sorry about that, ma'am."

"Air out your lungs if you feel the need, Mr. Hogg."

"You're most gracious, ma'am."

A minute passed, then another. . . . Hogg's knife dug deeper. . . .

"Damn it to hell's fire, I got it!" the scout yelled. "The son of a bitch is a .44-40 ball, unless I'm much mistaken."

Mary leaned over the bed. "How is he?"

"Sleeping. Or just unconscious." Hogg looked into the woman's eyes again. "He'll need care."

"I'll do what I can, Mr. Hogg."

The door swung open and Birchwood stuck his head inside. "I heard you yell that you'd recovered the bullet, Mr. Hogg. Now could you come outside at your earliest convenience and look at something?"

"What is it?"

"I was hoping you could tell me, Mr. Hogg."

The scout wiped his bloody hands on the cloth. "Be right there, Lieutenant."

"Oh, and ma'am," Birchwood said, "I have some questions for you."

He did not sound friendly.

Chapter 12

Lieutenant Steve Stryker woke to lamplight and a pounding headache.

He tried to sit up in the bed, but he was defeated by pains in his side and back that were living entities, clawing at him, warning that they would give him no rest.

He laid his head back on the pillow and a groan escaped his lips.

Suddenly Mary McCabe was at his side. She placed a small, cool hand on his forehead. "How are you feeling, Lieutenant?"

Stryker groaned again. "What did Joe Hogg hit me with? A rifle butt?"

Mary smiled. "No, just a jug of genuine Arizona busthead. Then he cut the bullet out of your back."

"Good. If Hogg's whiskey doesn't kill me, I can ride tomorrow."

Mary let that slide. "Hungry?"

"You know, I could eat something, hardtack and salt pork maybe."

Mary stepped to the stove where a fire burned.

She returned with a bowl and a spoon. "Beef broth," she said. "It will give you strength."

Stryker tried to take the bowl, but the woman moved it away. "You can't feed yourself. Let me do it."

Rather than argue, which in any case he did not have the energy to do, Stryker opened his mouth submissively and let the woman feed him. The soup was good, rich and hot, and Stryker ate the bowl empty and was wishful for more.

From outside drifted snatches of talk from the soldiers, and the scrape and clatter of tin forks. "Lieutenant Birchwood camped here," he said. "That makes sense. We'll move out at first light tomorrow." He looked at the woman. "You and your daughter will have to come with us, ma'am. The savages will be back."

"It's Mary McCabe."

"Yes, I vaguely remember. Then Mary McCabe it is."

The door opened and Hogg stepped inside, letting in the night that loomed dark and vast behind him. He smiled. "Still alive, I see, Lieutenant."

"No thanks to your whiskey."

"Numbed the pain though, huh?"

"That's what happens when busthead makes a man's heart stop."

"He has no fever, Mr. Hogg, and his wounds are clean," Mary said.

The scout turned to the woman. He seemed very big and shaggy in the lamp-shadowed gloom of the cabin. "Don't pay no heed to Lieutenant Birchwood, ma'am. Right now he's a mighty worried young man."

"I told him the truth, Mr. Hogg. My husband didn't tell me what he was doing and I never asked."

"But you saw the wagons."

"Yes, I did. I was ordered to stay in the house, but I could see from the window. There were six or seven men with the wagons, including an Apache. One of the men was called Williams, another, who seemed to be in charge, went by the name of Rake, or maybe it was Jake, I can't remember."

Despite his pain, Stryker struggled erect in the bed, his face intent. "Ma'am, Mrs. McCabe, was the boss's name Rake Pierce?"

"I didn't hear his last name, but, yes, he could have been called Rake."

Hogg looked at Stryker. "The dead man we found was the lady's husband. She identified him from the watch he was wearing."

"I'm sorry," Stryker said absently, his mind working, trying to drag his body with it.

"Don't be," Mary said. "He was a drunken, vicious brute who deserved to die." Her fingertips strayed to the savage scar on her cheek. "This is a lasting memento of my marriage to Tom McCabe."

"Ma'am," Hogg said, "you should have left him."

"And go where, Mr. Hogg? I didn't even have a horse. Maybe Kelly and I could have walked to a settlement, but he would have found us and brought us back." She smiled slightly. "And how could I make a living? Scarred as I am, I couldn't even become a whore."

"How did Rake Pierce meet your husband?" Stryker asked.

"Tom often visited the Army posts for whiskey and whores. He could have met Pierce, if that's who he was, at Fort Merit or Fort Bowie."

"Why would Pierce want him?"

"My husband knew this country like the back of his hand, Lieutenant. After he got sick of farming, which didn't take long, he hunted and prospected all over the Chiricahuas and as far south as the Perilla Mountains."

Hogg nodded. "Ol' Rake needed a scout, and good ones are mighty hard to find."

"Mrs. McCabe, when were the wagons here?" Stryker asked.

"Three days ago, I think. When a woman sees only cabin walls she loses track of time."

"Joe, we didn't see wagon tracks on the hogback."

"There's another way in and out of the basin, Lieutenant. It's a narrow, rocky canyon to the east of the cabin, but it's passable, even for freight wagons. I scouted over that way and found wheel tracks. That's how the wagons came and went, all right."

"Why didn't your husband go with them, Mrs. McCabe?"

"Lieutenant, it pleased him to beat me or rape me, depending on his mood. He didn't take me into his confidence when he was enjoying either activity."

Hogg's boots thudded on the hard packed dirt floor. He laid a hand on the woman's shoulder. "We buried him deep, Mrs. McCabe. He isn't coming back."

Mary nodded, looking up at him, but said nothing.

Stryker's mind was still racing. "Joe, why did McCabe split up from the rest of them?"

"Dunno, Lieutenant. Maybe McCabe left on a scout, agreeing to join up with Rake and the others at a certain place. Trouble is, he ran into traveling Apaches who shot first and asked questions later."

"Can we track those wagons?"

"We can track them."

Stryker swung his legs out of the bed and discovered that he was naked except for the bandage that circled his waist and looped over his shoulder. "Mrs. McCabe, could you avert your eyes?" He looked at the little girl who was standing close to her sitting mother's knee, regarding him with wide, solemn eyes. "And the child, if you please."

The woman smiled, but she and her daughter suddenly found something to do at the stove.

Stryker got to his feet, calling to Hogg to get his clothes.

Then a wave of pain and weakness hit him and he was falling headlong into a bottomless pit of darkness.

Chapter 13

"Lieutenant Stryker, you're shot through and through and you've lost a lot of blood," Mary McCabe said. "You're not fit to go anywhere."

The woman's face was an oval blur in the wan lamplight. "How long have I been out?" he asked.

"Not long, ten, fifteen minutes."

"Is Joe Hogg still here?"

"No. He left."

"Please tell Lieutenant Birchwood I want to see him."

When the officer stepped into the cabin, Stryker saw concern etched in the frown that had gathered between the young man's eyebrows.

"How are you, sir?" he asked.

"Well, I tried to get out of bed and fell down. Does that tell you something?"

Birchwood said nothing, but he shifted his feet uncomfortably.

"Tomorrow morning you will break camp before sunrise and proceed south to the Apache village.

Bring Yanisin and his people this far, then send Mr. Hogg to fetch me. Is that clear?"

"Yes, sir. I will leave a squad here to protect the cabin should the Apaches decide to attack again."

"No, you won't, Lieutenant. You might need all the men you have and then some." Stryker was tired and in pain. Looking at the fresh-faced Birchwood he suddenly felt old. "There's a possibility that the Apaches will turn north and attack Fort Merit. For that reason, you will send half the company back to reinforce the post garrison."

"I was not aware of that possibility," Birchwood said.

"I'm guessing, Lieutenant, and I know that trying to outguess Apaches is always a dangerous business. But if I'm right, Major Hanson can't hold the fort against Geronimo and Nana with just a single understrength company."

He shifted uncomfortably in the bed. Mary McCabe had put some kind of poultice on his wounds and now they itched.

"Joe Hogg says Yanisin is a tame Indian and he shouldn't give you any trouble. The big question is: How will his young men react? Listen to Mr. Hogg. He knows Apaches better than most. If you reach the rancheria and the young bucks show signs of a fight, get the hell out of there in a hurry. Do not engage them."

Stryker's eyes searched the younger man's face. "Do you understand your orders, Lieutenant?"

"I do, sir. Perfectly."

Stryker tried to smile and used the young man's name for the first time. "Dale, I'm sending you out with half a company of infantry when what you really need is a regiment. Just . . . just be careful."

"I will, sir, as far as my orders allow." He saluted smartly. "Sir, with your permission I'll see to my men."

"Yes, do that," Stryker said. God, he was weary. "Dismissed, Lieutenant."

Birchwood saluted again, turned smartly and stepped out of the door.

Stryker had the nagging feeling that he was sending the young man to his death.

Still weak and lightheaded, Stryker managed to drag himself out of bed to see the company leave. Mrs. McCabe was asleep in a chair, her daughter lying on a pallet on the floor.

As quietly as he could, he stood in the doorway, the chill desert night not yet giving way to the dawn.

The company moved out silently, marching toward the hogback. Birchwood saw Stryker, grinned and saluted. He then took his place at the head of his men.

Joe Hogg kneed his horse toward Stryker and drew rein opposite the door.

"You look like hell," he said.

"And I feel worse." Stryker's eyes sought the scout's face in the indigo light. "Bring them back, Joe," he said. "Every last one of them." He hesitated, then added, "And bring yourself back."

Hogg smiled. "Gettin' shot done you some good,

Lieutenant. You're suddenly full o' the milk of human kindness, as ol' Shakespeare says."

"You saved my life, Joe. Nobody else could have dug that bullet out of my back."

The scout nodded. "I think maybe yours was a life worth saving. I sure hope so." He looked beyond the cabin door to the darkness inside. "Take care of Mrs. McCabe, Lieutenant. Two scarred people should look out for each other."

He slid his Henry from the boot. "Take this; it's fully loaded. If you need more than sixteen shots, you'll be in a war you can't win anyway."

Stryker shook his head. "I can't take your rifle, Joe. You may need it."

"Hell, I'm surrounded by men with rifles. A Colt won't do you much good if the Apaches come back."

Stryker took the Henry, amazed at how heavy it felt in his weakened hands. "Ride easy, Mr. Hogg," he said.

The scout touched his hat, then turned around and cantered into the darkness. Soon there was no sound but the talk of the coyotes and the morning song of the desert wind.

"Both your wounds look much better," Mary McCabe said. "They're healing and I don't see any sign of an infection."

"What do you use on the bandage that works such wonders in just three days?" Stryker asked, smiling.

"A tea of chaparral and live oak bark. That and

the clean desert air keeps wounds clean. I've lived long enough in the wilderness to pick up a few things about Indian medicine."

"I still feel weak as a kitten."

"It will take time."

"I don't have time. Lieutenant Birchwood and his men will be here soon, herding an entire Apache tribe north."

"You will go with them?"

"Yes. You and Kelly and me. We're all going."

"Do you really think the Apaches will attack Fort Merit?"

"I don't know for sure. It depends on Geronimo. If he thinks he's strong enough, destroying an Army post would bring him much renown and respect among his people."

"How is the bandage? Is it as tight as you wanted?"

"It will do." The woman had helped him dress earlier, and now Stryker swung his legs over the side of the bed. "Bring me my boots, Mary."

He tugged on the boots, then said, "Now help me to my feet."

Leaning heavily on the woman, Stryker stood erect. Suddenly the cabin reeled around him and he reached out to the wall and closed his eyes, swaying, until the feeling had passed.

"You'll fall down," Kelly said, looking up at Stryker, her sad little face troubled.

"No, I won't," he said. He patted the child's head. "See? I'm feeling all better now."

Mary smiled. "She worries about you."

"I thought I might have scared her."

"Children can see past faces to what a person has inside, Lieutenant. Only adults are blind to that."

"Then thank God for children, huh?"

The woman nodded. "Kelly is the only good thing that came out of my marriage. I thank God every day for sending her to me."

Stryker buckled on his cartridge belt and holstered Colt. He picked up the Henry and it still seemed heavy. He slung a canteen over his shoulder.

"You should be in bed," Mary said, watching his face, pale under his weather-beaten tan.

"I know. But I need to find out what's happening."

"Lieutenant, nothing's happening. It's been quiet since the soldiers left."

"Yes, and that's what's troubling the hell out of me," Stryker said.

Chapter 14

Stryker stepped into the heat of the aborning day, his entire left side afire with pain. His saddle and bridle had been hung on the hitching post outside the cabin, but there was no sign of his dead horse. Joe Hogg had probably hauled it away somewhere.

Squinting his eyes against the sun glare, he looked to the west where the steep-sided hogback provided a formidable obstacle for a sick man.

Stryker began to put one foot in front of another—high and steep or no, the hogback was just another hill to climb.

He was even weaker than he'd thought. He climbed the slope one step at a time, pausing often to recover.

He was in no condition for a fight. If an Apache found him now . . .

Stryker shrugged off the thought. He was behaving like a frightened old maid who hears a rustle in every bush.

The crest of the hogback was still high above him

and the unrelenting sun gave him no peace. He was sweating heavily, the rifle in his right hand slick.

Still he climbed, using brush and bunch grass to help pull himself upward wherever he could. Above him buzzards were gathering, birds of ill omen who weighed him in the balance and didn't give much for his chances.

Stryker cursed the buzzards, cursed the heat, cursed the hogback and finally cursed himself. He'd been a fool to attempt this so soon after being shot. If Mrs. McCabe didn't find him, he could die out here.

Finally, through sheer strength of will, he gained the crest and started down the other side. This time the going was easier and didn't tax him as badly.

He found the game trail between the hills and followed it west, dropping five hundred feet lower until the far-flung reaches of the Sulphur Springs Valley came in sight.

Stryker took cover behind a clump of mesquite and looked around him. Out in the flat, away from the Chiricahua foothills, the land drowsed in the sun and made no sound. From a pile of jumbled rock close to Stryker's foot, an irritated rattlesnake shook its warning, then, its point made, slithered away. The buzzards still quartered the colorless sky, slowly drifting downward, wary, serene and patient.

Stryker used the Henry to help himself to his feet, then stepped into the open. North, in the direction of Apache Pass, nothing moved across the face of the vast land. To the south, a silent, sun-blasted emptiness told the same story.

The sand around Stryker was churned up by the passage of horses, unshod Apache ponies. The tracks headed north. Joe Hogg could have told him how many Indians had passed this way, but he guessed they were many.

It seemed to Stryker that the whole Apache nation was on the move, hurrying to join Geronimo and Nana. Fort Merit, with its tiny garrison, could be the only target. He was willing to bet that the adobes and jacals around the post were already deserted. The Mexicans had been fighting Apaches for hundreds of years, and if they were coming . . . they knew.

Then he saw the wagon tracks.

Two heavily-loaded freight wagons had passed this way, and very recently. Good businessman that he was, Rake Pierce was following his customers.

A mindless, primitive urge to kill resurrected in him, Stryker tilted back his head and drank from his canteen, splashing more of the water over the wreckage of his face. Only then did he notice that the buzzards had drifted away from him and were circling low about a hundred yards to the south.

He studied the land in that direction, willing to dismiss the dead or dying creature as a wounded antelope or the remains of a coyote kill. It would be a useless and foolish expenditure of his already depleted strength to investigate.

Yet . . . something about the buzzards troubled him, awakening in him an instinct for danger. He shook his head, angry with himself. He was scared, that was all, and a man's fear makes the wolf seem much bigger than he is.

Then he heard the choked, agonized shriek that made up his mind for him.

The dying creature was a man.

The thing that had once been human lay in a small clearing between a pair of mesquite juniper-covered hills that were bright with summer wildflowers. The man was spread-eagled beside the ashes of a fire, his wrists and ankles bound to stakes with strips of rawhide.

His eyelids had been cut off and fires had burned in his hands and on his groin. There was little left of either. His naked body was covered in small cuts and the desert fire ants had been busy on him.

The man raised his head, trying to see with black, burned-out eyes. There was a terrible fear in his quavering voice. "Who's there?"

"Lieutenant Steve Stryker."

A grimace that could have been a smile stretched the man's cracked lips. "Oh, thank God it's you! I'm saved."

Wearily, Stryker took a knee beside Sergeant Miles Hooper. He lifted the canteen from his shoulder and pressed it to the man's lips. Hooper drank deeply, then laid his head back on the ground.

"You've saved me, Lieutenant. Oh, please, I need a doctor bad. Get me to the post."

"What happened, Hooper?" Stryker asked.

"Rake . . . Rake Pierce. I . . . I asked him for 'elp and he threw me to the Apaches, like I was a piece of meat." Hooper raised his head again. "I can't see you, Lieutenant."

"Sun blindness. It will pass."

"He—Rake—laughed, Lieutenant. The Apaches were working on me, making me scream and he laughed. He's . . . he's not a man; he's a fiend."

Hooper tried to raise his head again. "My pisser," he croaked, "did they take my pisser?"

Stryker glanced at the blackened lump of burned flesh between the man's legs.

"No," he said, "it's fine."

"Thank 'eavens. I'll need that for the whores when I get well again."

"Where is Pierce headed?" Stryker asked. Silently he undid his holster flap and slid out the Colt.

"North, Lieutenant. That's all I know, following the Apaches." He moved his head. "Get the lads to cut me free and put me on a horse. I need a doctor real bad. I'm glad you saved—"

Stryker's shot slammed into Hooper's temple. He holstered his revolver and got to his feet, looking down at the dead man. Hooper had been a murderer, a deserter and a disgrace to his uniform, but nobody deserved to die as he'd done.

A sick emptiness in him, Stryker headed back toward the game trail between the hills. His steps were slow and halting, a dragging, agonized shuffle across the hot sand. Blood was seeping through his shirt, weakening him.

He gave up after twenty yards and collapsed into the thin shade of a juniper that struggled for survival in the narrow crevice of a fractured boulder. The sun rose higher in the sky, pounding the land into submission, and only the insects moved, making their small sounds in the bunch grass.

Stryker closed eyes that felt as though they were heavy with sand. He leaned his head against the rock and breathed through his mouth, grabbing at the thin air. Gradually he let not sleep, but a deep unconsciousness take him.

As the day shadowed into the lilac tint of evening and the stars set sentinels in the sky, an antelope trotted past the split rock, only to bound away when it caught sight of the sprawled human. A pair of hunting coyotes winded Stryker but quickly lost interest when they scented richer, closer and deader meat. . . .

His uneasy, restless slumber dragged on.

"Lieutenant! Lieutenant Stryker!"

Stryker's eyes flew open. Mrs. McCabe was calling into the darkness for him. He struggled to his feet just as the woman emerged from the gloom—leading a horse.

"When it got dark I grew worried," she said. "I thought . . . I thought maybe you were—"

"Dead?"

"Yes."

"Where is Kelly?"

"Asleep."

Stryker felt like he was a hundred years old. He stepped wearily toward Mary McCabe and studied the horse. "He's a criollo," he said. "I once saw a regiment of Mexican lancers mounted on them. How did you come by him?"

"One of the dead Apaches was riding him. I found him wandering under the cottonwood beside the cabin. I bridled him," the woman said. "He's not a tall horse. Can you get on his back?"

Stryker managed a smile. "Seems like I'll have to. I can't make it back to the cabin on foot."

It took him several attempts, but finally he managed to climb onto the little horse's back. The criollo was well-trained and had stood quietly while Stryker mounted him. Now Mary gathered up the reins and led the horse back toward the game trail.

On the way, Stryker told her about finding Sergeant Hooper. He did not tell her the man had still been alive and that he'd fired a mercy shot into his brain.

"The Apaches are heading north to join Geronimo," he said. "So is Rake Pierce, the man who beat me with a shackle chain."

When she turned, Mary's face was a pale blur in the gathering darkness. "You want to kill him, this man?"

"Yes, I do, Mrs. McCabe. I want to kill him real bad."

"I understand."

"You do?"

"I wanted to kill the man who abused me and cut me with a knife. I'm a coward who just never found the courage."

"You have courage, Mrs. McCabe. It's a quiet, womanly sort of courage that doesn't shout its name, but it's courage nevertheless. If you're a coward, I haven't seen it in you yet."

"No one has ever said anything like that to me, Lieutenant."

"A woman needs a man to say things to her, Mrs. McCabe. He should tell her about the way her hair catches the sunlight, the blue sky that lives in her eyes. True things."

"West Point taught you well, Lieutenant Stryker."

"No, life taught me well, or it's trying to."

"Hold on tight," Mary said. "We've reached the hogback."

Chapter 15

The McClellan saddle was designed to favor the horse, not the rider, and Stryker felt stiff and uncomfortable as he headed the criollo south across an endless brush desert cut through by dry creeks and wide, dusty washes.

He felt uncomfortable for another reason.

Mrs. McCabe and Kelly walked beside the horse, their only protection from the blazing sun a tiny white parasol that the woman had preserved from the time before her marriage. Stryker knew they were suffering, but neither uttered a word of complaint, a fact that did nothing to ease his conscience.

Mary knew that the lieutenant wasn't fit to walk a long distance and she'd accepted it. But again, that didn't make it any easier.

They'd left the cabin at first light that morning, planning to meet up with Birchwood and his infantry on the trail south. Stryker would then abandon Yanisin and his people to their own devices and use a series of forced marches to reach Fort Merit, hopefully before the Apaches attacked.

It wasn't a perfect plan, not even a good one, but it was all Stryker had, and at least he felt he was taking the initiative again.

He looked down at the woman. "How are you holding up, Mrs. McCabe?"

"It's hot."

Kelly's head was bent and her feet were dragging. She had earlier refused to sit on the horse in front of Stryker, but now he asked her again. This time the girl eagerly agreed, and he lifted her in front of him.

They had been walking for three hours and a look at Mrs. McCabe's face told Stryker that she too was growing exhausted. He drew rein, freed a stirrup and said, "Get up behind me, Mrs. McCabe."

The woman shook her head. "That's too much for the horse."

"He's a tough little bronc," Stryker smiled. "He can carry all three of us."

The woman had no argument left in her. She climbed up behind Stryker who kneed the criollo into motion. The horse's gait did not change and it seemed to handle the additional weight with ease.

Kelly leaned her head on Stryker's chest, lightly and tentatively at first, but then it grew heavier as the child slept.

The sky islands of the Chiricahuas soared above the three people on the little horse, dwarfing them into insignificance. Here and there eroded stone spires and columns rose out of thick tree canopies like the pillars of a ruined cathedral, ancient incense that smelled of pine still fragrant in the air. The sun had impaled itself on a peak and was motionless in the sky, unable to shake itself free. The entire vast land shimmered in the heat, distorting the way ahead, hard on the eyes, harder still on Stryker's stretched-taut nerves.

This was Apache country and no man who entered it, unless he was a fool, ever rode at ease.

And that was proved just thirty minutes later when three mounted Indians emerged from the shimmering landscape as though they were riding through a curtain of lace.

Over Stryker's shoulder Mary McCabe saw what he was seeing. She immediately slid off the criollo and lifted Kelly from the saddle. The girl was still asleep and her head rested on her mother's shoulder.

There was nowhere to hide, no time to run, but Stryker was a horse soldier and the woman knew that if it came to a fight she and Kelly would be an encumbrance.

Stryker racked the Henry and sat his saddle, waiting, his eyes fixed on the oncoming Apaches. He was still very weak, in no shape for a battle, but, as they had been for Mary, his options were limited.

All three of the Indians carried new Winchesters and they came on at a walk, unhurried, their flat, black eyes weighing Stryker, evaluating him as a fighting man.

Stryker quickly glanced around him. He saw nothing in the terrain that would give him an advantage.

Now that he'd looked at his hole card and didn't like what he'd seen, he gripped his rifle tighter and waited for the inevitable. No matter what, he would take his hits and survive long enough to fire two shots. Remembering what had befallen Hooper, he wouldn't abandon Mrs. McCabe and her daughter to the same fate.

The Apaches stopped ten yards away, and then one of them rode forward. He was young, stocky, bands of red and yellow paint across his nose and cheeks. At one time or another in his wild life, this warrior had been an Army scout.

Reining his pony alongside the criollo, the Apache stared hard into Stryker's face. Astonishment gave way to puzzlement and then to a wide grin. The warrior turned and enthusiastically beckoned the other two closer.

Stryker lifted the muzzle of the Henry an inch until it was pointed at the belly of the Indian closest to him. The man, still intent on studying the soldier's shattered features, didn't seem to notice. His head was inclined at an angle as he tried to imagine how the big officer had gotten that way.

As their leader had done, the other Apaches crowded around Stryker, staring at him in wonderment, excitedly discussing him in a language he did not understand.

One of the Apaches swung away and rode to where Mary and the child were standing. He studied the woman's face, then let out a wild yip of delight.

Stryker stiffened in the saddle. The reckoning had come, and he was ready.

The Apache slid off his horse, grabbed Mary's chin and turned her head so the others could see the terrible scar on her cheek. That immediately touched off a storm of laughter among the Indians that surprised Stryker. For some reason, Mary McCabe's scar was "a real thigh-slapper," as Joe Hogg would have said.

So far the Apaches had shown no hostile intent, and for now Stryker was content to let it remain that way.

The Apache let Mary go and mounted again. The warrior wearing the traditional war paint of the Army scout pointed to Stryker's face. "Ugly," he said. He pointed to the woman. "Ugh, same ugly." As his companions laughed, he said, "A good joke."

And with that, the three warriors rode away, heading north, their heads thrown back, still laughing.

Stryker felt the tension drain out of him. Hogg had once told him that Apaches were notional and that the white man did not share their sense of humor. Now, for some reason known only to themselves, a disfigured Army lieutenant accompanied by a scarred woman in the middle of the wilderness had struck them as funny.

Stryker didn't appreciate the joke, but he appreciated that it had saved their lives.

That night they camped two miles south of Rucker Canyon and its abandoned Army post. Sheltered by a narrow box canyon, Stryker built a small fire and they ate a hasty supper of broiled bacon and a few stale biscuits.

At first light, they were on the trail south again. And at noon they met up with Joe Hogg and Lieutenant Birchwood's depleted infantry company.

Chapter 16

Hogg was riding next to a huge man wearing a greasy buckskin shirt, his red hair falling in a tangled mass over his shoulders. A full beard covered his chest and when he looked at Stryker, then looked again, his black eyes were small and mean and full of malice.

Stryker smiled at Hogg. "Good to see you again, Joe."

"See you brung the whole family," the scout said.

Birchwood was a hundred yards behind Hogg. He cantered to Stryker and saluted. "Lieutenant Birchwood reporting, sir."

Stryker looked beyond the man and past the column of weary infantrymen. "Where are the Apaches, Lieutenant?"

The young officer shook his head. "We didn't find them, sir. The rancheria was abandoned, everyone gone."

"Did you encounter any Apaches?"

"No, sir."

"We did find this skunk, and a couple of others

with him who are now deceased," Hogg said. He leaned over in the saddle, shot out his booted foot and knocked the red-haired man off his horse.

The redhead hit the ground hard, raising a cloud of dust. He stayed where he was and cursed viciously at Hogg.

"His name is Silas Dugan," the scout said, smiling. "He's a scalp hunter by trade and a real good friend of Sergeant Pierce. In fact, Lieutenant, you might say they're partners."

Dugan got to his feet, spitting fury and hate. "I'm gonna kill you one day, Joe," he said. "You might be in bed with a whore or kneeling to say your prayers or singin' in the church choir, but I'm gonna walk right up to you an' scatter your brains, you son of a bitch."

Hogg shook his head and looked at the man. "Silas, all the time I've knowed you, you've talked big about what you was a-goin' to do to some white man or another. But all you've ever done is kill women and children and lift their scalps."

The scout laid both hands on the saddle horn and leaned into Dugan. "Now you shut your trap or I'll leave you to the first Apache warriors I come acrost. Know what they do to a scalp hunter, Silas?"

"That will do, Mr. Hogg," Birchwood said. "The prisoner will be delivered to Fort Merit"—he paused—"in one piece."

"You tell him, soldier boy," Dugan grinned.

Birchwood's head snapped around until he was looking at the man. "Dugan," he said, "shut your goddamned trap."

The scalp hunter shrugged, made a placating gesture with his hands and kept silent.

"This is a good time to rest your men, Lieutenant Birchwood," Stryker said. "We'll have a conference and Mr. Hogg, I want you to attend."

The scout swung out of the saddle as the infantrymen sought whatever shade they could find and lit their pipes. Hogg stepped to the criollo and helped Kelly down from the saddle, then Mrs. McCabe.

To Stryker's surprise, Hogg and the woman kissed tenderly, then clung to each other for a long while before parting. Finally the scout picked up Kelly in his arms and he and Mary held hands as he led them into the shade of some scattered junipers.

Stryker shook his head. He had always prided himself on being a perceptive man, but he had totally missed the budding relationship between Hogg and the woman. He smiled to himself. Joe Hogg was a good man, and Mary was a fine woman. They would be an excellent match for each other.

He swung stiffly out of the saddle and walked into the junipers, where Birchwood joined them. Hogg glanced back at the resting soldiers, and the young lieutenant smiled. "Don't worry, Mr. Hogg. Dugan is well guarded."

The scout nodded. "He's as slippery as a snake, Lieutenant. Don't trust him."

Stryker built a cigarette from his dwindling supply of tobacco and inhaled the smoke gratefully. Both Birchwood and Hogg were watching him, waiting for what he had to say.

What he really wanted to do was to interrogate

Dugan and force him to tell where he could find Rake Pierce, but more urgent Army business had to come first.

"Lieutenant Birchwood," he said behind a cloud of blue smoke, "the reason Yanisin's rancheria was abandoned is because the Apaches are moving north. That is why you didn't encounter any hostiles."

"Sir, you still expect an attack on Fort Merit?"

"Yes, if it hasn't already happened. Let the men have their rest now, because we are going to reach the post by a forced march. Your infantry will have to march day and night, rest little and live on water, cold bacon and biscuit. I want to be at the post within forty-eight hours, Lieutenant."

"My men can do it, sir."

"By God, sir, they'll have to do it."

Stryker looked at the soldiers who were sprawled in whatever shade they could find, talking quietly among themselves. Like all frontier Indian fighters, they were a ragtag bunch, but they looked bronzed and fit and their weapons were clean.

"Tell the men they have an hour to cook whatever salt pork they have left and soak their biscuit in the grease," he said. "It will serve as iron rations on the march."

Birchwood sprang to his feet and hurried away to carry out his orders, but Stryker's voice stopped him. "Oh, and Lieutenant, now would be a good time to boil up coffee. We won't have another opportunity to drink any for a while."

After Birchwood left, Stryker turned to Hogg. "Joe, bring Dugan over here. I want to talk to him."

The scout nodded, then said, "Here's what he won't tell you, but it's what I think, Lieutenant. I reckon Rake Pierce has no more guns to sell, but now he's trying to pick up the crumbs left on the plate. He and Silas are following the Apaches, preying on the women and children the warriors have stashed in canyons all over the Chiricahuas. An Apache scalp brings a hundred dollars in gold in Mexico and they ain't too picky about who once wore it, man, woman or child."

"You found Indian scalps on Dugan?"

"Eighteen, on his saddle and the saddles of the other two we kilt. A couple of the scalps could have been Mexican, but the rest were the genuine article."

"Do you think Dugan can lead us to Pierce?"

"Maybe. Ol' Silas will do anything to save his own skin, and he knows he's lookin' at twenty years in Yuma or worse."

"Joe, I'm not inclined to make a deal with the devil."

"Suit yourself, Lieutenant. But I'm just tellin' you how ol' Silas thinks." He smiled. "And you're right, he is the devil and he brings ten different kinds of hell with him."

Kelly was chasing a butterfly, wandering away too far, and her mother called her back. Hogg had been watching the child, and now he turned to Stryker again.

His voice was even, but gently chiding. "We have Fort Merit to consider, Lieutenant."

There was a time, very recently, when Stryker

would have snapped that he did not need to be reminded of his duty by a scout. But the people around him, the Apaches and the hard beauty and fierce dangers of the land itself were working small changes in him.

"You're right, I don't have time to chase after Pierce," he said. His fingers unconsciously strayed to the network of scars on his face. "Damn the man, damn him to hell."

"There might be a way, Lieutenant," Hogg said. "We can use Silas for bait, draw Rake Pierce in like a fly to shit."

Stryker's eyes held a question, and Hogg answered it.

"They got a partnership forged in hell and signed in blood and they need each other. Pierce is as mean and deadly as a rattlesnake, but he's not a patch on Silas. You take ol' Silas now—he says he'll cut any man, woman or child in half with a shotgun for forty dollars, and he's proved that plenty of times in the past. Killers like him are hard to find and Pierce won't let him go without a fight. That's just good business." Hogg shrugged. "Anyhoo, that's what I think."

"Joe, I know what Pierce thinks of his friends. He threw Hooper to the Apaches to play with." He shook his head. "Pierce won't risk his life to save Dugan."

"Lieutenant, Hooper didn't mean a thing to Rake. Back at Fort Merit they were drinkin' and whorin' buddies, but that don't go far once a man walks off the post. Pierce couldn't have cared less about the Englishman, but I reckon he worries a heap about Silas."

"How do we play it, Joe?"

"As much as I'd like Silas to hoof it, have him ride with you and Lieutenant Birchwood at the head of the column. That red beard of his is easy to spot, even at a distance."

"How many men do you reckon Pierce has with him?"

Hogg shrugged. "Scalp hunting is a dirty business and it can be dangerous, especially if the scalps you're hunting are Apache. He'll have gathered a bunch of renegades around him, all of them just as bad as he is."

"How many?"

"Enough to make a fight, Lieutenant, depend on it." Hogg got to his feet. "I'm going to see if the coffee's on the bile yet." His eyes shifted to where the criollo was grazing. "You found the Apache pony, huh?"

"Mrs. McCabe did." Stryker looked at the scout. "She's a fine woman, Joe."

"I know it." Hogg smiled. "Hell, for a spell there, I thought you was sweet on her your ownself. I was gettin' mighty jealous."

Stryker shook his head. "I had a woman. I don't want any other."

"You may change your mind one day, Lieutenant."

"Yes, the day my face goes back to the way it was. Maybe then."

Chapter 17

The column used up the rest of the daylight to cover eighteen miles, the men slogging through intense heat and clouds of biting black flies.

Already the sycamores, cottonwoods and flat-topped mesas of Turkey Creek were in sight. Mary McCabe rode behind Joe Hogg and Kelly was up on Stryker's saddle. The lieutenant had half-dozed for the past hour, exhaustion and the pain of his wounds sapping him.

Dugan, sullen and silent, rode between Stryker and Birchwood, his hands roped to the saddle horn, a noose around his neck. There was no one taking the point, adding honey to the trap Stryker hoped would lure Pierce.

Thirty minutes later, just as the light began to wane and the lengthening desert shadows crawled across the sand, the sky to the north turned a deep purple, a narrow band of burnished gold showing just above the horizon.

Thunder rumbled and ahead of the column lightning spiked. Searing bands of brilliant white bladed into the desert, throwing off forked tendrils that flashed across the looming cloud mass. Soon the whole sky, from horizon to horizon, seemed as though it were covered by the scrawled signatures of a demented god.

The wind rose, driving sand before it that ripped into the marching men like grapeshot fired from colossal cannons.

Then the rains came.

A few scattered drops at first were followed by a deluge, hammering from a sky as black as doom. The roars of thunder joined the clattering clamor of the downpour and the shriek of wind, dragging the day down into a cartwheeling pit of madness.

Soldiers, bent almost double, scattered into the foothills, seeking shelter wherever they could, the lightning, wind and rain eagerly stalking after them.

"Joe!" Stryker yelled. He was fighting his horse, and Kelly had buried her face in his chest. Beside him, Dugan tried to make his break, kicking his mount in the ribs. Stryker reacted instantly. He backhanded the man hard across the face and when Dugan reeled, he grabbed the end of the rope around his neck and yanked him from the saddle.

Suddenly Joe Hogg was beside Stryker, taking Kelly from him.

"Find shelter, Joe!" he shouted. "Get into cover!"

Hogg yelled something Stryker did not hear; then he vanished into the screaming maelstrom. Lightning struck close by, among the hills, the reverberating crash like the fall of giants. Terrified, the criollo reared and Stryker was thrown heavily to the ground.

For a moment the lieutenant lay still, gathering his wits and fighting pain. Then he climbed slowly and stiffly to his feet. He looked around him, his eyes scanning the reeling chaos of lightning and rain, but there was no sign of another living creature.

Stryker didn't see the rider until he was almost on top of him. The horse hit him a glancing blow and he staggered and crashed onto his back. Somewhere above the roar of the storm a rifle made a flat, emphatic statement, and then another.

Rising to one elbow, Stryker saw gun flashes among the foothills. He climbed erect, staggered on numb legs, then pulled his Colt. Rain pounded into his face and beat like a kettledrum on his hat.

A sudden lightning flash lit up the foothills and the rolling desert flatlands. It seemed to Stryker that the world was full of hurtling horsemen, shooting at unseen enemies among the hills.

Hooves pounded behind Stryker. He swung around and caught a fleeting glimpse of a half-naked Indian on a paint pony coming right at him, his feathered lance lowered for the kill.

Stryker moved to his right, but his ankle rolled on a rock and he fell, thumbing his Colt as he went down. The Indian pounded past, then slowly toppled off his horse.

Ignoring his pain, the lieutenant scrambled quickly to his feet. He fired between lightning flashes, marking his target's position. He had shot an Indian, but the enemies he was trying to kill were white men, and he was certain that Rake Pierce was leading them.

"Fire!" Birchwood's voice, coming from behind him.

Springfields crashed and a bullet split the air close to Stryker's head. He hit the ground as another volley venomously sang over him.

"Damn your eyes, Birchwood!" he roared. "Are you trying to murder me?"

"Advance!" the lieutenant yelled. "Fire at will."

A half dozen soldiers pounded past Stryker, and then Birchwood was kneeling beside him. "Sorry, sir," he said. "I took you for the enemy."

Now the fire from the foothills was steadier and Stryker was sure he could hear the staccato bark of Hogg's Henry.

Then, as quickly as it had started, the fight was over.

Hoofbeats receded in the distance and soldiers were firing a few last forlorn shots at shadows.

Birchwood rose to his feet. "Cease fire!"

The shooting staggered to a halt and soon the only sound was the racket of the rain and the grumble of thunder as the storm moved to the south.

Birchwood helped Stryker to his feet as Hogg emerged from the gloom. "It was Rake, all right, Lieutenant," he said. "I seen him clear and took a pot at him. Missed him clean."

Stryker nodded. "Over there, I downed an Apache."

Hogg shook his head. "He's Kiowa, Lieutenant. That's how come ol' Rake found us in the storm. A Kiowa can track damn near as good as an Apache and there are some who say even better."

"Where's Dugan?"

"Gone. An' three dead soldiers over there who tried to stop him."

"And Pierce's men?"

"The Kiowa dead and maybe a couple more of Rake's men winged, or maybe not." The scout hesitated a moment, then said, "They surprised us, Lieutenant, attacking out of the storm like that."

His failure to protect his men was a bitter pill to swallow.

Stryker turned on Birchwood. "Any other casualties?"

"I don't know, sir."

"Then goddamn you, Lieutenant, find out!"

His young face stricken, Birchwood saluted and strode away.

"How are Mrs. McCabe and Kelly?"

"They're fine." Hogg tried to find Stryker's eyes in the rain-lashed darkness. "A bit hard on the boy, wasn't you, Lieutenant? He did well, rallied his men under fire and mounted a counterattack."

Stryker smiled. "It doesn't do second lieutenants any harm to be reprimanded now and again. Don't worry, I'll make sure his actions are brought to the attention of Major Hanson."

Birchwood reported back a few minutes later. The news was bad. Three dead and one seriously wounded, a seventeen-year-old named Stearns who was shot through both legs.

Stryker was worried. This meant another delay, but there was no way around it. "We'll spend the night here, Lieutenant," he said. "At first light, rig up a travois for the wounded man. Use the Kiowa's pony."

Birchwood saluted and turned to go, but Stryker's sense of fair play would not let him remain silent. "By the way, Lieutenant, your behavior during the engagement was exemplary, and I will inform Major Hanson of this when we reach Fort Merit."

The young man smiled and saluted again. "Thank you, sir."

Watching Birchwood leave, Stryker wondered if he'd ever been that young. Then he realized he had once, when Millie had been in love with him. A thousand years ago.

Chapter 18

There was something wrong. . . . Seriously wrong . . .

Stryker again scanned Fort Merit with his field glasses. The adobes and jacals were deserted, but, given the threat of an Apache attack, that was to be expected. But there was no sign of life at the saloons or the hog ranch and the army buildings also seemed empty, a couple of barracks doors hanging open, moving back and forth in the wind.

No flag flew above the parade ground and one of the brass cannons was tipped over on its side.

"Damn it," Stryker whispered to himself, "where is everybody?"

He handed the glasses to Hogg. "Joe, what do you make of this?"

As Stryker had done, the scout studied the post for a couple of minutes, the glasses ranging all over the terrain and the mountains beyond.

Finally he lowered the glasses, his face troubled. "Looks like they left in an almighty hurry, Lieutenant."

"I don't see any sign of an Apache attack."

"Or Apaches either," Birchwood said, his own field glasses hanging on his chest.

"Mr. Hogg, let's ride ahead and take a look," Stryker said. "Lieutenant, if the coast is clear I'll wave you on, and you may bring in the company and Mrs. McCabe. If I don't show after thirty minutes, hightail it for Fort Bowie."

"Yes, sir."

Under a high, hot sun, Stryker and Hogg rode through the deserted jacals, and everywhere there were signs of a hurried departure. The tents of the infantry company had been struck and were nowhere in sight. Even the dogs that roamed around the post were gone.

Then they found their first dead man. The Mexican was sprawled outside the door to his adobe, facedown in the sand. A few silver coins were spilling out of his outstretched right hand and in his left he held an ornate crucifix. Blue flies buzzed around the bullet wounds in his back.

Sitting against the wall of a neighboring jacal was another body, this time one of Major Hanson's infantrymen. The man had died in the act of raising a canteen to his mouth and his eyes were still wide-open, staring intently into nothingness. There was a neat bullet hole between his eyes.

Hogg got off his horse and kneeled beside the dead soldier. After a while he looked up at Stryker. "Both his legs are broke, Lieutenant."

"What do you make of it, Joe?"

The scout shook his head. "I don't know. It could

be the work of Apaches, but I don't see any pony or moccasin tracks. Plenty of sign left by boots, though."

"How long ago?"

"Not long. Early this morning, maybe."

"Pierce?"

Hogg shrugged. "Your guess is as good as mine, Lieutenant."

"We'll check headquarters. Maybe Major Hanson left us a note."

Stryker waited until Hogg mounted, and then they rode slowly toward the parade ground. The scout had his rifle across the saddle horn, carried himself high in the saddle, and looked ready for anything.

It wasn't long in coming.

A shot rang out from the direction of the post hospital. A pause, then another.

Stryker pulled his Colt and kneed his horse into a fast canter. Beside him Hogg broke a little to the left, putting some fighting space between him and the lieutenant. The scout reached the hospital building first and leaped from his horse. Stryker watched him dash inside, then vanish from sight.

Hurting, Stryker swung stiffly out of the saddle. He turned and saw Birchwood and his men running across the parade ground toward him, rifles at the slant. His boots clumping on the hard-baked earth, Stryker stepped into the hospital—and almost tripped over a dead man.

Jake Allen lay on his back, shot twice in the belly at so close a range the skin around the wounds was blackened. He was unbuttoned and his pants and drawers had fallen down around his ankles. A combination of surprise and pain had already stiffened on his face and his eyes still held the horror he'd felt at the timing and manner of his dying.

Hogg and Birchwood stepped into the hospital at the same time. The young lieutenant saluted and said defensively, "Sir, your orders said nothing about gunshots, so I took it on my own initiative to come immediately to your aid."

Stryker smiled. "You did the right thing, Lieutenant."

Now he looked questioningly at Hogg and the scout said, "Something you should come look at."

All three men stepped out the rear door of the hospital. Beyond lay a hundred yards of sand, rock and cactus that gave way gradually to a low, mesquite and juniper-covered bluff. Behind the rise soared the vast bulk of a mountain peak, its upper slopes green with pine.

Hogg got down on one knee, and motioned to Stryker. "Take a look at that, Lieutenant."

Stryker bent and saw what the scout was showing him. It was a track, small, narrow, made by a woman's shoe.

"More of them heading toward the bluff," Hogg said. "I scouted over that way a piece, but didn't see hide nor hair of anybody. It's like the gal who left this track just vanished into thin air."

"Joe, who the hell is she?"

The scout shrugged. "White woman, slim, young enough to hightail it fast. That's all I can tell you."

"Lieutenant Birchwood, take some men and search the bluff. Find that woman, whoever the hell she is," Stryker said.

After the young officer left, he and Hogg walked back into the hospital building. The scout looked at the body. "Somebody sure saved me a bullet." His eyes ranged over the man's naked groin, and he smiled. "Ol' Jake sure is stiff, ain't he?"

Stryker nodded. "Before he rode two bullets into hell, he had the woman here." He shook his head. "What was Jake Allen doing at Fort Merit alone?"

"Maybe he wasn't alone, Lieutenant, at least not at first. For some reason he stayed behind."

"The woman?"

"As good a reason as any."

"It might help explain why he died, but it doesn't explain the deaths of the soldier and the Mexican."

"They're all tied together somehow, Lieutenant, and only the woman can tell us how."

"We'll find her," Stryker said. "Now it's time to take a look at the commanding officer's office."

Unlike the jacals and adobes around the post, the office showed no sign of a hurried departure. Everything was in its place and even the half-dozen sharpened pencils on the desk lay in a neat, soldierly row. A fresh sheet of paper was in the desk blotter and the coffeepot, empty and clean, sat on the stove.

Major Hanson had left no note.

"And why should he?" Stryker said to Hogg. "He figured we were heading for Fort Bowie with Yanisin and his people."

The scout nodded. "It looks like somebody higher up had a lick of sense and knowed Hanson couldn't hold Fort Merit with a company of infantry. I reckon he was ordered to pull out with the cavalry."

"But why leave a soldier behind?"

Hogg shrugged. "A deserter maybe, or a straggler from the half company you sent to reinforce the garrison?"

There was no answer to those questions and Stryker let them go. He glanced around him, not liking the echoing, ominous silence of the office, and stepped to the window. A couple of soldiers were pushing the brass cannon back on its wheels and a few more, their rifles at the ready, were checking out the saloons and general store.

After a while Stryker said, without turning, "We'll cross Apache Pass and head for Fort Bowie. I don't want the Apaches to catch us here."

This time he turned, smiling. "Joe, Mrs. McCabe and Kelly are walking across the parade ground beside the wounded soldier's travois."

"Will you excuse me, Lieutenant?" Hogg asked.

"Of course."

Stryker watched as Hogg and Mary embraced; then the scout put his arm around the woman's waist, took Kelly's hand and walked toward the post's married quarters. He felt a sudden twinge of envy that he instantly regretted. It was true that no one was ever glad at his coming or sad at his leaving, but that did not give him the right to be envious of the happiness of others.

Stryker turned away from the window, and built

a cigarette. He was lighting it when, to his surprise, Hogg stepped quickly inside. The man seemed agitated.

"Lieutenant, you can forget Fort Bowie, on account of how we're not going anywhere," he said. "There's talking smoke all around us."

Stryker didn't hesitate. "Call Lieutenant Birchwood and his men down from the bluff. I'm going to round up the others." He looked at the scout. "Hell, this is bad, Joe."

"About as bad as it gets," Hogg answered.

Chapter 19

"No sign of the woman, sir," Birchwood said, his face pale under his deep tan. "But I found out what happened to the relief column. For some reason Corporal Yates and twelve men made a stand on the bluff. They're all dead and stripped of their arms. I don't know what happened to the six others."

Stryker turned to Hogg. "Joe, I hate to ask you this with the Apaches so close—"

"I'll check it out, Lieutenant."

The scout left as he always did, silently, like a puff of smoke.

"How many effectives do we have, Lieutenant?" Stryker asked.

"Fourteen, sir. The wounded man, Private Stearns, you already know about."

"Where is he?"

"In the hospital."

"We'll have to move him. We can't defend the entire post."

"Sir, his . . . Private Stearns' left leg is black and it smells like rotten meat. I fear gangrene. It will have to be cut off if we are to save his life. I thought perhaps Mr. Hogg . . ."

"Perhaps. I'll have a word with him. In the meantime I want to look at the saloons and the hog ranch. One of them may be more defensible than any of the post buildings."

"What about the cannons, sir?"

Stryker smiled. "I don't think those relics have been fired since the war. Besides, Lieutenant, only white men stand in line and make themselves a target for grapeshot. The Apache fights a war of movement and he never stays long enough in one place for that."

Birchwood nodded. "You know a lot about the savages, don't you, sir?"

Stryker shook his head. "I don't know anything about Apaches, Lieutenant. But I do know, with a few men, we're being called upon to defend a military post against the best guerilla fighters in the world. Does that thought fill you with confidence?"

"No, sir."

"Me neither."

The Bull's Head saloon, where Stryker had first encountered Jake Allen, was a sod and canvas building and would offer no protection from bullets. The other saloon was a small, windowless adobe and was even less promising.

The hog ranch was farther out, a squat, adobe with an attached corral and to the right of that, a small barn, a chicken coop and an outhouse. There was also a well, usually dry.

Stryker and Birchwood walked in the direction of the ranch, their heads on swivels, constantly watching the smoke rising from the foothills on three sides of them. The Cabezas Mountains did not possess the same pillared majesty of the Chiricahuas, but they were raw and rugged, and the Apaches knew them well.

Stryker had the feeling he was being watched, that somewhere Geronimo was standing on a rocky plinth studying him with cruel, raven eyes that glittered with black fire.

It was not a reassuring sensation and it brought prickly beads of sweat to the lieutenant's scarred forehead.

The adobe had been built well, with thick walls and a sod roof that would resist fire. It had two windows to the front, one at the side facing away from the corral, and two at the back. There was a door leading to the outhouse and another at the front. Both were made of stout timbers to keep out the summer wind and the winter cold.

Inside, the single, dirt-floored room was partitioned into a half dozen tiny cells, each with a blanket for a door. A small bar stood at one end, the shelf behind holding a dozen or so bottles, and there was a rough pine table and benches.

Birchwood looked around him, his voice almost reverent. "So this is what a brothel looks like," he said.

"It's what a hog ranch looks like," Stryker said. "There are brothels and brothels, Lieutenant." He looked at the young man. "You've never been in one before?"

"Oh no, sir. I promised my betrothed on the day I graduated from West Point that I would not consort with fancy women and that my lips would ne'er touch whiskey. I stand by those promises."

"Well, I guess what you've never had you won't miss, Lieutenant." Stryker looked around him. "This place has excellent fields of fire and the walls are thick. We will make our stand here."

"A bit cramped, though, sir."

"With you, Mr. Hogg and me, we'll have seventeen defenders. Trust me, when the Apaches come at us in force and the bullets start flying, it won't seem so cramped."

"No, sir. I mean of course not, sir."

Stryker smiled. "Brothel fumes getting to you, Lieutenant?"

"I find the place a bit . . . unnerving, sir."

"Well, if you don't tell your betrothed that you're frequenting a bawdy house, then neither will I. Now get your men moved in here and bring as much ammunition as you can find."

"Yes, sir."

"And, Lieutenant, stay away from the bar. Suddenly you're inclining toward some mighty bad habits."

"Them boys up on the bluff were killed by Apaches, Lieutenant," Hogg said. "They were all scalped and cut up bad, and a few have arrows in them."

Stryker was irritated. "Why the hell did that corporal, whatever his name was, decide to fight up there?"

"Probably a sodbuster who didn't have the sense to know the Apaches could get around behind him an' attack every which way."

"Why didn't the Indians fire the buildings, Joe? Huh? Why didn't they fire the damned buildings?"

"My guess is they was scared off, or went after something else in a big hurry."

"But they're back, damn them."

"To finish what they started, maybe."

Stryker bowed his head in thought for a few moments, then lifted bleak eyes to Hogg. "It was Pierce. They went after Rake Pierce."

Hogg smiled. "You're stretching your mind out across some mighty big territory, Lieutenant."

"I know, but I've got a bond with that man, Joe. It was forged in the deepest fires of hell and nothing will ever break it. He's alive. Damn him, I can feel him, feel him—" Stryker made a grabbing motion with his right hand—"this close."

Hogg inclined his head. "Whatever you say. But one thing fer sure, Geronimo is back. As to the why of the thing, I don't know. It's hard to figure an Apache. He'll bamboozle you every time."

The first probing attack caught Stryker's men out in the open.

The lieutenant was watching Birchwood's infantry file toward the hog ranch when the Apaches struck, two dozen mounted warriors charging out of a narrow arroyo.

Hogg was bringing up the rear, carrying Kelly, his other arm around Mary McCabe's waist. Yet he fired first. In one fast, graceful motion he shoved the girl into Mary's arms, turned and drew his Colt.

In anyone else but Hogg, fanning the big revolver would have been a grandstand play, a fancy move full of sound and fury that signified nothing. But in the time it takes a man to blink, he hammered off five shots into the Apaches, killed a pony and sent the rider sprawling. The horse fell in a tangle of kicking legs and for a moment plunged the oncoming riders into confusion. Too close, another Apache mount got caught up in the dying pony's legs and went down, throwing its rider. The remaining Apaches swung wide, away from the wreck, and were firing their Winchesters from the shoulder. But those precious few seconds Hogg had gained gave the scattered soldiers time to deploy and unlimber their Springfields.

A short, sharp gunfight between Birchwood's men and the Indians followed, with no hits scored on either side. Then the Apaches were gone, leaving only a drifting cloud of dust to mark their passing.

The Apache who had been thrown by his dying horse had broken his neck and was as dead as he was ever going to be. The warrior who had collided with him had lost his rifle, but sprang to his feet, a knife in his hand, yelling his defiance. Stryker raised his revolver and cut him down.

Joe Hogg had been dead when he hit the ground, a bullet in the middle of his forehead. Mary McCabe, shot several times, lasted a few moments longer, gasping, her frightened eyes clouding in death even as Stryker kneeled beside her.

Kelly was unhurt, but she was hugging and kissing her dead mother, sobbing uncontrollably.

Birchwood stood beside Stryker, looking down at the dead. "Oh my God," he whispered, over and over again.

"Lieutenant, see to your men," Stryker snapped. "Occupy the adobe, then form a burial party."

It took a while, but Birchwood said, "Yes, sir."

"And Lieutenant, they had a few weeks of happiness. Maybe that's more than many of us are allowed."

"Yes, sir."

"Now go about your duties."

Stryker reached out and closed Hogg's eyes. He felt that he'd lost his good right arm, and more than that, he'd lost a friend. His only friend.

He looked to the mountains, now bathed in pale gold light as the sun dropped lower in the sky. The breeze brought the scent of pines and dust and of secret places where water tumbled and the gunmetal fish played.

Suddenly he felt very alone. Lonelier than the lonely land. Lonelier than the first man the day after Creation.

"God help me," Stryker said aloud.

Kelly turned, looking at him with tearstained eyes. But he had no other words, not for her or for himself.

Chapter 20

Before sundown, Stryker saw Joe Hogg and Mary McCabe buried.

Kelly was inconsolable, lost in grief that no child should be asked to bear. Crowded into the adobe, the soldiers did their best, rough and ready men who believed that if they only made the girl laugh, she'd feel better.

After a while they gave up, and Kelly retreated into a dark place they could not reach.

It was widely believed by Stryker and everyone else that Indians would not attack at night, fearing that if they were killed their souls would wander in eternal darkness. But Apaches were willing to fight at any hour, if they thought it would give them an edge.

Throughout the long night they fired probing shots at the adobe, and one of them coaxed cracked notes from a bugle and kept it up for a nerve wracking hour.

On the partition walls of the cells, the soldiers had found crude charcoal drawings of men and women engaged in various sexual activities, and, despite

Lieutenant Birchwood's prim disapproval, they became a topic of excited conversation and speculation until the men drifted off to sleep.

Birchwood had placed the bar off-limits to his soldiers, but Stryker poured himself a stiff drink and built a cigarette. To his joy he had found a supply of tobacco and papers at the general store, even though the Apaches had taken time to loot the place before they left.

Men were sprawled all over the floor and on the stained and odorous cots once used by the whores and their clients. Kelly was huddled in a corner, covered by a soldier's greatcoat, and seemed to be asleep. Private Stearns, his young face ashen, lay on the pine table, groaning softly, trying his best to be brave. Every now and then a soldier manning the windows stepped beside the youngster, trying to comfort him. Stearns' left leg was black from his toes to above the knee and would have to come off.

Stryker had brought a supply of knives and meat saws from the post kitchen and he would do the surgery at first light. He shook his head and whispered into the snoring darkness.

"Thanks, Joe, just what I needed."

The long night shaded into morning and outside birds began to sing. Men stirred and stomped their feet and pipes were lit. Birchwood gave his permission to light the stove just long enough to boil coffee, and Stryker silently approved. It was going to get hot enough in the crowded adobe as it was, and a burning stove would not help matters.

He had not slept. The constant Apache sniping

and the prospect of cutting off Private Stearns' leg had kept him awake throughout the night, though cigarettes and whiskey had helped.

Birchwood, exhibiting the resilience of the young, looked fresh and rested. He stepped beside the wounded soldier and his face fell.

"It's worse, Lieutenant, huh?" Stryker asked.

"Yes, sir. It has to come off soon." The young officer looked directly into Stryker's eyes. "It will kill him if we don't."

Birchwood had said "we." But Stryker knew there was no "we." There was only "you." What the boy was really saying was "It will kill him if *you* don't, First Lieutenant Stryker."

Back at the Point, this was called "the burden of command." He was the senior officer present, and it was his call. That's what Birchwood expected, and that's what the soldiers expected.

Stryker looked around him, searching the young, troubled faces that were waiting for him to say something, words of strength and wisdom that would reassure them. He gave up the search. There was no one else, only Steve Stryker. He had to do it.

"One of you men, bring a bottle of rotgut from the bar," he said. "I want this soldier good and drunk."

Stryker placed the flat of his hand on Private Stearns' heaving chest. "I have to take your leg off, son," he said. "There's no other way."

The teenager tried to smile. "I like to dance, sir. I was good at it back home in Tennessee. My . . . my sisters teached me, and my ma."

"One time at a cotillion I saw a man dance on

one leg," Stryker lied. "He did all right." He leaned closer to the youngster. "What's your given name, soldier?"

"Sam, sir. My pa set store by that name, said it was crackerjack."

Stryker smiled. "It sure is a crackerjack name, just like your pa said."

A soldier brought a bottle and with a rough, kindly gentleness raised the youngster's head. "Get this whiskey down you, Sammy, boy," he said. "I want to see you hymn-singing, snot-slingin' drunk."

A bullet shattered a window pane and thudded into the far wall, followed by a furious fusillade of fire that threatened to shred the adobe into Swiss cheese. The soldiers at the windows were shooting, but no hits were scored. Apaches moved like wraiths and were hard to kill.

A big, bearded trooper yelped as a bullet cut across his bicep and another got a faceful of splinters as a shot exploded the dry timber of the window frame.

Stryker watched Stearns try to drink, but the raw whiskey would not stay down and the youngster threw it back up, now tinged with scarlet blood. The inside of the adobe was thick with drifting gun-smoke, the stink of sulfur hung in the air and the amber light of the burning stove transformed the adobe into an antechamber of hell.

The coffee was boiling, but Stryker had a large, flat meat cleaver in the coals, the iron glowing dull red, and the fire stayed lit.

"Got one!" a soldier yelled.

"The hell you did!" somebody answered. "He's still running."

Birchwood had a half dozen men kneeling behind him at the door. He looked at Stryker who was standing motionless beside Stearns.

"Permission to sortie, sir," he said. "I can bring more of our rifles to bear."

Like a man waking from a dream, Stryker moved to a window. Outside, the Apaches were tightening the ring around the ranch, taking advantage of every scrap of cover. As Stryker watched, an Indian rose up, fired, and then disappeared again like a fleeting shadow.

A direct attempt to storm the adobe anytime soon was unlikely. The Apaches were playing a waiting game, trying to whittle down the number of men inside before launching an all-out assault.

Already two soldiers were wounded, both slightly, but the Apaches were finding the range and their fire was becoming more economical as they chose their targets.

Stryker stepped away from the window and raised his voice above the roar of gunfire. "Deploy in line, Lieutenant," he said, "and see if you can drive them back. A couple of volleys; then get inside again. For God's sake, don't linger."

He looked around him. "You men at the front windows, give Lieutenant Birchwood some covering fire." As the Springfields crashed, Stryker nodded to Birchwood and yelled, "Go, Lieutenant!"

The door swung open and Birchwood and his men dashed outside.

Immediately the tempo of the Apache fire increased, the flat bark of the Springfields a drumming counterpoint to the sharp ring of the Indian Winchesters.

There are times when a man does a wrongheaded thing and later he can't explain the why or the wherefore of it. Stryker knew he was in command, aware of the fact that he should not risk his life rashly and unnecessarily. Yet he drew his Colt and plunged from the adobe, his eyes seeking a target the instant he got outside.

Birchwood's men were kneeling in line, firing steadily. The Apaches, sensing the kill, had left cover and had formed into a loose arc, working their Winchesters.

Stryker emptied his revolver at an Indian wearing a red headband and fancy Mexican vest, and was sure he'd scored a hit. But the man vanished from sight and there was nothing to mark where he'd been but a wisp of dust.

An Apache fell to Birchwood's fire, and then one of his men toppled forward, his faced covered in sudden blood. A bullet tugged at Stryker's sleeve and a second kicked up dust at his feet. Another Apache went down, and they began to give ground, moving back, seeking cover again.

"Inside, Lieutenant," Stryker yelled. "We burned them."

He had reloaded his Colt and fired it dry before following Birchwood and his men into the adobe. The soldier who'd been shot was dead and they left him where he lay.

As he slammed and bolted the door behind him, Stryker's reeling mind betrayed him. Unbidden, the thought came to him, "Please, God, let Private Sam Stearns be as dead as the man outside."

Suddenly ashamed of himself, he stepped beside the young soldier. Stearns was still alive, his blue eyes huge and frightened in his ashen face. As bullets rattled into the adobe, Stryker spared a quick glance at Kelly. The girl was terrified, but she was still huddled silent in a corner and was unhurt.

The lieutenant turned his attention to Stearns' leg. Someone, probably Birchwood, had ripped the youngster's pants to allow for the gangrene's grotesque swelling. The leg itself was black, stinking, shining in the half-light like a gigantic, loathsome slug.

"Sir . . ." Stearns began. He could say no more, the words dying on his lips.

Stryker nodded. "I know, son. I know." He laid his hand on the boy's fevered forehead. "Very soon you're going to have to be very brave."

"Yes, sir, I know." His eyes were haunted as if he stood, trembling, at a door marked FEAR. "The trouble is, sir, I'm not very brave."

"Soldier, you're doing just fine so far," Stryker said. "When this is over I'm going to have Lieutenant Birchwood make you a corporal."

The boy managed a wan smile. "I'd like that, sir."

"Those stripes will be on your sleeve in no time." Stryker turned. "Lieutenant, I need two men." When the soldiers stepped to the table, he said, "Hold him down."

A bullet ricocheted off the iron stove, sang its vindictive song, then buried itself in a wall. At one of the windows a soldier fired, cursed, and fired again.

"You've got a good hold of him?"

One of the soldiers, yet another frightened youngster, nodded, pressing down hard on Stearns' shoulders.

"Then let's get it done," Stryker said. He picked up his instruments, a razor sharp kitchen knife and a bone saw. It was not yet time for the saw and he laid it aside.

Bending over, he poised the knife over Stearns' leg. Then he cut deep.

Chapter 21

Private Stearns' scream was immediately echoed by Kelly's terrified shriek. The girl was standing, her eyes transfixed on the body lying on the table. A soldier moved to comfort her, but she ducked away from him and cried out again.

Sweat beaded on Stryker's brow and his hands were crimson, slippery, slick, slimy with blood. Tears ran down the cheeks of the younger of the two soldiers holding down Stearns' arching body, and his lips moved in what might have been a prayer.

Green bile rising in his throat, Stryker sliced deeper, deeper still. Blood spurted from the soldier's leg, gushing fountains of red, splashing the front of the lieutenant's shirt.

The firing had stopped. The Apache, as curious as deer, looked at one another, wondering what was going on inside the adobe.

There! Stryker saw the white of bone.

He set the knife aside and picked up the bone saw.

The saw bit into green bone, skidding, making a

noise like grinding corn. Stearns was beyond screaming. His mouth was wide-open, but he made no sound.

Breathing heavily, Stryker worked the saw back and forth. He shook stinging salt sweat from his eyes.

My God, would the bone never cut?

Then he was through and he used the knife again. Now it was like cutting fatty pork, greasy and slick.

The leg was free. The stump was red, raw, pumping gore.

"Birchwood!" No time for the military courtesies. "Bring the cleaver."

The young lieutenant tried the wood and steel handle of the cleaver, jerked his burned hand away, then wrapped a rag around his hand.

"The cleaver, goddamn you!" Stryker yelled.

Stearns was screaming again, bucking wildly against the strong hands of the soldiers holding him.

The boy was in mortal agony, Stryker knew. But worse was to come. He knew that too.

Gingerly taking the hot handle of the cleaver, he quickly shoved the cherry-red steel blade against the raw, scarlet meat of the stump.

Stearns screamed into the sizzling silence. Only once. Then a ringing quiet.

The youngster's eyes were wide-open, filled with the memory of pain. The two soldiers, feeling the life go out of Stearns, lifted their hands off his shoulders.

Stryker opened his fingers and let the cleaver clang to the floor.

"Sir, his poor heart just give out," the older of the two soldiers said. "It couldn't take it no more."

Lifting bleak eyes to the man, Stryker said nothing. Now the bitter gorge was rising in him and his mouth filled with saliva that tasted like acid.

He turned away, bent over and retched uncontrollably. He threw up everything that was in his stomach, then gagged convulsively on its emptiness.

"Try this, sir." Birchwood was beside him, a cup of coffee in his hand. "It might help."

Stryker took the cup and with bloodshot eyes looked over the room. "You men," he said, "step careful over here. I made a real mess."

His thoughts turned inward. A mess of everything.

The coffee cup in his hand, Stryker stepped back to Stearns' body. Seemingly out of nowhere, slow black flies were angling above the bloody stump. He walked into a cell, dragged a blanket off the cot and spread it over the youngster's body. The soldiers were watching him, their eyes neither accusing nor sympathetic. Just . . . watching.

He felt he had to say something, anything. In the end, all he could manage was "I'm sorry." Words as inadequate as they sounded.

Stryker hadn't really expected "You did your best, sir," or "Sam was too far gone, sir," but what he didn't anticipate was total silence. It was not a hostile quiet and in its emptiness it did not apportion blame. Perhaps it was just dull resignation, that and the awareness that come night the moon would rise but they would not see it because they might all be as dead as Private Stearns.

Speaking into the vacuum, Stryker said, "I just wanted all of you to know that I tried."

This time there was no answering silence. Soldiers shuffled their feet, lit their pipes or stepped to the stove for coffee. The men manning the windows found sudden interest outside. Flies droned and gorged under the table amid the blood puddles. Kelly was sobbing quietly, but Stryker, who did not know how to comfort himself, could do nothing for her.

He looked at his hands, crusted in rust red. There was no water to spare to wash them. Stryker smiled a bitter little smile. Yes, he'd been caught red-handed, demonstrating his lack as a leader and as a man.

The early morning brightened and hard sunlight bladed through the windows, catching up flickering dust motes. In the cruel illumination Stryker's disfigured face was a fearsome parody of his once handsome features and men did not look at him, or, if they did, turned quickly away, shocked by what they'd seen.

He drank his coffee, his churning belly slowly settling.

Then the Apaches started firing again.

By noon, another soldier was dead and two were wounded, one with a sucking chest wound who could not live. As far as anyone could tell, since the sortie outside, not a single Apache had even been scratched.

The Apache fire was increasing as more warriors, coming up from the south, joined in the battle. As Indian confidence grew, Geronimo had sent in mounted attacks, the warriors boldly riding right up to the adobe. The soldier with the chest wound had been struck by a lance hurled through a window. And, as the whooping Apache rode away, he'd demonstrated his disdain for the marksmanship of those inside by showing them his bare ass.

Stryker could not fault Birchwood's infantrymen. They were green troops, hastily recruited and trained for the Indian Wars, and this was their first taste of fighting Apaches, a deadly, ruthless enemy much their superior.

Joe Hogg could have made a difference, but Joe was dead. His Henry was propped in a corner and Stryker, ignoring the bullets zinging through the windows, crossed the room and picked up the rifle.

If he could get to one of the saloons, he could lay down a good fire and attack the Apaches from the rear. That would give Birchwood another chance to try a breakout and catch the Apaches off guard. It was a slim chance, but it was the only chance any of them had. If he made it to—

The Apache fire suddenly ceased.

A soldier at the window closest to him was staring outside, his eyes wide, his jaw slack. "What the hell?" the man said.

Stryker stepped to the window and saw what the soldier saw. "Well, I'll be damned," he said.

Chapter 22

A red-haired woman was walking across the dusty, sun-splashed ground toward the adobe.

Her dress was stained and torn and her hair hung over her shoulders in dirty tangles. She walked purposely, neither looking to the left nor right, her eyes fixed on the building.

All Indians, but especially the Apache and Navajo, had a superstitious dread of madness, believing that sufferers had been possessed by a powerful, malevolent demon. One by one they left cover and shrank back from the woman, watching her with black, wary eyes.

She was a *nepotonje,* a bear watcher, since all understood that the demon often reveals itself in that guise. The more pragmatic Sioux would call her simply, *witkowin,* crazy woman, but the Apache knew better than that.

The flaming red hair was unmistakable and Stryker recognized her immediately as the silent, staring woman he'd rescued from the Apaches. He assumed she'd have left with the other women from the post, but, deranged as she was, she must have run away and hidden in the hills.

But Jake Allen had found her in the hospital, tried to force himself on her, and she'd killed him. That would explain the gunman's death, but it shed no light on what he was doing at the abandoned Fort Merit in the first place.

As he saw the woman reach the adobe and a soldier unbolted the door for her, Stryker felt a vague pang of disappointment. After Joe Hogg had found female tracks on the bluff, Stryker had harbored a flicker of hope that somehow Millie had come back, looking for him. He had not fanned the flames of that hope, knowing how foolish it was, yet now he realized that a feeble, dying spark had still lingered in him.

The woman stepped inside, looking around her. Her eyes showed no recognition of the soldiers, or any interest in where she was. But she did see Kelly. Without a word she crossed the room, her battered shoes clinking through the empty brass shells littering the floor, and sat beside the girl. Kelly looked at her warily, but the woman reached out and took her in her arms, laying her head on her breast.

"Sleep now, child," she whispered.

Those were the first words Stryker had ever heard her say.

Apaches didn't scare worth a damn and although the crazy woman had unnerved them, they soon resumed firing on the adobe.

"Mr. Birchwood," Stryker said. "A word, if you please."

The young lieutenant stepped beside him and, his breeding coming to the fore, tried to say all the right things. "Don't blame yourself, sir," he said. "No one could have done better." He looked at the blanketed body. "Private Stearns must have had a weak heart."

"There was nothing wrong with his heart, Lieutenant. Without ether or even whiskey, the pain was just too much for him to bear. I'm to blame. I'm a damned butcher, not a surgeon."

Birchwood would not be moved. "It had to be done, sir. It fell to you and you did your best."

Bullets thudded into the adobe. Stryker glanced out of a window and saw the Apaches massing for another mounted attack.

Stryker had intended to tell Birchwood about his plan to reach one of the saloons and catch the Indians in crossfire. He pushed that aside for now and stepped to the window. One of the soldiers moved back and Stryker took his place. He was aware of his limitations. A fair hand with the revolver, he barely passed muster at the Point in rifle shooting, coming in dead last out of a class of thirty-eight.

Now he steeled himself. The Henry wasn't a cumbersome model 1869 Cadet Rifle and maybe he could do better. He had to do better. He racked a round into the chamber and waited for the attack.

It never came.

The Apaches suddenly faded back into the hills, leaving behind them only emptiness and silence. As

Stryker watched, a dust devil spun across the parade ground and abruptly collapsed into a puff of sand. A piece of yellow paper, tossed by the breeze, fluttered around the adobe like a moth before rising higher into the air and vanishing from sight.

From behind Stryker, a man asked, "Why the hell did they pull back like that?"

No one answered him because no one knew.

Stryker walked to the door, stepped outside and looked around him. The peaks of the Chiricahuas were bathed in afternoon light, their lower slopes green. A bird called. The scent of cedar and sage hung in the air like a thin mist, as subtle and understated as the French perfume of a beautiful Washington belle. Deep in the bunch grass, crickets sawed tunes on their serrated legs, filling the morning with scratchy sound.

The riders came from the west—dirty, shaggy men mounted on small, wiry ponies.

Stryker had left his field glasses in the adobe. He took off his slouch hat and held it high against the sun, his eyes squinting in the glare, trying to make out the manner of these men.

He reached down and unbuttoned his holster flap.

If this was Rake Pierce and his renegades, he would do no talking. He would draw his gun and shoot the man dead. The chances were that he'd die right after, but it would be worth it if he could drag Pierce down into hell with him.

The men rode closer and Stryker was aware of Birchwood's dozen soldiers shaking out into a line

behind him. If a fight came, it would be up close and personal, and even green troops would not miss at that range.

And neither will I, Stryker promised himself. *Neither will I.*

Chapter 23

The three riders taking the point were all big men wearing dusty range clothes, pants tucked into scuffed boots that sported spurs as big and round as teacups. Each wore a Colt on his hip and had a Winchester booted under his left knee.

They drew rein when they were five feet from Stryker.

"Howdy," the older man said, "name's Abel Warden from over to Tucson way. I've got three hundred head of beeves for Fort Bowie coming up about half an hour behind me." He waved a hand to the man on his right. "This is my foreman, Arkansas Charlie Mullins, and this young feller here"—he nodded toward the man on his left—"is John Warden, my oldest son and segundo."

Abel Warden laid his hands on the saddle horn, his eyes ranging over the battle-scarred adobe and the dead soldier still lying in the dust in front of the building.

"You've been through it," he said.

Stryker nodded. "Apaches. They quit when they

saw you coming." He smiled. "I don't think that's going to be a permanent arrangement."

He introduced himself and Birchwood, then said, "You know Nana is out and joined up with Geronimo?"

"Heard that. Figgered they'd head south into Old Mexico, though. Back in Tucson, they say General Crook is headed for the Territory to lead another expedition against the Apaches."

"I hadn't heard that."

"Well, it's what they say. 'Lead another expedition,' was how it was put to me."

Arkansas Charlie and the younger Warden were staring at Stryker with that slack-jawed, rube-at-a-carnival-freak-show look he'd come to know so well. Abel, older and maybe wiser, didn't let it show.

The man's eyes ranged across around the post again, then to the dozen soldiers, then back to Stryker. "This all you got, Lieutenant?"

"This is it. Everybody else is at Fort Bowie."

Warden nodded. "Maybe you should come with us."

"How many drovers with you, Mr. Warden?"

"Us three and three others." He saw a flicker of doubt fleet across Stryker's face. "They're all good men, Lieutenant, and they've fit Indians before. Comanche mostly, and Kiowa. They'll stand."

Warden nodded in the direction of the cottonwoods. "The creek over there still got water?"

"Some. But three hundred head of cattle will drink it dry."

"Good. Then there'll be none left for the Apaches."

"One thing, Mr. Warden: I have womenfolk with me, a young girl and a crazy lady. And two wounded soldiers, one of them real bad."

"Can they walk? I got no wagon, only a pack mule."

"They can walk. The badly wounded man will die real soon."

Warden nodded. He turned to his foreman. "Charlie, you and John bring up the herd."

When the men had left, Warden followed Stryker to the adobe. He swung out of the saddle and set a foot inside, but quickly stepped back again, gulping air.

"Whoa, Lieutenant, no disrespect," he said, "but I can't stomach that stink. It could turn a man for sure."

"I have two dead men inside," Stryker said. He did not elaborate. "And it's hot."

"Kill any Apaches?"

"Maybe two. I don't know. The Apaches dragged them away."

"They'll do that. They always try to recover their dead."

Warden's gaze scanned the mountains around him. "Which way did they go?"

"North, back into the hills."

"How many?"

"Again, I don't know. Forty, fifty, at least."

"They'll be back." Warden thought for a while, then said, "I'll have the boys cut out a couple of head and leave them here. Apaches are always hungry and they may wait to fill their bellies before they come after us."

"They might," Stryker allowed.

"Or they might not," Warden said. "Comanches are notional, so are Kiowa, but they don't come close to Apaches in contrariness."

A half hour later, Warden's bony herd spread out along the creek. "They've been living on mesquite beans since damn near we left Tucson," the man offered by way of explanation. "I think every blade of grass is burned down to the roots between here and the Colorado."

The rancher's three other riders were just as shaggy and trail-worn as their boss, but they looked like tough and competent men and they kept their tongues still and rifles close.

While the cattle watered, Birchwood's infantrymen buried their dead, including the soldier and Mexican from the jacals, both of them already badly decomposed.

"Sir, we have a problem," Birchwood said, saluting.

To Stryker's surprise, he'd found all three of their horses still in their stables. It seemed that the Apaches, confident of victory, had left them there to be picked up later.

Now he stroked the criollo's nose, enjoying the relatively cool gloom of its stall and he looked at Birchwood, his eyes asking a question.

"It's about Private Carter, sir. The chest wound."

"What about him?"

"To be brutally frank, sir, he's not dead yet." The

young officer hesitated and then said, "I don't want to leave him behind for the Apaches."

"Nor do I, Lieutenant. We'll use the travois again. Mount it behind one of the horses."

"He won't survive the journey to Fort Bowie on a travois, sir, and he'll be in great pain. He's already suffering dreadfully."

Suddenly Stryker was irritated. "Then what do you suggest I do, Lieutenant? Shoot him?"

"No, sir. Private Carter is one of my men. I'll shoot him. But I need an order from you to that effect."

Irritation turned to anger. "Mr. Birchwood, you wish to salve your conscience with the excuse that you were only following my order. You're right. Carter is one of your men. If you plan to shoot him, then the responsibility lies with you."

"I was neither trying to evade my responsibility nor salve my conscience, sir," Birchwood said stiffly. "Since you are in command, I thought you should give the order."

Stryker's anger died. Birchwood was right; he was in command and he was the one to give the order. Besides, he already had blood on his hands. He'd shot Hooper after the Apaches had gotten to him and one mercy killing was much like any other.

But it shouldn't be like this. It was not meant to be like this. He had never intended to make these life-and-death decisions.

Stryker's future career had been all mapped out for him, a handsome tin soldier who married the colonel's daughter and would make an excellent career for himself in Washington. He shouldn't be here, in a stinking stable in the middle of a stinking desert, listening to a boy second lieutenant ask him for his permission to kill a man.

"Mr. Birchwood," he said, not looking at the lieutenant, his expression empty, "If Private Carter does not show much improvement by the time we leave for Fort Bowie, I order you to shoot him, to spare him from further suffering and to prevent him from falling into the hands of the enemy."

Now he looked at Birchwood. "Would you like that order in writing?"

For a moment the lieutenant seemed scandalized. He had grown up in a society where a gentleman's word was his bond and was never questioned. To doubt Stryker, an officer and a gentleman by writ of Congress, would be to betray his own class and everything it held dear.

"That, sir," he said, his face pale and tight around the mouth, "will not be necessary."

Stryker understood perfectly and did not press the matter. "Very well, Mr. Birchwood, carry on."

The young man saluted sharply and left. Stryker looked around the shadowed barn and whispered aloud, "Where the hell are you, Joe? I need you."

The only sound was the stomp of Birchwood's bay as it shook off flies and a distant shout from one of Abe Warden's drovers.

Stryker walked into the bright sunlight and his eyes moved to the hills where the Apaches waited. . . .

Waiting for what?

Chapter 24

"I figure to drive the herd right through Apache Pass, taking the old military road, then swing south to Fort Bowie," Abe Warden said. "We should arrive there by nightfall if the pass ain't grazed out, we don't get a prairie fire and the Apaches don't stampede the cattle."

"How about water on that route?" Stryker asked.

"There's water at Apache Springs, Lieutenant, and grass. We can rest the herd there for a spell."

"Then we should move out immediately. Where do you want my men?"

"My drovers will stay close to the herd. Maybe a couple of sod'jers out on the point and the rest can bring up the drag."

"I'll ride point, Mr. Warden."

"Suit yourself, Lieutenant. Just give me plenty of warning if you bump into hostiles."

"There will be cavalry patrols in the pass. I believe the Apaches will stay clear."

Warden nodded. "Well, sir, I don't put that much stock in the Army or the Apaches. Both will do as they please. And, in the case of the Apaches, the last damn thing a man expects."

The rancher's eyes lifted over Stryker's shoulder. "Charlie!" he yelled. "Start moving 'em out. We're heading for the pass." He glanced at Stryker. "If you'll excuse me, Lieutenant . . ."

"Of course."

As Warden bustled away, Stryker walked to the adobe and stepped into its stench. The wounded soldier lay on a cot in one of the rooms, Birchwood standing over him.

"How is he?" Stryker asked.

It was an unnecessary question. Private Carter's chest bubbled blood and fluid with every labored breath and lilac death shadows were gathering under his eyes and in the hollows of his unshaven cheeks.

"He's dying, sir. But not fast enough."

"We're moving out, Mr. Birchwood. Your men will follow the herd and flank it where the terrain allows."

"Yes, sir." Birchwood was only half listening.

Stryker stepped into the cabin and looked down at the red-haired woman, who seemed much younger than he'd first thought. Kelly was still in her arms, her eyes frightened. "What is your name?" he said, trying to pitch his rough voice in a softer tone.

To his surprise, the woman answered him, her green eyes on his. "My name is Fedelia Lacy. I am twenty-three years old."

"Can you ride a horse, Fedelia?"

"Yes."

"Good. We're headed for Fort Bowie. I'll give you a horse and you will ride with Kelly. Do you understand?"

"Kelly is nice, but she's so sad. Her mother was killed by the Apaches."

"Yes, I know. Now you must come with me and I'll saddle your horse."

The woman rose to her feet and held Kelly close to her. "Will you hang me?"

Stryker was taken aback. "No, of course not. Why would I do such a thing?"

"I killed a man. Over there in the hospital. He wanted to touch me and I've been touched by too many men. His gun was in his holster and I grabbed it and I shot him."

"Fedelia, he was a bad man. You were only defending"—Stryker almost lapsed into a false, gentlemanly language and said, "your honor," but instead he said—"yourself."

"He killed the soldier who had stayed behind to look for me. The soldier was asleep on a cot and the bad man broke his legs with an ax. He dragged the soldier away and later he shot him while offering him water. Then he said he'd killed a Mexican who'd begged him for his life. He said he'd killed the Mexican just for fun. He said the same thing would happen to me if I wasn't nice to him and be his whore."

"Then you shot him and ran away into the hills?"

"Yes. The Apaches left me alone."

"Fedelia, the bad man's name was Jake Allen. I don't know why he came back here."

"He said he was going to kill a cavalry scout. He was looking for him."

Gently, Stryker took the woman's arm, but she cringed away from him. "Sorry," he said. "Let's go get your horse."

He turned and saw Birchwood standing at the door to the cell, his Colt in his hand.

"I'll saddle your bay, Mr. Birchwood."

The young lieutenant said nothing, his eyes empty.

Stryker was halfway to the stables when he heard the shot.

Two different ecological systems collide in Apache Pass. The high, hot Chihuahuan Desert of New Mexico to the east weds with the lower, and much hotter, Sonoran Desert to the west, and barbarous bouquets of prickly pear, agave, yucca, sotol and cholla mark the union. Mountain mahogany, piñon, wild oak and juniper grow higher in the canyon, completely covering its raw, rocky slopes.

Stryker had been riding for an hour and the herd was a mile behind him. He was learning from bitter experience that the Apaches were a formidable, merciless enemy, desert fighters who had no superior. He feared them greatly and he knew he was right to do so.

He rode the criollo at a walk, Joe Hogg's Henry across his saddle. Here in the pass it was very hot and there was not a single cloud in a sky the color of bleached-out denim. His eyes constantly scanned the ridges, but he saw no movement, and there was no sound but the steady hoof falls of his horse and the creak of saddle leather.

He had seen no cavalry patrols.

Smelling water, for Apache Springs was not far ahead, the criollo tossed its head, the bridle ringing, and was eager to go. Stryker held it back, his uneasy eyes studying the land around him.

He found partial shade under a rock overhang and drew rein. He built a cigarette and lit it, liking the harsh, dry taste of the tobacco. He was still weak from his wounds and very thirsty, tormented by memories of the foaming steins of Anheuser-Busch beer that were always on hand for the enlisted men when Fort Merit celebrated holidays.

Stryker finished his smoke and stubbed out the butt against the heel of his boot. He kneed his horse into motion and headed for the springs.

As he'd expected, the only water source for miles around was guarded by a reinforced infantry company, and the officer in charge kept him in his field glasses until he rode closer and could be identified.

Stryker sat his horse and saluted the infantry captain. "Sir, I'm bringing in twelve infantry from Fort Merit under Second Lieutenant Dale Birchwood. Those, and three hundred head of cattle and six drovers."

The captain looked beyond Stryker back to the pass.

"They're about half an hour behind me, sir, depending on how fast those beeves walk."

The captain was small and slender with a trimmed,

spade-shaped beard. Stryker thought he looked prissy, a spit-and-polish soldier. He felt shabby and dirty by comparison. "Lieutenant, we were under the impression that you were bringing in old Yanisin's people, to be returned to the San Carlos," the captain said.

"Skedaddled," Stryker said, purposely using one of Joe Hogg's words. "Every last one of them had gone to join Nana and Geronimo."

"Did you pursue?"

Stryker looked around him. The spring, crystal clear, bubbled out of the earth and fell into a rock basin shaded by juniper and wild oaks. Emerald green moss clung to the rocks around the basin's rim and among the exposed roots of the oaks. The air smelled clean, of wet fern and of the water that splashed with diamond brightness into the tank.

Finally he said, "No, Captain. All the signs showed the Apaches heading north and I suspected they planned an attack on Fort Merit. I sent half of my infantry company ahead, and later we reached the post by a forced march. Unfortunately, we were in turn besieged by the Indians."

"And you decided to march here."

"Yes, sir, that's what I decided."

The captain was silent for a while; then his flitting eyes moved to Stryker's face, quickly sliding away as though they'd been burned. "All things considered, Lieutenant, you could have done better. But you can explain your actions to General Crook."

"You weren't there, Captain. Neither was he."

Anger flushed in the officer's sallow face. "Don't

be impertinent, sir!" Before Stryker had a chance to answer, he said, "Dismount. Have yourself a drink, then come look at this."

Stryker swung out of the saddle, accepted a canteen from a soldier and drank deep. He then followed the captain to a low rise just east of the spring. The officer pointed. "Your Apaches passed that way not an hour ago, headed into the Chiricahuas. I sent a message to the fort to report the movement and I have no doubt General Crook will pursue the hostiles immediately."

"Did you engage them, Captain?"

"My orders are to guard the spring, not to engage the enemy."

"Still, you could have slowed the Apaches and given the general some time to mount an attack."

"I repeat, those were not my orders."

Stryker nodded. "Maybe, but all things considered, Captain, you could have done better. But you can explain your actions to General Crook."

The officer looked like he'd been slapped, his cheekbones rouged with rage. "Damn you, sir, you are impertinent. Report immediately to the general and know that I plan to inform him of your insubordination. I will direct the others when they get here."

Stryker saluted smartly, turned on his heel and swung into the saddle. As he rode toward the fort he felt the captain's eyes burn into his back. He had just made an enemy.

Chapter 25

"Lieutenant Stryker?"

General Crook's startled question hovered in the air like a wounded moth.

"Yes, sir."

"Jesus Christ, man, I hardly knew ye. What happened to your face?"

"A shackle iron, sir."

"Explain."

Stryker did and Crook fell silent afterward. Crook did not look like a soldier, in his shabby canvas jacket and battered pith helmet. His beard split at the chin into two forks that hung on his chest; he could have been a slightly deranged poet, not a famous Indian fighter.

"And the girl you were to marry, that Colonel What's-his-name's daughter?"

Stryker touched his face, but said nothing.

"I see. Better off without her in that case."

He waved a hand. "Sit down, Lieutenant, and make your report. Be brief; I don't have much time."

Going into a little more detail than he had with the captain, but using as few words as possible, Stryker told of his failed mission to bring in Yanisin's tribe and his fights with the Apaches.

He then mentioned the former sergeant and murderer Rake Pierce and his gun-running and scalp-hunting businesses.

"I believe by now he's back in the Chiricahuas somewhere," Stryker said.

Crook nodded. "Interesting. And a pity about Yanisin. He's about as tame as an Apache can get." He sat back in his wicker chair and stroked his beard, thinking. Finally he said, "Lieutenant, I feel there is little to criticize in your actions. You did as well as can be expected with the limited force at your disposal. You will give me your report in writing, of course."

"Yes, sir."

A tap-tap on the office door. "Enter!" Crook yelled.

Colonel Mike Devore stepped inside and Stryker sprang to his feet. The colonel stuck out his hand. "Good to see you again, Lieutenant, and all in one piece."

Stryker took the man's hand and smiled. "I was carrying Apache lead for a while, sir. But I'm on the mend."

"You'll have to tell me about—"

"Yes, yes, Colonel, I'm sure Lieutenant Stryker will later. Is your regiment ready to leave?"

"Yes, sir."

"Then keep in close contact with Geronimo and his people. I'll follow on with the infantry and mountain howitzers."

"Yes, sir." Devore hesitated, then said, "Did you sign the authorization for Lieutenant Stryker's promotion?"

Crook looked baffled.

"I left it on your desk, sir."

Crook glanced at the piles of papers scattered across his desk and shook his head. "That will have to wait, I'm afraid."

Stryker grinned. "Probably just as well, sir. The captain in command of the detail at the spring plans to report me for insubordination."

"Ah, Captain Forrest," Crook said. "Damn that man—he's forever reporting people. I'll give him a hearing, as I always do, and then forget I even spoke to him." He looked at Devore. "I'm sure you're anxious to lead out your regiment, Colonel."

"Yes, sir." Devore smiled at Stryker, silently made the word, "Sorry," with his mouth and emphasized it with a roll of his eyes.

After Devore left, and as Crook buckled on his cartridge belt and holstered Colt, Stryker said, "Sir, I'd like to join the expedition. I am willing to serve in any capacity."

Crook, slender, wiry and well over six-foot tall, smiled. "Thank you for volunteering, Lieutenant, but the answer is no. You look like hell, standing there like a bent old man. You will therefore remain here at Fort Bowie and recuperate from your wounds. I'm sure Captain Forrest will find tasks for you."

"But, sir—"

"Rest and recuperate, Lieutenant. That's an order."

"Yes, sir." Stryker was weighed down by a sense of defeat. Rake Pierce would head south with Silas Dugan, trailing Geronimo like coyotes on the edge of a buffalo herd. The man would not come near Fort Bowie where he was known and would be arrested.

Stryker cursed his luck. All he could do now was loaf around the post, as useless as tits on a bull.

First Lieutenant Steve Stryker stood to rigid attention in Captain Forrest's office while the man read, or pretended to read, the contents of a large manila envelope.

Four days had passed since Crook had left with three regiments and seventy-five Apache and Navajo scouts. Since that time, Stryker had supervised the unloading of supplies, inspected the feet of the remaining soldiers, managed the kitchen to ensure the proper preparation and presentation of food, and spent the last two days watching over a detail of six ham-handed infantrymen strip and clean the temperamental steam engine that powered the fort's well.

The railroad clock on the office wall ticked slow seconds into the room and the rough pine boards under Stryker's feet creaked when he shifted his weight even slightly. Outside, a dog barked incessantly and the sun pounded the post's adobe, stone and wood-frame buildings with merciless heat.

Stryker was hot, sweat trickling down his back, running on his cheeks, and the thick air inside the captain's office felt and tasted like long-baled cotton.

Finally, Forrest lifted his eyes. "I have another detail for you, Lieutenant. You and . . . damn, I've forgotten his name. Ah yes, Second Lieutenant Birchwood."

The captain saw Stryker lift an eyebrow in surprise. He said, "He's a troublemaker, hitting the bottle too much and threatening others. I should have him court-martialed, but he comes of a good Boston family and I'll give him this one last chance to redeem himself."

"Sir, Mr. Birchwood promised his betrothed that his lips would ne'er touch whiskey. I very much doubt—"

"I don't give a damn what he promised his betrothed. He's drinking whiskey now, and I want him off the post and away from the sutler's store."

Stryker's heart sank. That could only mean guarding the spring, Forrest's way of getting rid of both troublemakers at once.

The captain's eyes were filled with acid. "You will help Second Lieutenant Birchwood onto his horse. Then you will scout to the south. I want to know if there are any hostiles within striking distance of the fort. Understand?"

Stryker's heart leaped. "How far south, sir?"

"Damn it, use your initiative, Mr. Stryker. As far south as you deem is necessary to ensure the safety and well-being of Fort Bowie."

Forrest waved a hand, signaling his boredom.

"Pick up whatever supplies you need; then roust Mr. Birchwood from the sutler's."

"Yes, sir."

The captain bent his head to the papers on his desk again, perhaps convincing himself that First Lieutenant Stryker no longer existed.

Stryker got his supplies from the cookhouse. The sergeant cook was overjoyed that the horribly disfigured officer who had stood over him and watched his every move was leaving. The man was so relieved that he sacked up enough bacon, biscuits and hardtack for a regiment.

After saddling Birchwood's bay and the criollo, Stryker tied the sack to the saddle horn and led the horses to the sutler's store.

Second Lieutenant Dale Birchwood was stinking drunk.

He was draped over the bar, a bottle and glass beside him. Stryker stepped over to him and shook his shoulder. "Mr. Birchwood, I need you for a detail."

The young officer turned and considered Stryker with bleary, bloodshot eyes. "Go to hell, Stryker," he said, and turned away. His trembling hand reached for the whiskey, but Stryker snatched it away and smashed it on the floor.

"How long has he been like this?"

The sutler was a big man with the arms and shoulders of a blacksmith. "Days. Since he rode in with the drovers."

"You always let your customers get drunk like this?"

"Mister, when a man's got a gun on his hip, threatens to draw down on you and don't much care if he lives or dies, you serve him as much whiskey as he wants."

"Help me get him on his horse."

"Hell, in that condition, he ain't going anywhere on a hoss."

"He'll have to, won't he? Now give me a hand here."

"Suit yourself, but he's gonna go ass-over-rain-barrel first chance he gets."

The sutler was a strong man and he easily man-handled Birchwood into the saddle. The young officer lay on the horse's neck, then threw up a vile-smelling stream of stale whiskey. Strings of saliva hung from his mouth and his cherry-red eyes popped out of his head like a pair of rotten eggs.

"Stryker, you dirty son of a bitch!" Birchwood yelled. He made to swing out of the saddle, but the sutler grabbed his leg and stopped him. "Let me down from here, you goddamned—" The Lieutenant launched into a stream of curses that a boy from a good Boston family should never have known.

As Birchwood's curses grew louder, Stryker glanced hurriedly around him, saw no one in sight, and grabbed Birchwood by the front of his shirt, pulling him closer. He drew back his fist and hit the foaming, raving lieutenant a hard, sharp rap on the jaw.

Birchwood's body went slack and Stryker draped him over his horse again. He turned to the sutler. "What did you see?"

The man smiled. "I seen you punch him."

A note of irritation in his voice, Stryker repeated his question. "What did you see?"

"The officer fell asleep on his hoss."

Stryker nodded. He swung into the saddle, grabbed the reins of the bay and turned south. Ahead of him lay a thousand square miles of towering sky islands cut through with deep, shady canyons, thick with cottonwoods, mesquite, willow and wild oak. The lower slopes of the mountains were shaggy with walnut, alder, sycamore, maple and juniper. Higher, there grew ponderosa pine and Douglas fir, their lofty canopies silhouetted like arrowheads against the hard blue sky.

Somewhere in this wilderness lurked Rake Pierce, a needle in a vast haystack. Stryker had no real reason to believe he could find him, but at least he was trying, better than sitting on his ass in the officer's mess in Fort Bowie or carrying out Forrest's petty and vindictive orders.

Stryker followed a winding game and Indian trail through Bear Spring Pass. At nearly six thousand feet above the flat the air thinned and he rode through thick forests of walnut, sycamore and pine.

Riding due south he dropped down to a timbered plateau and passed between a couple of craggy mountain escarpments before coming up on Pinery Canyon. He took a switchback route to the canyon floor, and stopped once to allow a black bear to amble through a thicket of ponderosa and Apache pine just ahead of him.

Only then, perhaps wakened by the sudden start

of his horse when it scented the bear, did Birchwood wake up.

He lifted himself upright in the saddle and looked around, blinking like a puzzled owl. "Wha . . . wha the hell?"

Stryker smiled. "Welcome back to the land of the living, Mr. Birchwood."

"Where . . . where the hell are we?"

"In the mountains, hunting Apaches."

The young officer glanced behind him, then at Stryker. "Where's the company?"

"There is no company. Just you and me."

Birchwood worked his jaw, then felt the bruise on his chin. "Did somebody sock me?"

"No, you fell down."

"I need a drink."

"Like hell you do."

"Damn you, Stryker—" He got no further than that. Suddenly his eyes rolled in his head and he toppled sideways off his bay.

Stryker shook his head. There were still hours of daylight left, but Birchwood was in no shape to travel. He swung off his horse, grabbed the young lieutenant by the shoulders and dragged him into the shade of the trees.

They would camp where they were and move out at first light in the morning.

Stryker was loosening his saddle girth when he heard a noise. He stood perfectly still, listening into the silence. Nothing.

"I'm imagining things," he said aloud.

But suddenly he felt as though he was under a

glass dome and somebody was studying him. That noise he'd heard had sounded like a man in pain.

He looked around him, at the sunlight splintering through the trees, the shimmer of the deep creek that ran through the canyon, even this long after the snow-melt.

All right, now he needed Birchwood; if for nothing else, he wanted Birchwood to share his anxiety. Stryker untied the sack from the saddle, took out the coffeepot and filled it with water from the creek. He stood in front of the sleeping lieutenant and threw the water into his face.

"Wake up you drunken officer and gentleman," he said. "Nap time is over."

Chapter 26

Birchwood spluttered and tossed his head, an action he obviously instantly regretted because he groaned from deep in his belly and kneaded his temples.

His eyes lifted to Stryker. "Why did you do that, damn you?"

"We've got work to do."

"Get away from me, Stryker. You're the devil."

Stryker smiled. "All right, that's it." He grabbed Birchwood by his shirtfront, hauled him to his feet and stuck his face close to his.

"I'm not a forgiving man, Lieutenant, but I've been willing to let things slide because you were drunk. From now on, you address me as sir, or Lieutenant Stryker, whatever you please. But if you ever call me only by my last name again, I'll beat the shit out of you. Do you understand me?"

Birchwood nodded, his mouth hanging slack. "Yes."

"Yes, what?"

"Yes, sir."

Stryker's eyes were merciless. "You're full of self-pity because you had to kill a dying man. Well, we've both had to kill dying men. You get over it, Mister. You don't crawl into a whiskey bottle and try to forget that it ever happened. Once you do that, you'll have to stay inside the bottle for the rest of your miserable life, looking out from behind the glass."

Birchwood was sobering fast. He tried to grab Stryker's wrist and push it away from him, but the lieutenant was too big, too strong and too angry to be moved.

The young officer gave up the struggle and said, "Sir, don't talk to me of self-pity. You wrote the damned book on that, sir. Your face was smashed up and you've been grieving for yourself ever since, sir."

Stryker expected his gorge to rise, but it did not. "Mr. Birchwood, you're correct. I did write the book on self-pity, but I crawled into myself, not the bottle. And I admit, one is just as bad as the other. But I'm trying to break out of me because I don't like what I see in there. It's a dark place where slimy things crawl. If you don't do the same, your military career is over and so are you. And, like me, you'll lose the woman you loved and you'll never find another."

"I . . . I told her my lips would ne'er touch whiskey," Birchwood whispered, half sober, but still drunk enough to be maudlin.

"She doesn't have to know."

Stryker's big hand had the young man pinned to a tree like a butterfly in a case. But he managed to struggle erect. "You have orders for me, sir?"

Stryker let him go, his arm falling by his side. Suddenly he was very tired, his wounds catching up to him like phantoms in the darkness. "I thought I heard a man cry out," he said.

"A bird?"

"Maybe. We're going to find out."

As he was about to turn away, Birchwood's voice stopped him. "When I shot that soldier, his brains flew out the other side of his head. They . . . they looked like the oatmeal a little child eats. Gray, like that, but mixed with blood and bone."

"That's what happens when you shoot a man up close, Lieutenant. Mr. Colt designed his revolver with that very thing in mind, to scatter a man's brains. But the Apaches would have killed Private Carter just as surely, only much more slowly."

"Sir, I don't think they came back."

"Then death would have taken Carter in its own good time, and it can be crueler than any Apache."

"Sir, was I right?"

Stryker nodded. "You did what had to be done, Mr. Birchwood. I regard your action at Fort Merit justified and even commendable."

The young man was silent for a moment, and then said, "I'm sorry, sir. I mean about the drinking and—"

Weary, aware that Birchwood was anxious to worry his guilt like a hound dog that had just caught a jackrabbit, Stryker said, "Let it go, Lieutenant. Just . . . let it go."

The young officer heard the finality in Stryker's

voice and wisely didn't push it. "One more question, sir: Why the hell are we here?"

Stryker's eyes ranged over the canyon, resting on the spot among the trees where he had heard the man's voice—if that's what it had been.

He turned his attention to Birchwood again. "Captain Forrest ordered us to scout the mountains to the south. He wishes to ascertain if Geronimo poses any threat to Fort Bowie."

Birchwood was trying to think in a whiskey fog and it took him a while. "Sir, I don't see any logic in that order. We can't scout the whole Chiricahua mountain range."

"Then try this logic, Lieutenant: The captain wanted us the hell off the post."

Birchwood smiled. "Bad apples."

"Correct. The baddest in the barrel."

To the east, the canyon rose gradually, passing through thick groves of hackberry and yucca, then into stands of mesquite and juniper. Here the rock walls directed heat into the bottom of the canyon like molten bronze pouring into a mold. The sunlight broke apart as it filtered through the trees and splashed like white paint on the underbrush. There was no wind.

Stryker sweated as he made his way through the trees, his Colt in his hand. Beside him Birchwood was laboring, his breath coming in groaning gasps, a hangover punishing him.

Lifting his hand, Stryker signaled a halt. He listened. Higher, above the canyon where the tall pines grew, a breeze rustled, but there was no other sound. The heavy air smelled of decaying vegetation, pine resin and the heady scent of wildflowers that grew in profusion everywhere. A dragonfly, as iridescent blue as a gas flame, hovered in front of Stryker for a few moments, then darted away into the trees.

He motioned Birchwood forward. Then he stopped as a shower of gravel rattled from the canyon wall.

Birchwood's gun came up and he fired twice, the echoes of the shots racketing around the canyon like a granite ball rolling down a marble corridor.

"Goddamn you, boy! You tryin' to kill me?"

A man's voice, creaky with age and orneriness.

"You up there, come down here, real slow!" Stryker yelled.

"Cain't do that, soldier boy. Got me leg stuck in a damn hole."

"We'll come up there."

"Yeah, you do that. Seen you comin' for a ways, crashing through the trees like a herd o' damn buffalo. If'n I'd been an Apache, I'd have both your scalps by now."

Stryker holstered his gun and after a search found a place where he could climb the canyon wall. Birchwood following behind him, he scrambled onto a scrub-covered mesa.

The old man was sitting on a rock, his left leg buried to the knee in a hole, part of a narrow fissure that cracked across the limestone rock. A canteen and a seven-shot, .52 caliber Spencer carbine lay beside him.

"Didn't see the damn thing," he said, his eyes lifting to Stryker. "Stepped right into it an' got caught somehow. I don't know if my leg is broke or not."

Stryker kneeled beside the rift. "What the hell were you doing here?"

"What I always do. Followin' my nose." He shook his head. "Been prospecting these hills for nigh on twenty year and the Apaches always left me alone. Then, 'bout a week back, five young bucks holed me up in a cave down to Black Mountain way. Finally they got bored an' left, but they kilt my burro." The old man turned quizzical eyes on Stryker. "Why for would them Apaches kill my burro? He was blind in one eye, mean as a Tennessee wildcat and wasn't worth spit. But me an' him had prospected for a long time and I set store by him."

Stryker shook his head. "I don't know. Apaches are notional."

"There's a lot o' truth in that." He stuck out a brown, gnarled hand. "Name's Clem Trimble, by the way."

Stryker shook the old man's hand and introduced himself and Birchwood.

"You the young feller that took pots at me?" Trimble asked.

"Sorry, sir."

"You take me fer an Injun?"

"I didn't see you. I heard gravel fall and shot."

"You heard gravel fall because I thowed it, young feller. I heard you tromping through the brush and knowed fer damned sure you was white men, but I didn't want to holler and wake up every Apache in the territory. 'Course, now you gone an' done that very thing fer your ownself."

"Have you seen other Apaches since those five bushwhacked you, Clem?" Stryker asked.

"Nary hide nor hair. Seen some white men though."

Stryker's interest quickened. "What manner of white men?"

"The kind you don't meet at a church social, Cap'n. The one them I recognized right off was Silas Dugan. He's a scalp hunter and afore that the Messkins paid him to take poxed blankets into Navajo an' Comanche villages. He's bad 'un, all right, and he's killed more'n his share o' white men."

Stryker leaned forward, his eyes revealing his excitement. "Clem, listen to me real well, where—"

"Damn it, Cap'n, git my leg out of this hole an' then we can talk," Trimble said. "Unless you was plannin' to ride off an' leave me here."

"Oh, yes. Of course."

The old prospector's ankle was jammed into a ragged break in the rock shelf and was bent over at an odd angle. It took the combined efforts of Stryker and Birchwood thirty minutes to free him and both were sweating heavily from the merciless sun that blasted the mesa.

Trimble gingerly tried moving his ankle. He winced a little, but said, "Well, she ain't broke. Punishing me some, though."

"Think you can make it down into the canyon?" Stryker asked. "I don't like being out in the open like this."

The old man rose to his feet and tried his weight on the injured leg. "I can make it." He looked at Stryker. "You got coffee at your camp? I could sure use some—haven't had a cup in days. When the Apaches kilt my burro, he fell into a ravine an' took everything I own with him."

"We've got coffee."

"Grub?"

"Got that too."

"Then what are we waitin' fer?" Trimble hesitated, then said, "Cap'n, I got to ask. Did Apaches do that to your face?"

Stryker shook his head. "Rake Pierce, one of the men you saw with Dugan, rearranged it with a shackle chain."

"So that's why you was so all-fired interested in them white men." The old prospector shook his head. "I'm a plainspoken man, Cap'n, and I'll say my piece: The man who done that to you hit you so damned hard and so damned often, that you don't even look human no more. Man like that deserves to die. And if'n you want me along, I'll help you hunt him down."

Stryker smiled. "Thank you, Clem, but this is my concern."

Trimble nodded. "Suit yourself, Cap'n, but judgin' by the way you an' the young feller there crash around in the woods, you'll never find him without me."

Chapter 27

Clem Trimble had eaten his fill of biscuits and bacon and now he sighed and rested his back against the trunk of a cottonwood.

He knuckled his forehead, looking through the firelight at Stryker. "Best grub I've et in days, Cap'n. 'Course, it's the only grub I've et in days."

Stryker paused, tobacco and cigarette paper in his fingers. "Where are the Apaches headed, Clem?"

"If Uncle George is after them like you say, then Geronimo is hightailing it south to the Madres. The Apaches already had a bellyful of Crook and they ain't exactly hankering for more."

"Why are Rake Pierce and Silas Dugan still here?"

"Nosin' around, seeing what they can pick up. There are homesteads in these hills, to say nothing of wandering Apache women and young 'uns. If he tries, a man like Dugan can do well for hisself."

"Have you any idea where they are?"

"Cap'n, I can take you to the place I last seen them and you can track 'em from there. But since you don't want my help, that ain't gonna work."

"I'm rethinking that, Clem."

The old man nodded. "Good idea, Cap'n. A man shouldn't walk around with all kinds of notions set hard in his head like cow flops in the sun."

"How many men does Pierce have with him, sir?" Birchwood asked.

"I can't answer that, young feller, since I got no acquaintance with that gentleman. Now, if you was to ask how many men Silas Dugan has with him, I'd say an even dozen." He smiled. "Beggin' your pardon, but against you two pilgrims, I reckon that's more'n enough."

Birchwood stiffened. "Sir, both Lieutenant Stryker and myself have fought Apaches before."

"You ever fit the likes of Silas Dugan and them hard cases he has around him afore?"

Birchwood nodded gleefully, like a man about to say check in a chess game. "Yes, we did. Rake Pierce attacked us in an attempt to free Dugan from our custody."

"An' did he?"

Reluctantly Birchwood said, "Yes. But we killed one of his men in that engagement, an Indian."

"And how many men did you lose, young feller?"

Before Birchwood could answer, Stryker said, "Clem, I want you with us. We'll pull out at sunup and follow your back trail. Then you'll find Pierce and Dugan."

"I'll do my best fer ye, Cap'n, but gettin' to them two won't be easy."

"Let me worry about that."

Trimble nodded. "When a man believes he's in

the right, it can make him stubborn, Cap'n. Just don't let that stubbornness get you kilt. From where I was hid, I took the measure of them hard cases with Dugan. Now, most were the kind of border riff-raff men like him attract, but a couple were gun-hands, read that plain enough." He waited a moment to let that sink in, then said, "I ain't sure, but I thought I seen Billy Lee in the bunch."

That name did not register on Stryker's face and Trimble said, "He's a gunman and bank robber out of El Paso, Texas. He claims to be kin to old Robert E., but I don't know about that. But I'll tell you true, he's killed a bunch and he's hell on wheels with a hogleg."

Stryker poured himself coffee, motioned with the pot and Trimble stuck out his cup. "As I told you before, Clem, let me worry about Lee and the rest."

"Anything you say, Cap'n." Trimble had burned his fingers on the cup and was shaking them. "Just don't let worry share your blanket tonight. That can weaken a man."

Stryker built a cigarette and lit it with a brand from the fire. Yellow flared on his shattered face giving him the look of a stage demon in limelight.

Seeing what had happened to Trimble, he held his cup by the rim and drank. The old man was right about worry weakening a man, wrong about not letting it share his blanket.

Later, stretched out near the fire, he racked his brain, trying to come up with a plan, a strategy, anything.

After an hour, he gave up. He had no plan. All he could do was throw his fate to the winds and hope they blew in his direction.

That thought brought him no comfort. No release.

Trimble told Stryker he was a couple of hours north of Black Mountain when he saw Dugan and his bunch. Now they rode in that direction, the old man, who was favoring his ankle, up behind Birchwood.

The mountain was a rocky, volcanic peak visible for miles, its steep slopes covered with mesquite and cactus.

"There's old ruins up there on top, Cap'n," Trimble said, "walls an' sich. As to who built them, nobody knows. But it was way before the Apaches' time."

"Can I get a good view of the country from the peak?" Stryker asked.

"Sure you can, Cap'n. From there a farsighted man can see clear to Old Mexico."

Stryker stored that away. If they didn't pick up Pierce's trail, he'd climb the mountain and scout the land around him with his field glasses. A wisp of smoke or the glint of sunlight on a horse bridle could reveal the man's location.

The sun rose higher in the sky. It was not yet noon, an hour shy of it, yet the heat was building, promising the day would be an inferno.

Black Mountain right ahead of him, Stryker led the way across a ridge that gradually sloped downward and opened onto a small, grassy meadow, bright with wildflowers. A small stream, lined with cottonwood and willow, was just visible behind thick brush and here they stopped to water the horses and let them graze for a while.

Stryker found shade under a cottonwood and stretched out his legs. He ate a strip of cold bacon and biscuit, then smoked a cigarette before stepping to the stream for a drink.

He chose an area free of brush and lay on his belly, splashing cool water onto his face and neck. He bent his head to drink directly from the stream when the water suddenly erupted to meet him. At the same time he heard the slam of a rifle shot.

Rolling to his right, Stryker crashed into the brush and lay still, his Colt in his hand. There was no sign of Birchwood and Trimble, and he assumed they had already taken cover.

"Birchwood! Trimble! You all right?"

"We're all right, Cap'n," the old man yelled. "Who took a pot at us?"

"Damned if I know!"

Another bullet kicked up dirt close to Stryker, a second rattled through the brush just above his head. He was pinned down, nailed to the ground by someone who knew how to use a rifle.

Was it Pierce and his men?

He dismissed that. They would have all fired at once. This was one man. A lone bronco Apache? That was more likely.

"Hey, Maryann, eat this!"

Trimble's voice was drowned out by the bellow of

his Spencer. It was a probing shot that went nowhere.

And it was immediately answered by a flurry of rifle fire that crashed bullets all around the area where Birchwood and Trimble lay hidden.

Stryker heard the old prospector's laugh, a high-pitched, "Hee-hee-hee!" that chased itself around the meadow. "Damn me, boy," he yelled, "but that was good shootin'."

A pause, then, "Are you white men?" A woman's voice.

"Hell, do we sound like Apaches to you?" Stryker yelled.

"Identify yourself!"

Irritation flared in Stryker. He had no desire to bandy words with a bushwhacker, female or not.

An impatient bullet spurted a V of dirt in front of his face.

"Identify yourselves."

Stryker shook his head. This was developing into a Mexican standoff. He justified his surrender by telling himself he was only being polite to a lady.

"First Lieutenant Steve Stryker, United States Cavalry. Those two in the bushes are Second Lieutenant Dale Birchwood and Clem Trimble, the crazy old coot with the Spencer."

"An' I'm right pleased to make your acquaintance, ma'am," Trimble called out, apparently unfazed by Stryker's comment.

"Step into the open where I can see you," the woman said.

"That won't work, lady," Stryker said. "You show yourself first."

"You're a white man all right," the woman yelled. "Always wanting me to show myself." There was a moment's pause; then the woman stepped out into the meadow. "This enough show for you?"

Chapter 28

Stryker rose to his feet and the others did the same.

The woman, dressed in canvas pants and a man's collarless shirt that hung loose on her thin frame, carried a Winchester in her hands. She was young, with a thick mane of beautiful blond hair, but her face was overlaid with a veneer of hard years that had browned and wrinkled her skin and put flint into her eyes. She had a rash all over her face and neck that looked angry and red as though she'd been stung by hornets.

Stryker made to step toward her, but the rifle came up fast, the muzzle unwavering on his belly.

"Stay right there, soldier boy," she warned.

"I can offer you food," Stryker said, stopping right where he was.

"Coffee," Trimble said, smiling. "I can bile you up some, ma'am." His smile grew wider. "You're a right pretty gal, an' that's a natural fact."

"Horseshit, pops. Save it for somebody who cares." The woman motioned to Stryker with the rifle. "You, soldier boy, what the hell did you do? Walk face first into a band saw?"

Stryker smiled. "Something like that."

"You in charge?"

"Yes." He waved a hand in the direction of his companions. "This is my command."

"Well, we're camping here and I want you and your men to move out."

"We?" Stryker asked.

By way of reply, the woman looked over her shoulder and yelled, "It's all right, Maxine. Bring the wagon."

Two mules hauled a small wagon with a canvas top into the meadow. A woman was handling the reins and two others walked beside front wheels. They all seemed young, but unlike the first were wearing dresses, stained, ragged and dirty, but store bought and once expensive.

Trimble's eyes twinkled and he smiled and smoothed his ragged beard. "Welcome, ladies," he said, stepping toward the wagon. "A thousand warm welcomes."

"Clem, stay back!" Stryker yelled, panic edging his voice.

The old prospector halted in midstride and turned to Stryker. "What the hell, Cap'n?"

"Look at their faces!"

Trimble did, and the aborning haze of desire fled quickly from his eyes.

The woman with the rifle spoke to him. "The soldier boy is right, old timer. We're poxed."

Looking aghast, Trimble took a step back, his hand on his chest. "What kind of pox?"

"Smallpox, you idiot. Now just stay away from us. I have one dying in the back of the wagon if she isn't dead of fever already and time's running short for the rest of us." She looked around the meadow, at the trees and then to the creek that ran clear over lilac-colored pebbles. "I figure this is as good a place as any to die, and better than most."

As though to put an exclamation mark on the woman's statement, Maxine suddenly groaned and slumped over the reins. The two other women helped her down from the seat and laid her on the grass.

Stryker shook his head in disbelief and spoke to the woman with the rifle. "What in God's name are you women doing here in the middle of an Apache uprising?"

"And that's exactly why we're here, soldier boy. We came up from Sonora in Old Mexico. Had a house in a settlement just across the border. But business dried up." She turned. "How is Maxine?"

A woman shook her head, her fevered eyes telling what her mouth did not.

"I don't know what happened to them boys down there," the woman with the rifle said, speaking again to Stryker. "Maybe they got religion or the Apaches scared them, but they stopped coming round. Then we were told by a Texas drover that General Crook was gathering an army in the Pedregosas and that he was camped on Big Bend Creek with three regiments. He told us how to get there, so we packed up the next day and headed north, following the soldiers."

"Ma'am, the general established his headquarters at Fort Bowie to the north," Birchwood said.

"Don't you think we know that by now, sonny?" the woman said. "We were told wrong was all."

Birchwood flushed and said nothing.

Again the woman glanced behind her. "Fetch me a canteen, Selina."

She filled the canteen at the creek and walked back to Maxine. She lifted the dying woman's head and tried to make her drink, but Maxine refused, coughing weakly.

Stryker had never seen smallpox before, but somewhere he'd read that you had to stay at least ten feet from a victim or risk being infected.

"Mount up, Mr. Birchwood," he said. "We're moving on."

"Yes, sir," the young lieutenant said, glad to get away from that place of death.

But Trimble, inquisitive, or revealing an old man's concern about his health, said, "Ma'am, beggin' your pardon, but did you get the pox around these parts?"

The woman laid her rifle against the wagon and stood facing him, keeping her distance. "I know where we got it, pops. South of here. We were camped about two miles north of the Big Bend, right close to a mountain."

"Sounds like the Packsaddle to me, ma'am," Trimble said. He nodded. "We'll ride around them parts, I reckon."

"It wasn't the mountain that gave us smallpox, Mister. Two men came riding into our camp. Big men and well armed. They'd brought whiskey with them and stayed for the night and we girls showed them a real good time. Then, at first light, they came to me and said they'd no money. But the bigger of the two, a man wearing buckskins who called himself Silas—"

Stryker was suddenly alert. "Ma'am, was his last name Dugan?"

The woman shook her head. "Since when does a man give a whore his last name? He called himself Silas and the man who was with him Rake."

"When was this?" Stryker asked.

"Nine days ago. The smallpox took us real fast."

Stryker and Birchwood exchanged glances, and Trimble stepped into the silence. "Ma'am," he said, his voice hollow, "he didn't give you blankets, did he?"

"He said he was camped nearby and he'd stashed away food and blankets to hide them from the Apaches. He said blankets were better than money, because we'd need them if we planned on heading for Fort Bowie. He said the nights get cold in the Chiricahuas. He brought us the blankets and some food and right after that, we all got sick."

Suddenly Clem Trimble looked old. "Ma'am, the Mexicans pay Silas Dugan in gold to spread disease among the Indians. I reckon he aimed on doing it to the Apaches, but they went on the warpath, broke down their rancherias and spoiled his plans. He spreads smallpox with infected blankets because he had the pox once hisself and it can't trouble him a second time."

For the first time the woman acted like the girl she was. Tears started in her hot eyes and she said, "We drank his whiskey and done everything for him a man could daydream about. Why would he do that to us?"

His voice clicking in his throat, Trimble said, "Because he's Silas Dugan and he thought it was a funny joke to play on you, ma'am."

"Can a man be that evil?"

"If you'll forgive me for sounding like a preacher, ma'am, evil is at war with the entire creation. That's how ol' Silas thinks of hisself, a man at war with God hisself and the rest of humanity."

A silence followed that grew, then stretched taut, and Stryker decided to break it. "Mount up," he said.

He swung into the saddle of the criollo and then kneed the horse toward the woman, keeping his distance. "Is there anything I can do for you, ma'am? If I meet up with General Crook's command, I could send a doctor back here."

The woman shook her head. "Thank you, but we'll be dead by then." She lifted her eyes to Stryker. "Have you whiskey?"

"Sorry. I don't have any."

"No matter; we'll just die sober." Her fevered gaze softened and Stryker was no longer looking into the hard eyes of a whore but of a woman in pain. "Lieutenant, my name is Stella Parker. Will you remember that?"

"Do you have kinfolk I can contact, ma'am?"

"No, no folks. Just say my name sometimes. I mean years in the future, will you say, 'Stella Parker,' now and then?"

Too overcome to speak, Stryker nodded.

"Thank you," the woman called Stella said. "Thank you most kindly."

Chapter 29

Stryker and the others rode due south, in the direction of Packsaddle Mountain. Riding through rugged, difficult terrain, they crossed Box Canyon and were within two miles of High Lonesome, yet another forbidding chasm, when thunderheads began to build above the Swisshelm Mountains to the west.

Within minutes the clouds had turned black and the air smelled of ozone and of the pines that were already tossing their heads, worried by a rising wind.

"Big blow comin' up, Cap'n," Trimble told Stryker. He winked. "We don't want to be caught in no canyon when the rains come; a man can drown quicker'n scat that way."

Stryker was irritated, not at the old man but at the volatile temperament of the desert summer. He was praying that Pierce was still camped close to the Saddleback and had not already slipped south into Mexico.

"Look for a likely place to hole up," he said. He looked around himself, but saw nothing that promised shelter. Trimble was right; there was always a danger of flash floods in the canyons and arroyos. They would have to reach higher ground.

Now the scowling clouds above them were black. Thunder banged and lightning flashed skeletal fingers that clawed the face of the sky. Rain hammered down, falling like a cascade of stinging steel needles.

Stryker turned in the saddle. "Up ahead!" He had to yell over the noise of the storm. He waved the others forward.

He pushed the little criollo up a steep, pine-covered rise and headed toward a limestone overhang, jutting out from the lower slope of a shallow peak. The overhang was low, no more than six feet, holding up a detritus of fallen rocks, whitened tree limbs and rubble. But it covered a deep gash in the slope that went back fifteen feet, gradually sinking lower until it petered out at a rock face. It would shelter both men and horses until the storm passed.

The wind ravaged through the trees like a shark, shredding pine needles, cartwheeling them into the air. Lightning blazed and thunder roared in the voice of an angry god.

"Hell," Trimble said, throwing himself off the back of Birchwood's horse, "it's like the end of the world."

Stryker and Birchwood led their mounts into the shelter of the overhang. The horses were frightened, their eyes showing arcs of white, but they stood where they were, preferring even that meager shelter to what lay outside.

Stryker stepped deeper into the cleft, found a place to sit and built a cigarette. He wondered how the women were faring back at their camp. Huddled in the wagon probably, waiting for death to take them.

"Stella Parker," he said aloud.

Birchwood looked at him strangely, but said nothing.

"The woman with the rifle," Stryker said. "Her name was Stella Parker."

"Oh," Birchwood said.

Stryker glanced up at him. "Yes, that was her name all right."

After the storm passed, they mounted again and rode south and that night camped in the looming shadow of the Packsaddle.

As though ashamed of its temper tantrum, the desert compensated by putting on a show. The violet sky was clear, glittering with far-flung stars, and a bright moon rose, braiding the pines with mother-of-pearl light. A soft breeze rustled, heavy with the scent of damp moss, and out in the darkness the waking coyotes shook themselves and sprayed from their coats water that haloed around them like beads of silver.

Stryker sat by the fire, drinking coffee and smoking. Opposite him, Birchwood was deep in thought, his young face crimsoned by the flames.

"Something troubling you, Mr. Birchwood?" Stryker asked. "You still tearing yourself apart over your whiskey bender?"

The young man shook his head. "No, sir. My betrothed can't hear me, I know, but I've made another vow that I will not enter houses of ill repute and that my lips will ne'er again touch whiskey."

"Very commendable, Mr. Birchwood. I'm sure your lady would be pleased to know that her cavalier has sworn off whores and strong drink."

Birchwood looked sharply at Stryker, but the lieutenant's face was empty.

After the time it took him to light another cigarette and sample his coffee, Stryker said, "So what's sticking in your craw?"

Birchwood poked a stick deeper into the fire, throwing up a shower of sparks. "I think we should head back to Fort Bowie, sir. We've followed our orders and ascertained that there are no Apaches within miles of the post. Now it's time to go back."

"We will, just as soon as I settle with Rake Pierce."

"We have no orders to that effect, sir."

"Mr. Birchwood, the man is a deserter, a murderer, a gunrunner and a scalp-hunter. He needs killing. I don't require orders to that effect."

"Sir, have you noticed that there are only two of us?"

"Trimble doesn't count, huh?"

"He's out of it. This isn't his fight."

"Or yours, Mr. Birchwood?"

The young officer hesitated, then said, "You asked me what was troubling me. Well, sir, it's the right or wrong of going after Pierce that troubles me. I don't know where my duty lies. But I doubt that giving my life for my senior officer's personal vendetta should be a part of it."

Birchwood's comment had stung, and Stryker felt molten steel scald his insides. "Your duty, Lieutenant, is to follow orders and I'm giving you one now. You will join me in the pursuit of the deserter and renegade Sergeant Rake Pierce. Have I made myself perfectly clear?"

The young officer's face was stiff, the iron discipline and respect for authority of the frontier army presenting him with an impassible barrier. "Yes, sir. Perfectly, sir."

"I'm very glad to hear that, Mr. Birchwood," Stryker said.

Suddenly Trimble was beside him. "Don't look now, Cap'n, but we got comp'ny," he said.

Chapter 30

Stryker unbuttoned his holster flap as he rose to his feet. Two men sat their horses in the shadows, black outlines against the moon-raked night. Some primitive instinct warned him of danger and he felt a malevolence gather around him, as though the air had suddenly grown colder.

"Hello the camp!" one of the riders yelled.

Stryker stepped out of the firelight. "Come on ahead." Somewhere to his left he heard Trimble cycle his Spencer. Birchwood had faded to his right, half in shadow.

He watched the riders come, aware that he'd not been alone—Clem and Birchwood had sensed the brooding danger as he had.

The two men stayed beyond the rim of the firelight. "Smelled your coffee," the man to the right of Stryker said. "We could sure use a cup."

Before Stryker could answer, the rider looked beyond him into the gloom. "Clem Trimble, is that you I see skulking back there? I know I heard your Spencer."

The old prospector stepped out of the gloom. He let his rifle hang loose in one hand and knuckled his forehead with the other. "Yeah, it's me, Billy. Ol' Clem Trimble as ever was."

The man called Billy smiled. "You loco old coot, I thought your hair would be hanging in some Apache buck's wickiup by now."

"Apaches never troubled me none, Billy. Until lately, that is." He grinned. "It's real nice to make your acquaintance again, Billy. I don't recollect meeting your compadre there."

"This here is Tom Diamond from up Denver way," Billy said. He was talking to Trimble but his eyes were trying to pin Stryker to the darkness.

"Right pleased to meet you, Tom," Trimble said. "Last I heard o' you was when you gunned ol' Shep Shannon down Abilene way."

Diamond's head turned slowly, like a lizard. "Shut your trap, old man," he said. "I'm tired of hearing you talk."

Trimble nodded, smiling, saying nothing.

The old prospector looked afraid, and Stryker reckoned he had every right to be. There was an air of malice and threat about the two riders and an aura of danger that seemed to wrap them both to the eyes in a sinister black shroud.

"Still want that coffee?" Stryker asked.

The man called Diamond answered. "Sure we do, but we'll get it ourselves . . . afterward."

"Cap'n, this here is Billy Lee, the man I was telling you about if you recollect, him being kin to ol' Bobby Lee an' all."

Trimble was warning him, Stryker knew. He was stretched tight, his mouth dry, a cold sweat on him.

Lee nodded. "The old coot's right. Cousin kin to the great man himself. And that's why I don't cotton to Blue bellies, especially ugly ones like you." The man grinned and turned to his companion. "You ever in all your born days see an uglier Yankee than that 'un?"

Diamond shook his head. "Can't say as I have."

"Know your enemy" was a saying at the Point, and Stryker took time to study the two riders. Both were dressed like Texas drovers, but they wore guns, belts, boots and spurs that no cowhand could afford. That's where their similarities ended.

Lee was short, thin, with the eyes of a snake. Like any westerner who laid even a tenuous claim to manhood, his top lip was covered in a downy fuzz that did nothing to conceal a small, cruel mouth. He was poised, eager and ready to kill.

By contrast Diamond was a tall, handsome man with a thick dragoon mustache, black hair falling to his shoulders in glossy ringlets. He wore two Remingtons strapped to his chest in shoulder holsters, a gun rig Stryker had never seen before. At first glance he looked like a thinking man, but that was an illusion. Diamond was a mindless killer, and now he wore that brand on his face like a mark of Cain.

Lee was talking. "What are you soldier boys doing here?"

Stryker began, "My name is—"

"I know your damned name. I asked you what you're doing here."

Anger flared in Stryker. "If you know my name, then you know what I'm doing here."

"You tell me, soldier boy."

"We're scouting for Apaches." This from Birchwood, who looked like a towheaded farm boy in the ruddy firelight.

"You're a damned liar," Lee snarled. "You already know Geronimo is being chased into the Madres by Crook. You two are looking for a man. A man by the name of Rake Pierce, a real good friend of ours."

"As the lieutenant told you, we're scouting for Apaches," Stryker said.

"What is this, a goddamned liars' meetin'?" Lee asked. "Stryker, we got us a Mescalero breed who's been trailing you. He seen you talk to them poxed whores, then followed you here." The gunman smiled. "The only reason you're at the Packsaddle is because the whores told you Mr. Pierce had a camp close by." He grinned like a death's head. "Well, them whores won't be talkin' to anybody else."

"Her name was Stella Parker," Stryker said.

"What the hell are you yapping about?"

"One of the women you killed. Her name was Stella Parker."

"Like I give a shit."

"Here's my offer," Stryker said, a terrible anger in him. "You tell Pierce and Dugan to surrender themselves up to me by noon tomorrow and we'll head back to Fort Bowie where they will receive a fair trial and benefit of clergy."

Lee laughed. He turned to Diamond. "Did you hear that? He's making us an offer."

Diamond did the lizard turn of his head. "Billy, you talk too much. Let's get it done."

Then his hands streaked for his guns.

Stryker was drawing.

During a gunfight, thoughts don't proceed through a man's mind in an orderly fashion. They flash into his head instantly, fully formed, like images at a magic lantern show. As they now did for Stryker.

I'm slow. Way too slow.

My body is already weakened. I can't take another hit.

Dive! Hit the ground!

Both Lee and Diamond were firing.

Stryker hit the dirt hard, rolled and came up on one knee.

The two gunmen were fighting their skittish horses, Lee turning backward in the saddle to get off a shot.

A bullet cracked past Stryker's head. He fired. Missed.

Trimble's Spencer boomed. Diamond's saddle horn disintegrated and the man jerked backward.

Birchwood was on his belly, his Colt straight out in front of him, grasped in both hands. He was firing steadily, methodically, running out his five-shot string.

Stryker fired at Lee. A hit. The gunman's thin chest seemed to cave as he bent over, blood on his lips, his shoulders pushing forward.

The Spencer blasted another shot. Diamond was hit hard. He was firing both his Remingtons, the big revolvers rolling with the recoils.

Trimble yelped in pain and his rifle thudded to the ground. He was out of the fight. Birchwood was trying to reload, his fumbling fingers dropping shiny brass rounds onto the grass.

Stryker rose to his feet. He raised his Colt and fired at Diamond. A clean miss. He fired again. But the gunman was already sliding from the saddle. He hit the ground with a thud.

Like Trimble, Billy Lee was out of the fight.

Slumped over and still, Lee let his horse carry him toward the surrounding trees at a walk. Birchwood was on his feet. He assumed a target shooter's pose he'd been taught at the Point, his revolver held high at arm's length, left foot tucked behind his right heel. He fired, thumbed the hammer, then fired again. Lee rolled slowly from the saddle.

Thick gray gunsmoke twined through the clearing, silvered by moonlight.

Stryker turned. "Clem, are you hit?"

The old man cackled. "Ol' Tom clipped a finger off'n me, Cap'n. Cut her as clean as a whistle."

"Mr. Birchwood?"

"Unhurt, sir." The young officer stepped to Stryker and looked him over. "You seem to be all of a piece, sir."

Stryker nodded, amazed that all three of them were still alive.

Trimble, holding a bloody left hand, offered the reason. "We was lucky, Cap'n. Green horses and men who had killed too often and too easily. That breeds carelessness and they was only half trying. Then they suddenly knowed they wasn't dealin' with pilgrims, but by then it was too late for them." He shook his head. "It's a real shame, because Billy Lee was one of the best around, an' him bein' close kin to ol' Bobby an all."

"Let me see your hand," Stryker said.

The ring finger of the old man's left hand was gone, blown off clean at the knuckle. "The trigger was shot off'n my Spencer," Trimble said. "Gonna need a gunsmith afore she's right again."

"We have to do something with your hand," Stryker said. But just what, he did not know.

"Cap'n, I'll find me some willow bark for pain, bile me up some sage to keep the stump clean, an' I'll be good." He cackled. "Did you see ol' Tom jump when I blowed off his saddle horn, huh? Sceered the shit out of him, like he'd just seen a boogerman. I reckon he didn't know that I'm too old a cat to be played with by a kittlin'."

"Can you ride, Clem?" Stryker asked.

"Of course I can ride, Cap'n. Learned how when you were still in knee britches." Trimble's face took on a crafty look. "You want me to go after Dugan and Pierce with you."

Stryker nodded. "I need your skill with a rifle, Clem. Even if you fire one-handed, you'll be better than me."

"Don't you worry none about that, Cap'n," Trimble said. "I can still shoot." He looked at Stryker, anticipating his unasked question. "Cap'n, when them boys don't come back, ol' Dugan will do one of two things: He'll scamper for the border or he'll come lookin' fer us. Either way, I'll ride with you, Cap'n."

"What will he do, Clem? Run or fight?"

The old man thought for a while, then said, "Silas Dugan don't scare worth a damn."

"So he and Pierce will come hunting us?"

"Damn right they will."

Chapter 31

As Trimble wandered off into the night, seeking his remedies, Stryker and Birchwood stepped over to the dead men. Lee was on his back, his eyes wide and his mouth full of blood, and Diamond's last defiant snarl was frozen on his lips.

They had been riding young horses. Apache ponies by the looks of them, and that had saved all of their lives.

Stryker stripped the dead of their guns and carried them back to the fire. He poured himself coffee and lit a cigarette with a trembling hand. It had been a close business. Too close. He knew that if Lee and Diamond had taken the trouble to dismount before getting their work in, he'd be cold and dead by now, looking up at stars he could no longer see.

"Sir?" Birchwood squatted beside him.

"What is it, Lieutenant?"

"Sir, I suggest we find a defensive position and provision it as best we can. I don't know how many men Pierce will bring against us, but I believe we'll be badly outnumbered." Birchwood took a sip of his coffee. "Whatever happens, we can't let him catch us out in the open."

"The reason Pierce sent those two gunmen after us tonight is because he's scared," Stryker said. "He knows I can put his head in a noose and he'll do anything to stop us taking him back to Fort Bowie."

He smiled. "A siege might suit him just fine. That way he can kill us at his leisure."

"Then what do you suggest, sir?"

"We're going after him, Mr. Birchwood. We'll keep at him, wear him down and eventually he'll get careless and make a mistake. When he does, he'll find me waiting for him."

"Sir, there's three of us, and old Clem is wounded."

"Even wounded, Trimble is ten different kinds of hell in a gunfight."

"Sir, we still can't face Pierce in an open engagement."

"You're right; we can't. Stealth will be our ally, Mr. Birchwood. We'll pick off his men at a distance, then fade back into the hills. Under no circumstances will we stand and fight." Stryker grinned at the young officer. "In other words, Mr. Birchwood, we will become Apaches."

Stryker saw the puzzled expression on the lieutenant's face as conflicting thoughts worked through his brain. He smiled, sure he was reading Birchwood right. The young man's superior officer had just advocated they become like the very enemy he despised. That had knocked him for a loop.

"People change, Lieutenant," Stryker explained. "A

man's attitude shifts slowly, until one morning he wakes up and sees the world differently."

"I see, sir. So you have grown to like the Apaches, as General Crook does."

Stryker shook his head. "Mr. Birchwood, General Crook doesn't like Apaches, but he respects them as fighting men. I don't like them either, but I've also come to respect them. They fight well, and they die well. I think that's a fine epitaph for a people that will all be gone in a few short years."

Birchwood nodded. "The world is changing, sir, and the Apaches can't change with it. If they can't, then they must be swept aside."

"Indeed, Lieutenant. But our little corner of the world hasn't changed, and it won't until barbarians like Pierce and Dugan no longer cast their shadows on it."

At first light, Stryker and the others made a hasty breakfast of bacon and coffee, then saddled their horses, Trimble choosing the buckskin pony that Billy Lee had been riding.

The old man had bound up his left hand in a bandage torn from his shirt, giving himself an even more ragged appearance. He picked up a new Winchester and a belt of ammunition and assured Stryker that he could still shoot as good as ever.

Birchwood took the Winchester that had been carried by Diamond and he tucked the man's Remingtons in his belt.

"You any good with a rifle, Mr. Birchwood?" Stryker asked.

The officer nodded. "I came first in my class in rifle shooting at the Point, sir."

Stryker felt a little niggle of jealousy. "I finished dead last."

There was no diplomatic way to comment on that, so Birchwood settled for, "Is that so, sir?"

"Yes, Mr. Birchwood," Stryker snapped, irritated, "that is so."

The young lieutenant suddenly found that he had urgent business elsewhere. Stryker shoved the spare Colt into his waistband and shook his head.

What was it about rifle shooters that made them so damned . . . uppity?

Despite his wound, Trimble insisted on riding point as they headed due west. The old man had spent hard years in the mountains and he was enduring, as tough as a knot in a pine board.

Stryker and Birchwood followed a trail that rose gradually, passing through forests of pine, juniper and mountain mahogany. The sky was a clear blue, not yet scorched colorless by the sun, and a few bands of gossamer cloud rode so high a close-sighted man could not have seen them.

The silence and emptiness of the land grated on Stryker's nerves. He was suspicious of the morning, his eyes scanning the terrain around him. This was bushwhacker country, a wilderness of trees and rock where a man could shoot, shoot again, and then vanish completely, as though he had never been.

Beside Stryker, Birchwood rode with the Winchester across his saddle horn, his face calm. But there was tension in the way he held his head and shoulders, as though the country they were riding through were whispering warnings.

The tobacco hunger in him, Stryker led the way into a stand of trees, the forest floor carpeted thick with pine needles. He built, then lit, a cigarette while Birchwood dismounted and stretched his legs.

Finally Birchwood looked up at Stryker and said, "Clem's long in coming back, sir."

"Uh-huh," Stryker said. "I believe he may have crossed some sign."

"Well, we know he's not been ambushed. The sound of rifle shot would travel for miles through these rocks," Birchwood said, looking around.

Whether he was attempting to reassure himself or both of them, Stryker could not tell. He nodded to the trail. "See the bald ridge up there? We'll cross that, rest up in whatever shade we can find on the other side and wait for Trimble."

Birchwood swung into the saddle and gathered up the reins. "If I live through this, sir, which I'm beginning to doubt, I'm going to ask for a transfer to Kansas where there's nothing but flat, long-riding country for as far as a man can see."

Stryker stubbed out his cigarette butt and nodded. "You'll do all right in Kansas, Mr. Birchwood. That is, if you can stay away from whorehouses and whiskey."

An hour later, as Stryker and Birchwood waited in a copse of pines, Trimble showed up, sitting his horse at a walk.

Stryker waved the old man over and then waited for him to speak.

"I found 'em, Cap'n," Trimble said. "An' they're real close." He nodded. "Camped in a valley over yonder."

"How many, Clem?"

"Speakin' for myself, Cap'n, I'd say too many."

Chapter 32

They rode west, away from the bald ridge, with Trimble leading the way. After ten minutes the old man drew rein. "I reckon we best walk from here, Cap'n," he said.

They had entered a round, shallow basin about ten acres in extent, thick with good grass, especially among the cottonwoods that fronted a stream bed. The water had all but dried up, reduced to a series of unconnected puddles only a few inches deep.

Around them rose rugged mountain slopes, and to Stryker's surprise, a narrow ledge of snow still clung to one of the peaks.

They led the horses into the cottonwoods, and Trimble slid his rifle from the boot. "Ready, Cap'n?"

"Lead on, Clem," Stryker said. Butterflies were dancing in his stomach.

Trimble led Stryker and Birchwood out of the basin; then he swung south along the lee of a low ridge. They were making their way through country made rough by close-growing juniper, mesquite and jumbled rocks when, after fifteen minutes, Trimble stopped. He motioned Stryker into a narrow arroyo, choked with brush and stands of low-growing prickly pear.

The old man's voice dropped to a gravelly whisper. "Up there, on the ridge, Cap'n, we can see Dugan's camp. The arroyo goes back a ways, maybe half a mile, then curves around and heads back to the place where we left the horses. It's hard going, but we'll be well hid when Dugan's men come lookin' fer us."

Stryker had an idea. "Clem, can we get through the arroyo in the dark?"

"Sure, Cap'n. We'll get our asses tore up by cactus, but we can get through."

"They'd have more trouble finding us in the dark," Stryker said. "If they even try."

Trimble glanced at the sky where the sun had not yet reached its highest point. "Then we got us a wait."

"In the meantime, we'll get onto the ridge and take a look."

The climb was steep with few handholds and patches of loose gravel hiding among the brush and grass. Coming down would be a lot faster and Stryker consoled himself with that thought.

Lying on his belly between Trimble and Birchwood, Stryker made his way to the rim and looked down at the valley below. Its slopes were thickly covered in timber and a fair-running creek ran along its entire length.

Pierce and his men were camped near the tree

line, behind an arc of yellow sand. A single tent stood near the creek and two wagons were parked close to the pines, beside them the horse line where eight mules and a dozen saddle horses were tethered.

Stryker glanced at the sun. It was still behind him and he raised his field glasses, sure that there would be no flash of sunlight on the lenses.

He swept the camp, counting nine armed men coming and going near the fire and its smoking coffeepot. He saw no sign of Pierce or Dugan.

Then something happened that started his heart hammering in his chest and made a desert of his mouth.

Rake Pierce, big and hairy, wearing only the bottom part of his long johns stepped out of the tent. Dugan, bigger and even more hairy, came out behind him.

Pierce held a naked Apache girl by her upper arm. He looked around, scratched his belly, then raised a leg and broke wind, the fart so loud it sounded like a rifle shot. Beside him now, Dugan slapped his back and laughed.

The girl was struggling to get away, but Pierce held her in a vice grip. He looked around again and beckoned to a man to come closer. The man, tall and lanky, wearing greasy buckskins, stepped in front of him and Pierce threw the girl to him. He said something to the lanky man that made Dugan guffaw and slap his thigh again, and the man grabbed the girl, laid back his head and howled like an animal.

As Stryker watched, the man in buckskins dragged

the naked girl under the wagon, pulled down his pants and rolled on top of her. Pierce watched for a while; then he and Dugan stepped back into the tent.

But it wasn't over. Horror was about to pile atop horror. Stryker's glasses filled with the image of the buckskinned man reaching his climax, then collapsing his whole weight on top of the girl. Finally he rolled out from under the wagon, pulled up his pants and dragged out the Apache. He looked around the camp and hollered, "Anybody else want a taste?"

Getting no takers, he casually took out his knife and cut the girl's throat. Then he put his knee on the small of her back and scalped her. Brandishing the bloody scalp above his head, the lanky man ran around the camp, whooping like an Indian. His compadres stopped what they were doing and looked and laughed. A couple of them even joined in the demented cavort, jumping over the dead girl's bloody body.

Sickened, numbed by what he had just witnessed, Stryker edged down from the ridge. He lay on his back and rested his head on the slope, breathing hard.

He looked at the red-hot coin of the sun, at its molten light that spread from horizon to horizon and burned out every trace of color from the sky, reducing it to pale white ashes.

Stryker closed his eyes, red flashes dancing in their lidded darkness. Something akin to guilt, and to grief, its bastard child, curled in his belly.

He could have killed Rake Pierce but didn't.

All he had to do was tell Clem Trimble to shoot

him. Bad hand or no, the old man could have put a bullet in Pierce's brain pan and it would have been all over.

It would have been easy . . . too easy.

Death would have come clean and fast to Pierce. He wouldn't even have felt the bullet he straddled into hell or known who was killing him.

He needed to know. Stryker wanted the man to despair at the manner and timing of his death. He had to look into Stryker's eyes, burning in their crushed sockets, and know he was in the presence of his judge, jury and executioner and that there was no mercy in him. Only then would Rake Pierce's debt be paid in full and the reckoning be over and done.

Trimble slid down the slope on his back and came to a halt beside Stryker. "Cap'n, if we're waitin' until sundown, we'd best get off this ridge."

Stryker looked at him and blinked, like a man waking from sleep. He held fast on the old man's eyes, thinking about the Apache girl and the terror she must have felt in her last moments. And he recalled the lanky man who murdered as casually as he'd kill a rabbit, without thought or a pang of conscience.

A crazed recklessness rose in Stryker. He was damned if he'd scuttle into the brush and cower like a frightened animal, hiding until dark. He would not give Pierce that satisfaction.

"Clem," he said, "let's dust the bastards."

The old man smiled. "Cap'n, that don't sound like soldier talk."

"No, it's war talk." Stryker smiled without humor.

"Then you're speakin' my language, Cap'n." Trimble looked over at Birchwood, who still seemed to be in shock over the murder of the Apache. "You game for it, sonny?"

Shaken as he was, the young officer stood on his dignity. "Please address me as Lieutenant, Mr. Trimble."

"Sure thing, Lieutenant. Well, sonny, are you game for it?"

Birchwood sighed, then smiled. "Damn right I am."

Stryker looked from Birchwood to Trimble and grinned. "Then let's open the ball, gentlemen."

Chapter 33

Pierce's camp seemed unchanged, until Stryker scanned the horse lines. Two ponies and a mule were missing. He felt concern ball up inside him. Had Pierce and Dugan ridden away for some reason?

No, it could be any two of the renegades. Maybe a couple of men who had left to hunt or were off scouting somewhere.

But Stryker felt uneasy. Pierce and Dugan had the instincts and inclinations of wolves. Had they sensed danger of some kind and fled?

Edging close to Trimble, Stryker told him what he'd seen. The old man nodded, then turned. "See them two teeth I got there on the bottom, Cap'n?" He opened his mouth.

"I see them," Stryker whispered. "They're the only two you have."

"Uh-huh, an' they're what I call 'Indian teeth.' They start to punish me when Apaches are close."

"They punishing you now?"

"You bet, Cap'n. An' hear that? All the birds have gone quiet."

Stryker listened into the afternoon. There was no sound, not even the scratching of insects in the brush. The men in camp seemed not to have noticed. Ten of them had gathered around the fire to eat and a few had lit pipes. No one had bothered to cover the body of the Apache girl and she still lay where she'd fallen. The sunlight gleamed on the polished dark skin of her arms and legs, as if she were still alive and full of health.

Another whisper from Trimble. "I don't see ol' Silas, nor that feller Pierce either."

Stryker bit his lip, his mind working. Finally he said, "Shoot up the tent, Clem. Force them out. Mr. Birchwood and I will concentrate our fire on the men by the fire."

The old man nodded and Stryker turned to Birchwood. "Ready?" The young man raised his hand, his rifle against his shoulder.

"Let's get it done," Stryker said.

He pushed out his Colt and opened up on the men around the campfire, Birchwood's rifle blasting next to him. The renegades jumped up and scattered, all but one who lay stretched out on the ground.

The tent canvas ticked as Trimble's bullets thudded into it. But there was no sign of Pierce or Dugan.

Men were milling in confusion around the camp. Someone, Stryker thought Birchwood, had scored another hit. He saw the lanky man running for cover in the trees, fired at him and missed.

Now the renegades were getting more organized

and bullets were kicking up dirt around Stryker and the others. A man firing at an uphill target tends to shoot high, but Pierce's men were finding the range.

Firing as they came, a half dozen charged for the ridge. Trimble dropped one, and the rest took cover.

Birchwood yelped as a shot kicked gravel hard into his face. He laid down his rifle, knuckled his stinging eyes . . . and missed the start of the Apache attack.

Two dozen riders swept into the camp like hawks attacking doves. With incredible speed and violence, the Apaches gunned down men as they scrambled for cover or ran for their horses. A few of them, unlucky enough not to die, were clubbed to the ground, including the lanky man in buckskins.

It was over as suddenly as it had begun. Six dead men lay sprawled around the camp and the remaining four were herded against a wagon, their hands in the air. Stryker read the fear in their faces, each of them well aware what was in store for him.

Some of the Apaches gathered around the body of the dead girl. One of them stepped away, clubbed his rifle and drove it into the skull of the lanky man. The man's head exploded in a scarlet halo of blood and brain, but the Apache kept clubbing him, even when he lay dead on the ground.

One of the others dropped to his knees. Raised his hands as though in prayer and loudly pleaded for his life. This amused the Apaches highly, until one of them kicked the man into silence.

There was no sign of Pierce and Dugan. As wary

as barn rats, they'd pulled out and left their men to face the Apaches.

Trimble wriggled closer to Stryker. "Cap'n, we'd better skedaddle. The Apaches—"

He never completed what he had to say. The rifle muzzle pressing into the back of his head stilled the words in his mouth.

Stryker turned, looked up and found himself looking into cruel black eyes, glittering in a lined, weather-beaten face, an iron lance blade at his throat.

Trimble found his voice again, looking at the Indian with the lance. "Hail, great chief Geronimo," he said. "I'm right pleased to make your acquaintance."

The Apache, his face emotionless, motioned with his lance, and Stryker and the others got to their feet. Their guns were taken from them and they were pushed down the slope of the ridge.

"Cap'n," Trimble whispered, "I don't have a real good feelin' about this."

Stryker nodded. "I don't need your teeth to tell me that."

Stryker knew that to be taken prisoner by Apaches was to admit to yourself that you were already dead. He recalled that the sign above the gates of hell read, *Abandon hope all ye who enter here*, and he could read words to that effect in the merciless eyes of the warriors around him. They were writ plain enough.

Yet he felt one small glimmer of hope.

They were not herded together with Pierce's men, but ordered to sit near the campfire. Trimble noted looked at him with disdain. "You have the same easy way with lies as all white men." His eyes hardened. "You are a soldier. Why do you come to take our land?"

"That is not my reason for being here," Stryker said. "I hunt a man called Rake Pierce and another called Silas Dugan."

"Why?"

Stryker touched his face. "This, and other reasons."

Geronimo was silent for a few moments, reading Stryker's eyes.

The Apache had a keen intelligence and would not be easily fooled. Stryker knew only truth would satisfy this man. He would detect a lie as easily as a diner spots a fly in his soup.

"I too hunt Pierce and Dugan," Geronimo said. "They've killed and scalped many of my people." He waved a hand. "But they are gone from here."

"Yes, but they were here, and then they rode away."

"They scented the Apache, as the antelope does the wolf."

"That is so."

"What will you do when you find these men?"

"Kill them."

Again Geronimo was silent. Then he said, "It is said that the enemy of my enemy is my friend. I will think on this." His eyes swept the three men. "You may live or you may die. I will decide."

He turned on his heel and walked away.

Birchwood looked at Stryker. "Well, sir, I think that went rather well."

Trimble stated what was in Stryker's mind. "Sonny," he said, "if you think that, you're a damned eejit."

Chapter 34

The day slowly stretched into late afternoon and the heat grew. An Apache brought a bladder of water and tossed it at Stryker's feet. Over at the other side of the camp, men were shrieking, a sound that put Stryker's teeth on edge.

If things turned out badly and the torture began, could he resist screaming and instead curse his enemies? Could he die well?

The cries of men in mortal agony that echoed around the valley convinced him otherwise. They were dying like dogs, and so would he. The Apaches knew how to kill a man slowly and in great pain. Sometimes the torment would last for hours, other times for days.

The women were the worst, or so he'd been told, but there were no women here. That thought brought him little solace.

Birchwood was sitting, his chin on his drawn-up knees. He glanced at Stryker. "Where the hell is he? Let's get it over with."

"Geronimo will be here in his own good time,"

Trimble said. "An Apache don't like to be rushed into a thing."

A scream ripped through the fabric of the afternoon; then another, and another, tearing loose from a man's throat. The Apaches, their faces solemn, were roasting meat on a small fire that had been lit on the man's belly.

Birchwood was very pale. "I won't let them kill me like that," he said. "I'll try to take one of the bastards with me."

Both Stryker and Trimble looked at him, but said nothing. Then the old man said, "Cap'n, you in good with God?"

"No. Are you?"

Trimble shook his head. "We're not exactly on speakin' terms." He looked at Birchwood. "How about you, Lieutenant?"

Stryker answered for him, his voice flat, like a man making a joke on the gallows. "Mr. Birchwood has recently become much taken by whorehouses and strong drink. No use asking him." He looked at Trimble. "Why the sudden interest in God?"

"Because now's a time for prayin', if you catch my drift, Cap'n. Except that nary a one of us is a prayin' man an' that's surely a disappointment to me."

"I can pray, and sing all the grand old hymns," Birchwood said.

"Is that a fact?" Trimble said. "Well, let 'er rip, boy."

The young man waited until a wild, agonized shriek ended in bubbling sobs, then said, "I don't feel much like it."

Stryker passed Birchwood the water bladder. "Take a drink, Mister," he said. "Your throat sounds dry."

Geronimo stepped out of the trees and walked to where Stryker and the others were sitting. The lieutenant rose to his feet.

"I am Goyathlay, the one the white men call Geronimo," the Apache said. "Where I walk, I leave no tracks. I can make rivers run backward and I can still the rising sun in the sky. I am able to do these things because my medicine is strong."

Stryker waited. He felt his heart thud in his chest.

"I have thought long and hard about what I must do, and then the Great Spirit made it clear to me. Crook presses us close and my people must hide in the Madres. Two of you will go after Pierce and Dugan and you will kill them for us. The one who remains must die. You will choose who this man is to be, and tell me."

"Hell, Cap'n, I'm the oldest and it should be me," Trimble said. "I've lived my life and—"

"Clem, shut your fucking mouth," Stryker snapped, angry beyond all measure. He stared into Geronimo's black eyes, his own blazing. "All three of us go, or none of us. We will not choose and we will not leave one of our own behind to be tortured."

"Well," Trimble sighed, "that sure enough thow'd the hog fat on the fire."

Geronimo was silent for a long time, his face still, revealing nothing. Then he said, "If you had chosen otherwise I would have killed all of you. You have spoken like a man and in so doing purchased your lives. You will leave now and kill our enemies."

"How will you know that the thing is done?" Stryker asked.

"I am Goyathlay. It will be written in the wind and I will know." He turned to the warriors around him and said something in his own tongue. The Apaches brought Stryker and the others their guns and then their saddled horses.

Geronimo waited until the three white men had mounted; then he said, "Pierce and Dugan will ride south into Mexico. They have many Apache scalps to sell for gold."

Stryker nodded. He looked across the camp where bloody, broken things were still screaming, but more weakly now. He swung his horse away and the others followed.

He felt Geronimo's eyes on his back until he was swallowed by the shadows of the hills.

They had crossed Big Bend Creek and were heading due south in the direction of the Perilla Mountains before anyone said a word. Predictably it was Trimble, who would speak even when he'd nothing to say.

"That was close, Cap'n," he said. "In all my born days I never come nearer to losin' my hair. 'Course, if a man's gonna get scalped, better it's by ol' Geronimo. It'd give a man the feelin' that the cuttin' had more class, like."

"Clem, I don't want to be scalped by anybody," Birchwood said.

"Just so, Lieutenant. Just so."

They camped that night in Saddle Gap, then crossed into Mexico early next morning, riding into rolling country just south of where the peaks of the oak- and pine-covered mountains of the Sierra Madres brushed against the sky.

For an hour they followed a military road that cut through shaggy oak forests, and then stopped at a wicker and adobe village that had spread itself along both banks of a creek.

It was just short of noon, but the heat was intense and the village seemed deserted as its inhabitants sought shelter from the raking sun.

A cantina, consisting of a single adobe building with an adjoining outhouse, stood at the end of the main street, the name *El Lobo Rojo* painted on the wall to the right of the door.

Stryker and the others looped their reins around the hitching rail and stepped inside. Away from the pitiless sun, the interior of the cantina felt shady and cool. A bar stood in a corner, an array of bottles on its shelves. There were a few tables and chairs, and a doorway, covered by a blanket, led into another room.

Stryker stepped to the bar and ordered tequila for himself and Trimble. He nodded in Birchwood's direction. "He'll have milk if you have it, water if you don't."

"I have no tequila, Senor," the bartender said. He was small and very dark, with quick brown eyes. He shrugged. "Only mescal."

"Then that will have to do."

He put fingers to his bleeding lips and wailed, "Why did you do that?"

Stryker smiled. "Because you have no cojones."

He walked out into the bright sunlight, Birchwood and Trimble grinning beside him. They swung into the saddle and rode south.

Behind them Felipe stood at the door of the cantina and aired out his lungs, throwing curses at them in Spanish and English.

"I think you upset that little feller, Cap'n," Trimble said.

"Serves him right," Stryker said.

Chapter 35

For the remainder of the day they rode through the foothills of the Madres, avoiding the high desert country that stretched almost three hundred miles to the east. That night they camped in an arroyo and made a meager supper of the last of their bacon and some stale biscuits.

The next morning Trimble picked up sign—the tracks of shod horses—but lost them again in the canyons and the oak, juniper and piñon forests that covered much of the mountain country.

"I reckon we're two hundred and fifty miles north of Chihuahua, give or take," Trimble said. "It's a lot of country to cover, Cap'n."

"We'll catch up to them sooner than that," Stryker said. "They're close; maybe only a few miles ahead of us."

"And Geronimo is right behind us," Birchwood said. "Sir, do you think he'll be looking over our shoulders to see that we do what we promised?"

Stryker shook his head. "I doubt it. My guess is

that he's already shaken off General Crook, crossed the border and is heading for his old stomping grounds in the eastern Madres. From there he can strike deep into central Mexico and raid into Texas and New Mexico."

Trimble nodded. "The Apaches have their women and young 'uns stashed in the mountains. Nothing an Indian does makes sense and he'll fool you every time, but I think you got it right, Cap'n."

"I sure hope so, Clem," Stryker said. "I don't want to meet up with Geronimo again, unless it's to take his surrender."

"An' that's the day pigs will fly, Cap'n," the old man grinned.

At noon they rode into another village and managed to barter one of their spare Colts for tortillas, beans, bacon and a small sack of coffee.

The village mayor said that he had not seen the two *americanos* and that in all his life he'd never even met a man with red hair and a red beard.

He also asked if the United States was at war with Mexico to bring Army officers so far south.

Stryker realized that the blue blouses and officer's shoulder straps worn by him and Birchwood were too conspicuous. Further bartering obtained them a couple of baggy cotton shirts. After they left the village, he and Birchwood changed, stashing the uniform blouses in their blanket rolls.

Trimble, who'd been watching closely, could not let that go without comment. "Well, Cap'n," he said, "you two look like a couple of Messkin peasants an' no mistake. Now you don't have all that gold braid on your shoulders, maybe I should start callin' you Pancho instead of Cap'n, huh?"

Stryker turned to the old man. "See that rifle under your knee, Clem?"

"I see it."

"Call me Pancho just once and I'll shove it right up your ass."

Trimble cackled and slapped his thigh, as if it were the funniest thing he'd ever heard.

A horseman traveling from here to there leaves a scar on the country, even in the mountains. The mark made by Pierce and Dugan was the death they left in their wake.

The day was fading into dusk when Stryker and the others rode up on the abandoned coach. They had been following a well maintained wagon road that curved around an outcropping of rock and had hidden the coach until they were almost on top of it.

Its four horses were still in the traces and had pulled the coach toward a patch of grama grass growing beside the road. But one of the rear wheels had wedged between rocks and the horses had been brought to a halt. They stood with their heads low, too tired to kick at the flies that clouded around their legs.

Stryker swung out of the saddle and stepped closer to the coach. There was a dead man slumped in the driver's seat. He wore the fancy trappings of a vaquero, embroidered short jacket and silver-studded pants. His ivory handled Colt was still in the holster.

An older man was sprawled inside the coach, gray-haired and distinguished looking. He'd been shot several times. The man was impeccably dressed in the highest fashion, but by the disarray of his clothing it looked as though he'd been robbed of his jewelry and watch and chain.

"Over here, Cap'n!"

Stryker answered Trimble's beckoning arm and walked to the side of the road where he was standing. "Take a look," he said. "She says it all."

The woman had been young, dark and exceedingly beautiful. She lay on her back, stripped half naked, her legs forced open. She'd been raped, and then her throat had been cut. The middle finger of her left hand had been cut off, probably to get at a ring she'd worn.

Stryker looked at Trimble. "Pierce and Dugan?"

"Who else, Cap'n?"

"This is a private coach," Birchwood said. "It's got a fancy coat of arms on the door and the words 'Hacienda Cantrell.'"

"Some rich rancher's rig," Trimble said. "Probably belongs to the man inside. I reckon this was his wife or daughter."

The vaqueros came from the south, eight men riding hard in a cloud of dust. Before Stryker could react, he and the others were surrounded, steady guns pointed at them.

One of the vaqueros looked down at the dead woman and said something in Spanish to Stryker. He shook his head. "*Americano,*" he said.

An emotion that could have been pity crossed the

vaquero's hard, lined face. "This is very bad for you," he said.

"We found the coach and the bodies," Stryker said. "These people have been dead for hours."

The vaquero made no answer. He turned his head and looked as a handsome young man riding a magnificent palomino stallion galloped beside them. The man savagely drew rein, the horse's haunches slamming into the ground.

He leaped from the saddle and ran to the dead woman. He kneeled, cradled her in his arms and raised his face to the sky, letting out a scream of loss, grief and despair that splintered apart the hush of the evening and sounded barely human.

The vaquero who had first spoken to Stryker had dismounted. He stuck his gun into the lieutenant's ribs and whispered, "I think, very bad for you now."

Stryker knew it was useless to protest his innocence again, and he held his silence.

After that one primitive scream, the young man held the woman in his arms, sobbing, his head bent over her. Minutes passed; then one of the vaqueros, older than the others, stepped beside him.

He quietly said something in Spanish to the man, then nodded toward Stryker.

Their eyes met; the young man's were full of death.

He rose to his feet and looked into the coach, standing motionless for several long moments. Now he turned again to Stryker. After the initial shock of seeing the lieutenant's crushed face, he said quietly, evenly, almost without anger, "It will take you a long, long time to die, my friend."

Stryker had feared Geronimo, and now he feared this man. But he came quickly to anger, figuring he had been pushed around enough and had nothing to lose.

"I'm an officer of the United States Army, and I did not kill these people," he said. "We found them just before your men arrived."

"That's the God's honest truth, your worship," Trimble said. "But we've been hunting the men who did this."

The young man's eyes ranged over Stryker, taking in his sky blue breeches with their yellow stripes and the knee-high cavalry boots.

Sensing the man's dawning doubt, Stryker stepped to his horse and removed his and Birchwood's shirts. He threw the young lieutenant his, then held up his own where the shoulder straps could be seen. "First Lieutenant Steve Stryker, United States Cavalry, at your service."

The vaquero who'd been holding a gun to Stryker's ribs said something to the young Mexican, who reached out and grabbed the lieutenant's hands. After a while he dropped them and said, "Pedro is right, you have no blood on your hands."

"We have no blood on our hands, nor do we have the jewelry that was taken from the bodies," Stryker said. "You may search us if you have a mind."

The young man thought long and hard, then shook his head. "That will be unnecessary, Lieutenant. If you were the guilty ones, you would not have lingered at the scene of your crimes." He shoved out his hand. "My name is Don Carlos Santiago Cantrell. The man in the coach is my father, and yonder lies my wife. They were returning from the mission in the village of Playa Vicente where my wife prayed that the Madonna would bless us with a child. But she gave us no child, only death."

Stryker shook the young Mexican's hand, then Cantrell's black eyes flicked to the dead man in the driving seat. "I should have ridden with the gun, not that cowardly *hijo de puta.*"

He looked back to Stryker. "I am honor bound to invite you to my hacienda, Lieutenant. But tonight no lamps will be lit in my home and my people will wail in mourning. It is not a place where you would wish to be."

Stryker looked at the sky, at the darkness crowding closer, shadowing the vast land. "We will camp farther down the trail tonight, Don Carlos," he said.

The man nodded. "I will join you with my vaqueros tomorrow before the noon hour. Together we will hunt the men who did this. Give me their names."

"Rake Pierce and Silas Dugan. Pierce is a deserter from my regiment, and both are murderers and rapists. They rob and kill without conscience, as they did here."

Cantrell repeated the names, then said, "Be ready to ride tomorrow, Lieutenant. If I must, I will hunt those men to the ends of the earth."

The man turned on his heel and swung into the

saddle. A vaquero carried his dead wife to him and placed her reverently in his arms.

The vaquero named Pedro closed the coach door and then gave the reins of his horse to another man. He climbed into the driver's seat and kicked the dead guard to the ground.

He slapped the lines and the coach bumped over the rocks and lurched into motion, the other vaqueros following, surrounding their grieving *patrón*.

Stryker waited until the Mexicans were out of sight, then mounted his horse. "Clem, you can see better in the dark than I can. Ride on ahead and find us a place to camp for the night," he said.

The old man cackled, then nodded. "I've got cat's eyes, an' no mistake, Cap'n. And lately, I've come to believe that atween us, we got us ourselves more lives than a cat."

Stryker smiled. "Maybe, but if we do, I think we're fast running out of them."

"A truer word was never spoke, Cap'n." Trimble grinned, knuckled his forehead and rode into the gloom, the first stars of night glittering high above him.

"The old man is right, sir," Birchwood said. "That was a damned close-run thing."

"And it's not over yet," Stryker said. "I have a feeling our troubles are just about to start."

Chapter 36

Trimble found a camping spot in an oak grove near a thin rock spring. The old man fried bacon and wrapped the greasy strips in tortillas, a supper Birchwood, with his youngster's appetite, declared a "crackerjack meal."

Trimble sat opposite Stryker across a hatful of fire, and froze his coffee cup to his lips, speaking quietly around the rim. "Don't look around right now, Cap'n," he said, "but there's somebody in the trees."

"Maybe it's a bear," Birchwood said. He opened the cotton shirt and undid his holster flap.

"My teeth are aching like hell," Trimble said. "It's an Injun fer sure."

He rose slowly to his feet, both hands up and visible on his cup. "Come right on in, big chief," he said, talking into the black wall of the night. "We've got coffee on the bile."

A few tense moments passed; then the darkness parted and a man carrying a rifle stepped into the camp. He wore white cotton pants tucked into high moccasins, a shirt of the same color and over that a blue vest, decorated with beadwork. His hair was cropped short with no attempt at style and the top half of his face was painted black.

He was looking at Trimble, but his eyes missed nothing, especially the slow rising of Stryker and Birchwood.

"He's Comanche, by God," Trimble said. "I haven't seen one o' them in nigh on twenty year." The old man raised his hand, smiled and said, "*Maruawe*, great chief."

The man ignored the traditional Comanche greeting and looked around the camp, his eyes resting briefly on Stryker's face.

Trimble had run through all the Comanche he knew and now he said, "I see you have cut your hair and blackened your face. You are in mourning, great chief."

"My name is Thomas, and this you will call me. I mourn the death of Donna Maria Elaina Cantrell. She was my friend."

Stryker was on edge. Did the Comanche believe they were guilty of the girl's murder? Was he about to push it?

Birchwood was obviously thinking along the same lines, because his hand was close to his Colt, his eyes fixed on the Indian.

"I will drink coffee now," Thomas said. He squatted right where he was, waiting.

Birchwood forced himself to relax. His hand dropped from his gun and he said, "You speak English very well, Thomas."

The man nodded. "The Texas Rangers taught the Comanche to speak English pretty damn quick."

He accepted coffee from Trimble, then fished a pipe out of his pocket, which he lit from the fire.

After a couple of minutes of silence, Stryker said, "Thomas, we did not kill Mrs. Cantrell."

"I know you did not. If I thought otherwise, you'd all be dead."

The man was silent again, then took something from his pocket. He held up a small silver locket. "I found this on the trail a mile south of here. It was given to Donna Maria by her mother when she was a child. She wore it around her neck all the time. Don Carlos would laugh and say, 'I offer you diamonds, but you will wear only a cheap silver locket.' And Donna Maria would say, "Husband, this locket is more precious to me than diamonds.' Yes, that's what she would say. I have heard her say that many times."

The Comanche was quiet again, deep in thought; then he said, "The men who murdered Donna Maria threw the locket aside as having no value, as they considered her life of no value. Soon they will curse the day they were born and the mother that bore them."

Thomas drained his cup, then rose to his feet. He looked at Stryker. "You ran afoul of a cougar or a bear?"

"No, this was done by Rake Pierce, one of the men we are hunting."

The Comanche nodded. "Then him I will leave for you."

He turned away and let the darkness swallow him.

"Right nice feller," Trimble said. "A talkin' man, fer an Injun."

"I'm glad he's on our side," Birchwood said.

"He's on his own side," Stryker said, staring into the night. "I hope he does what he said and leaves Pierce for me."

The sun had not reached its highest point in the sky when Cantrell and four riders met Stryker and the others on the trail. The man had swapped the flashy palomino for an ugly, hammerheaded mustang that looked like it could run all day and then some.

Stryker told Cantrell about his meeting with the Comanche, but the man showed no surprise. "He had to see you for himself," he said. "Thomas makes his own judgments."

"Where is he, your worship?" Trimble asked. "I was just saying last night that he looks like a real nice feller."

"He is ahead of us. He will find the men we seek." Cantrell looked at Trimble. "Thomas has killed seventeen men, eight of them on my order. He is not 'a real nice feller' as you say, old man. He makes a terrible enemy."

As they headed south along the ragged edge of the foothills, Stryker fell in beside Cantrell. After sorting out in his mind the order of his words, he said, "Are your wife and father laid to rest?"

The man nodded. "Yes, in our family mausoleum. One day I will rest beside them."

that as well, because he was smiling and nodding at the Apaches, though they studiously ignored him.

Birchwood seemed scared, and that was no fault in him. But he held his head high, preparing to die like an officer and a gentleman and bring no disgrace to his regiment or family.

An hour passed. The Apaches reverently wrapped the body of the dead girl in a blanket and carried her into the trees. The three remaining captives were stripped naked and spread-eagled on their backs, their ankles and wrists bound with rawhide to stakes. The man who had begged for mercy was whimpering, and one of the others, who could have been the breed Billy Lee had mentioned, told him to shut the hell up.

The Apache that Trimble had identified as Geronimo stepped in front of Stryker. There was nothing about him to suggest he was a great war chief. He wore a white Mexican shirt, breech cloth and buckskin moccasins to his knees. His head was bound in a black headband and he carried a new Winchester '73 in his hands.

"Who speaks for you?" he demanded.

Stryker rose to his feet. "I do."

Geronimo looked at him closely, with the wide-eyed curiosity of a child. "Broken Face. I have heard your name spoken many times."

"And I have heard the name of Geronimo many times. And always men say you are a great chief, a brave warrior and mighty hunter."

If Stryker thought flattery would get him everywhere, he was quickly disillusioned. The Apache

"I'm sorry, Don Carlos. I thought I might find the words, but I can't."

The young man was silent, a frown on his handsome face. "It is done, Lieutenant, and all the words have been said." He turned bleak eyes to Stryker. "I should have ridden with the gun. Instead, as my wife was being raped and murdered, I was on the range, to see how the summer rains had improved my grass. That is something I will live with forever."

"The Apaches are far to the east; how could you expect there would be danger?" Stryker asked. "Wild beasts like Pierce and Dugan are few and, like wolves, seldom encountered."

Cantrell nodded. "You speak well, Lieutenant, and I know it comes from the heart. But the sin is mine and words will not wash it away."

The trail stubbed its toe on high, broken country and the way south became difficult. Oak and pine forests continually barred the way and deep, brushy arroyos cut across their path. Stryker looked longingly at the scrub desert to the east, mostly flat-riding country, its hazy pink mesas rising like dismasted ghost ships on a shifting yellow sea. But there was little water in the desert and what there was was hidden deep and hard to find. It was a place where determined men might endure, but not horses.

After two hours, Trimble, again riding point, began to find sign left by the Comanche: two deep cuts in a tree trunk or a couple of rocks laid in the middle of the trail. Thomas had Pierce and Dugan's scent, and he was following them close.

The trees thinned again, and Stryker could see

half a mile of trail ahead of them. It led through a rocky canyon, then climbed abruptly among scattered juniper and piñon toward a high plateau.

The flurry of shots came from beyond the tableland. Then there was a lull, followed by several more.

Trimble came down the slope at a fast canter, drew rein and pointed behind him. "The cornered rats are fighting back, Cap'n. I reckon the Injun is in a world of trouble."

Stryker kicked his horse into motion, Birchwood beside him. Followed by Cantrell and his men, he hit the slope at a run and drew rein at the top of the plateau. Level ground stretched away for a hundred yards, then began a gradual descent into a wide forested valley. There the mountains intruded, and a sheer V of raw rock at least sixty feet high jutted into the valley floor. The trail ahead curved around the mountain and then was lost from sight.

The sound of two more shots crashed headlong into the quiet of the day, followed by a ringing silence.

Stryker drew his Colt and charged down the incline, the rest thundering after him. He swung around the rock outcropping at a gallop, then found himself in the south end of the valley. Here timber-covered peaks soared skyward on each side, and a mountain drain-off cut across the valley floor. On the far bank of the creek, half hidden by cottonwoods, sprawled a tangle of ancient volcanic rock. Thomas was sitting on one of these, blood staining the front of his shirt.

There was no sign of Pierce and Dugan.

Chapter 37

Stryker splashed across the creek, flanked by Birchwood and Cantrell. The Mexican had waved his men forward and they'd galloped off to the south with Trimble. But Pierce and Dugan could easily lose themselves in this country and it would be a useless pursuit.

A bullet had plowed across the Comanche's left shoulder, near the neck, a bloody wound that had turned the front of his shirt crimson.

"The two men we hunt were hidden in the rocks," Thomas said, addressing Stryker. "One of them fired too soon and"—he motioned to his shoulder—"gave me this. I rode into the trees and fired back. They did not wait around long."

Cantrell stepped closer to the Indian, his face concerned. "Can you ride, amigo?"

"Si, *patrón,*" Thomas answered. "I would ride with more serious wounds than this."

He turned away and foraged among the trees for willow leaves and wildflowers. When he returned to the waiting men his shoulder was padded and the bleeding had stopped.

Thomas looked at the sky, clear blue with no cloud in sight. "Thunder is coming," he said, "and much rain. There is an abandoned village ten miles to the south and it is my mind that the men we chase could seek shelter there." He nodded. "Maybe so."

A look of horror flashed in Cantrell's face and he hurriedly crossed himself. "I know that village, Thomas. *El Pueblo de la Muerte* is a place of evil. We cannot go there." He looked at Stryker. "It was a plague village, many years ago, and the ghosts of the dead still walk there."

"Don Carlos, maybe there are things that scare Pierce and Dugan—I don't know, but I doubt that ghosts are one of them."

"The men we chase will not go to the village, Lieutenant. No one goes there."

"They might, if they don't know its reputation."

"My vaqueros are simple men and so superstitious they will ride five miles around a place where a vaquero was struck by lightning. They will not enter the pueblo." As the Comanche had done, Cantrell looked at the sky. "Besides, there will be no storm."

Thomas shook his head. "Your pardon, *patrón*, but the thunder is coming."

Stryker turned to Birchwood. "Are you afraid of the boogerman, Lieutenant?"

"No, sir."

"Thomas, you will enter the village?"

"I do not fear spirits."

"And Trimble will make four of us." Stryker looked at Cantrell. "Don Carlos, you and your men can stay at a distance and seal off the approaches to the village from the north and south. Pierce won't head east into the desert and his way to the west is blocked by the mountains."

"Five of us will go, Lieutenant. It is my duty. I will post my vaqueros around the pueblo as you say."

Cantrell's men returned an hour later. They'd seen no sign of Pierce or Dugan. Cantrell spoke to them, about the death village and the task he had for them.

Reading the expressions of the vaqueros, Stryker saw that they had no desire to get close to the place. Years before, men like these had passed on their fears of haunts and ghosts to the Texas punchers, who were now among the most superstitious group of men on earth.

One by one, a few of the older riders among them spoke up, their brown faces concerned, even frightened. All of the vaqueros had faced Apaches, outlaws and cattle rustlers without thought for their own hides. But these were men who believed that bad luck would follow if you used the same iron on an animal twice, placed your left foot in the stirrup first or put on your hat in bed. The supernatural was very real to them, and the evil reputation of the plague pueblo realer still.

In the end, and after what seemed to be a lot of convincing, the vaqueros agreed to cover the north and south approaches to the village—at a safe distance.

"They will let no one in or out," Cantrell told Stryker.

"If a big rain comes as Thomas says, Pierce and Dugan will have reached the village before us," Stryker said. "We'll go in real quiet and easy, and on foot."

Cantrell nodded. "If they are there, we will find them."

Stryker smiled. "Or they'll find us."

Because of the threat of another ambush, both Trimble and the Comanche took the point. After clearing the valley, the trail along the mountains climbed upward and the country became more rugged.

Stryker calculated that they were at least eight thousand feet above the flat, and the juniper and piñon began to give way to high timber, mainly ponderosa and lodgepole pine, cut through by thick forests of oak.

As Thomas had predicted, the sky lowered on the riders like a lead roof and a stiffening breeze gusted off the mountains. It was not yet three in the afternoon, but the day was growing dark and a few splashy drops of rain were being tossed around in the wind.

Behind Stryker the vaqueros were talking among themselves and he was sure the death village and its malignant spirits was the sole topic of conversation.

It was also uppermost in Cantrell's mind. He edged his mustang closer to Stryker. "Lieutenant, it has been said by those few who have visited the village and survived that on days like this the souls of the dead can be heard wailing, lamenting their fate. I have heard that the plague killed a hundred people in less than a week. Another week passed, and by then everyone was dead."

Stryker smiled. "The wailing is the sound of the wind tangled in the trees, Don Carlos."

The young man shook his head. "No, the wailing comes from the village, not the trees." Thunder rumbled in the distance, and Cantrell said, "On days like this, the spirits walk. You will hear them, and see them."

"Don Carlos, right now I'm more afraid of Pierce and Dugan than I am the ghosts of dead peasants."

"We will kill them, Lieutenant, never fear. The spirits of my wife and father are already reaching out to me. Their spirits will not rest until they are avenged. That is what they are telling me."

Stryker looked at him and said, "That time is close, when we'll kill Pierce and Dugan or they'll kill us. One way or another, the reckoning is at hand. For me at least, it's been a long time in coming."

"How are you with the *pistola*, Lieutenant?" Cantrell asked.

Stryker smiled. It was a shade late for that question. "Fair," he said.

The young Mexican tapped the handle of his Colt in its fancy gun rig. "I'm less than fair. I use this to string wire and hammer nails."

"Please, Don Carlos," Stryker sighed. "Don't give me any more good news."

"I just thought you should know," Cantrell said. He did not smile when he said it.

Chapter 38

The monsoon season comes early to northern Mexico, by mid-June, but it lasts well into the summer months. Its broad fronts push into the southwestern United States and reach as far as California, bringing torrential rains and savage winds.

One such front was stalking Stryker and the men who rode with him. The sky was dark, ugly and mean, the day swirling with rain, and the light had disappeared among the tall timber. Thunder detonated with a sound of dynamite, deafening and intimidating, and lightning cracked open the clouds like eggs.

Stryker rode with his head lowered against the downpour. The relentless rain rattled against his hat and soaked him to the skin, bringing with it a chill.

He didn't see Trimble until the old man was almost on top of him. His face streaming, he yelled above the racket of the storm, "Village a mile ahead, Cap'n."

Stryker abbreviated his speech. "Pierce?"

Trimble shook his head.

Cantrell heard the exchange and went back to talk with his vaqueros.

"Lead on, Clem," Stryker yelled.

He tried to build a cigarette, but wind and rain batted tobacco and paper from his fingers. Disappointed, he gave up and threw away the shredded remains.

After a few minutes the trail dropped lower, losing a hundred feet, until it opened up on a wide, grassy valley, studded with oaks and pines that ticked rain and shimmered like silver columns in the lightning flashes.

Stryker saw four of Cantrell's men drop out of the column and ride east until they disappeared into the gray curtain of the rain. The pueblo must be close.

Trimble swung east, motioning Stryker and the others to follow. The remaining vaqueros rode on to stake out the village from the other side. Thomas rode out of the darkness and swung his horse beside Stryker. The black paint on his face ran down his throat and chest and mingled with the rusty stain of blood on his shirt. He was quiet and withdrawn and said nothing.

The village consisted of adobe houses clustered around a central plaza where there was a church, stores and a well. Most of the buildings were ruined and the church roof had caved in years before. The shop fronts were crumbling, though a couple still had the tattered remains of canvas awnings that flapped in the wind. To the south of the village, beyond a stand of timber, lay an ancient lava flow, most of it as tall as a man on a horse. A few bushes and bunches of scrub grass struggled for life on its top, adding to the rain-swept bleakness of the place.

Stryker found shelter in the trees, then swept the pueblo with his field glasses, pausing constantly to wipe rain from the lenses. Several of the adobes still had roofs and if Pierce and Dugan had sought shelter here, they would be in one of them. No horses were in sight, but they would have taken their mounts inside with them or stabled them in another adobe.

Wordlessly, he passed the glasses to Birchwood; then he motioned Cantrell, Trimble and the Comanche closer. "The adobe on the left, under the oak. We'll take the horses inside there, then sweep the village on foot." He looked at Trimble. "Clem, how is the hand?"

"I'll manage, Cap'n."

Stryker waited until a thunderclap rolled across the sky, then said, "Both these men are good with guns, but Silas Dugan is better than most. Be careful, and keep another man in sight at all times." He looked around at his four companions. "Any questions?"

There were none and Stryker said, "Then we'll ride on in."

They had to cross fifty yards of open ground, but the day was so wild and the visibility so bad that Stryker was confident they could pass unnoticed. That proved to be the case because they reached the adobe without drawing fire.

The house was small, but it was large enough to

accommodate the horses and it still had most of its roof.

Trimble loosened the girth on his mount, then wiped rain off his face with his sleeve. "What do we do now, Cap'n? Start kicking in doors?"

"Thomas can see and hear better than any of us." He turned to the Comanche, rain dripping from his hat onto the mud floor. "Can you find them?"

The Indian nodded. "If they are here, I will find them."

"We'll do some searching ourselves," Stryker said. "But if you find out where they're at, come looking for us. Don't try to take them by yourself." He looked into the man's eyes. "Do you understand?"

Thomas nodded, but said nothing. He turned on his heel and stepped outside the door. An instant later he was dead.

Stryker heard the two shots, close together and louder than the roaring of the thunder. He ran for the door, his Colt in his hand.

Rain whip-lashed through the village, and searing lightning flares followed one after another. Thomas lay sprawled on his back, splashed with mud from his fall. Rake Pierce stood ten yards away.

The man's long black hair tossed across his bearded face and he was grinning.

"Pierce, you bastard!" Stryker screamed, all his pent-up fury turning his voice into a rabid shriek of rage. He raised his gun and fired at Pierce, who was starkly outlined by a shimmering lightning flash.

Pierce fired back, then ducked behind a low wall.

Stryker followed, his boots splashing through mud, mouth open in a soundless roar. He reached the wall, the downpour hissing around him. But Pierce was nowhere in sight.

Then, from somewhere ahead of him, unseen behind the spinning maelstrom of wind and rain, came the man's roaring voice. "I'm gonna kill you, Lieutenant Stryker. Goddamn you, we'll end it here today."

Chapter 39

Boots pounded behind Stryker and he turned quickly, his gun coming up fast.

"Don't shoot, Cap'n!" Trimble yelled. "It's us!"

The three men ducked behind the wall and Birchwood said, "We tried to head him off, came round behind the adobe, but he was gone."

"He fired at me, then ran away, damn him," Stryker said.

Trimble nodded. "Ol' Rake likes an edge, Cap'n. Standin' out in the open that way, he figgered he didn't have one."

"Was that the man Pierce shouting, Lieutenant?" Cantrell asked.

"Yes, that was him."

"He's trying to get you good an' mad, Cap'n," Trimble said. "In a gunfight, an angry man is a dead man."

"He's succeeding," Stryker said.

His mind was working. As Trimble said, Pierce would look for an edge. But what kind of an edge?

His eyes moved across the plaza to the three ruined stores. Each had an open front where goods had been displayed, leaving a wall about four foot high under them. Unlike the windowless adobes, a man could shoot from concealment there.

Was that where Pierce and Dugan were holed up?

The range was too great for his Colt. He turned to Birchwood who was white-knuckling his Winchester in both hands.

"Lieutenant, dust along the store fronts over yonder and we'll see what happens. You too, Clem."

Both men rose and fired at the stores, working their way along the open fronts. Bullets thudded into adobe or rattled through the stores, followed by sounds of shattering pottery and glass.

"Cease fire!" Stryker yelled.

He did not have long to wait for a reaction.

Both Pierce and Dugan rose from behind the low wall of the middle store, working their rifles. Bullets chipped Vs of adobe along the top of the wall, and Birchwood, a split second too late in getting to cover, was hit, a round opening up his left cheekbone.

Stryker turned to him. "You all right, Lieutenant?"

The young man looked at the fingers he'd touched to his cheek, now streaming with rain and blood. "I believe so, sir," he said.

"A battle scar to show your betrothed," Stryker grinned.

Birchwood nodded. "I sincerely hope it's the only one."

Cantrell stuck his gun over the adobe wall and shot at the store. But return fire drove him behind the wall again.

"Lieutenant," he said, "we know where they are and they know where we are, so how do we get to them?"

"The short answer is 'not easily,'" Stryker said. He looked at Birchwood. "I guess you know you're bleeding like a stuck pig."

The lieutenant nodded, the blood running down his cheek intermingled with rain so it had taken on a pink cast. "I've always been a bleeder, sir, ever since I was a boy. One time I remember—"

"Stryker!"

The voice from the store front was not Pierce's. It was Silas Dugan's harsh rasp.

Stryker turned to Trimble. "Clem, see if you can do something for Mr. Birchwood's wound." He got closer to the wall and yelled, "Dugan, you sorry piece of shit, what do you want?"

"Harsh words, Lieutenant. A thing I'll keep in mind. It could make the difference atween you getting it in the belly or the head."

"I asked you, Dugan, what the hell do you want?"

Thunder shook the village and lightning scratched across the black sky. The wind had turned ferocious, baring its teeth, ratcheting up the rage of the raking rain.

"Stryker!" Dugan yelled. "Are you still there?"

The lieutenant glanced at Birchwood. Trimble had torn a strip off the white cotton shirt he was wearing and had wound it under the young man's chin and tied it at the top of his head. It seemed to have stopped the bleeding, at least for now.

"I'm here! What do you want?"

"See, me and ol' Rake are getting soaking wet and we got the coffee hunger. So what do you say we have it out, us against you four? Step into the plaza and so will we, and then we can go to our work and end this thing."

"Clem," Stryker asked, "can we take them?"

The old man shook his head. "Not a chance in hell, Cap'n."

Stryker bit his lip, thinking. Rain dripped from his hat in strings that got caught up in the wind and scattered into the roaring day.

"Clem, give me your rifle," he said.

Doubt in his eyes, Trimble handed over the Winchester. Stryker stood and fired at the store where Pierce and Dugan were holed up.

After he ducked back again, grinning, Trimble asked, "Hit anything, Cap'n?"

Stryker shook his head. "No, that was just my answer to Dugan's proposal."

A moment later, his voice angry, the gunman yelled, "Now you get it in the belly, Stryker."

Long minutes ticked past and the rain and wind grew in intensity, driving mud and stinging pine needles into the four men crouched behind the wall.

"Anybody hear that?" Birchwood asked, his face stiff with unease.

Trimble nodded. "Yeah, Lieutenant, I've been hearing it for quite a spell."

And so had Stryker. A thin, eerie wailing rose and fell in the wind; a lost, lonely sound, as poignant as a widow's tears.

Cantrell crossed himself hurriedly. "It is the cries of the dead," he whispered. "They walk abroad in the storm."

Trimble looked hard at the young Mexican. "Don Carlos, I don't know what's scarin' me more, Rake an' ol' Silas, or you!"

"Be very afraid, old man," Cantrell said. "Many people have come to this village seeking plunder, and few have ever returned."

The wailing carried in the wind like smoke, shredding into what sounded like long, drawn-out sobs.

Stryker prided himself in being a practical man, but he felt shivers finger up and down his spine. He had been taught many things at West Point, but dealing with the supernatural had not been one of them.

Then it seemed that Pierce and Dugan had missed that particular lesson themselves.

"Stryker!" Dugan yelled. "Who's doing all that damned screaming?"

"It's all the people you've murdered, Dugan," Stryker called out. "Those are dead Apache women and children coming back for your dirty scalp."

He waited a moment and hollered. "Surrender now, Dugan, and we'll protect you."

"You go to hell!"

Bullets chipped along the top of the wall and whined into the gloom.

Trimble shook his head. "I never took ol' Silas for a scaredy-cat when it comes to ha'ants an' sich."

"He has a right to be afraid," Cantrell said.

Stryker latched onto that. Had the wailing unnerved the superstitious Dugan so much that he might have grown careless?

Now was the time to do something, a course of action better than waiting for night, when he and the others could slink away like whipped dogs.

"Mr. Birchwood," he said, his mind made up, "I'm going for my horse. You and the others will lay down a covering fire."

The lieutenant had been trained not to question orders, and said simply, "Yes, sir."

But Trimble was not a soldier and had no such qualms. "What the hell you plannin', Cap'n?"

"Clem, when you hear shooting from across the plaza, just come a-running."

"Cap'n, you're—"

But Stryker was already moving, crouching low through the wind and rain as he ran for his horse.

Chapter 40

Stryker reached the adobe without drawing fire. He was relieved, but at the same time he felt a twinge of concern. Even amid the gloom of the storm he'd been visible to Pierce and Dugan for a couple of seconds.

They were expert marksmen, so why the hell hadn't they shot at him?

He had no answer to that, and put the thought out of his head.

The criollo was standing on three legs, its head lowered, dozing. The little horse objected strongly to being led out into the storm and fought the bridle. But eventually it accepted its harsh fate and allowed Stryker to lead it outside.

Windblown rain hammering into him, he stepped into the saddle and swung the horse around the side of the adobe. Here the wind was cut by the building and even the downpour seemed less.

He kneed the horse forward, but immediately drew rein as Silas Dugan stepped around the corner, a grin on his lips and a gun in his hand.

The man's buckskins were black from rain and his wild red hair tossed in the wind, his beard matted against his chest.

In that moment, Stryker had a flash of insight: This was what death looked like.

"Get off the damned horse, or I'll blow you right out of the saddle, Stryker," Dugan said. His gun was up, steady on Stryker's chest.

He had to play for time. His Colt was in the holster and he was no fast-draw artist.

Stryker swung out of the leather, and Dugan said, "Step away from the nag. Well away. I told you I'd give it to you in the belly and I want a clear shot."

"We can talk about this," Stryker said desperately.

"All my talking is done, Stryker. Now it's killing time." He smiled. "You really didn't think we was stupid enough to let you get behind us, huh? I could have shot you when you made your run from the wall, but I didn't. I wanted to watch you die, see, kicking your legs in the mud and screaming like the ugly pig you are."

Dead men have few options, but Stryker was left with one: defiance.

"Dugan," he said, slowly and evenly, "you're a squaw-killing son of a bitch and I hope I see you roast in hell."

The gunman grinned. "Now you get it, Stryker, one right in the belly."

The hammer of his gun triple-clicked as it was thumbed back.

Stryker was about to go for his Colt, but the wind saved his life.

A tremendous, shrieking gust blasted over the roof of the adobe, carrying with it the wails of the dead.

Dugan's eyes flickered and his jaw went slack. For an instant, fear danced in his eyes, and he instinctively raised his head to the wind.

Stryker took his chance.

He dived to his left, drawing his gun before he splashed into the mud. He and Dugan fired at the same instant. Momentarily unnerved, the gunman's bullet went wide, burning across Stryker's ribs. But Stryker's shot parted Dugan's beard at the point of his chin, driving his shattered jawbone into his throat.

Dugan's scream was a gurgling screech of pain and terror. The gunman staggered back, holding his gun high. Stryker fired again, missed, and fired a third time. This bullet crashed into Dugan's left shoulder and he dropped to his knees, his lower face a scarlet mask of blood, teeth and bone.

Stryker rose to his feet. He stepped in front of Dugan, raised his boot and used the sole to kick the man's face. Dugan fell on his back, still alive, his terrified eyes looking into Stryker's.

Wails braided through the wind, swelling, waning, and swelling again, like howls from the lowest regions of hell.

"Hear that, Silas?" Stryker said. "They're coming for you."

Lightning flashed, flickering white on Dugan's shattered face, gleaming in his scared eyes.

Suddenly sick of it, Stryker raised his gun. "You've

an appointment to keep in hell, Silas," he said. "I don't want to hold you up."

He fired into the man's forehead. Dugan's body jerked and all the life that had been in him left.

"The trouble with you, Dugan, is that you lived too long," Stryker said.

He reloaded his Colt and shoved it back in the holster only to draw again as footsteps thudded behind him. He turned and saw Birchwood, his face bound up and tied on top of his head like a dead man in a coffin.

The young lieutenant looked at Dugan, then at Stryker. Anticipating Birchwood's question, he said, "His luck ran out. Now I'm going after Rake Pierce."

"He's gone, sir. As soon as the shooting started between you and Dugan, he ran for his horse and fled the field."

Stryker smiled inwardly at Birchwood's choice of words. You can take the boy out of West Point . . .

Trimble stepped through the teeming rain to Stryker's side. "Cap'n, ol' Rake's skedaddled. Left Silas to face the music." He then saw the body sprawled behind Stryker and Birchwood. "You killed him, Cap'n?" His voice held a note of disbelief.

"I got lucky," Stryker said. "He didn't."

He looked at Cantrell. "That's one of them down, Don Carlos."

The Mexican nodded silently, an awareness of the emptiness of revenge in his eyes. The gunman was dead, beyond suffering. There was nothing more to be done with him.

"I'm going after Pierce," Stryker said.

Trimble was horrified. "Cap'n, ol' Rake knows mountains like an Apache. He'll lay up somewhere an' kill ye fer sure."

"Maybe my luck will hold."

"Let me go with you, Cap'n. I'll smell him out for you."

Stryker shook his head. "This is personal, Clem, between Pierce and me. I have to do it alone."

He reached into his saddle roll and pulled out his blouse. Indifferent to the rain streaming over his bare chest and shoulders, he removed the cotton shirt and dragged the blouse over his head.

"If I am to fall," he said, "I'll fall as a soldier."

"Sir, I respectfully request that I accompany the lieutenant."

"You're wounded, Mr. Birchwood. I'd say you've already done enough. You will remain here until I return."

"But, sir—"

"That is an order."

Birchwood looked disappointed, but said only, "Yes, sir."

Stryker swung into the saddle and looked down at Cantrell. "I'll kill him for you, Don Carlos."

"It is my duty to go with you, Lieutenant."

Stryker smiled. "I appreciate the offer, but you shoot even worse than me. I'll do this alone."

"Then go with God, Lieutenant."

"Clem, south you reckon?" Stryker asked.

"He's draggin' a pack mule, Cap'n. Rake badly wants to sell his scalps, especially now when he can keep all the profit."

Stryker touched his hat and kneed the criollo around the adobe and into the snarling storm. The day was shading darker, shadows gathering on the mountain crevasses and rock ledges, and the wind ravaged through the tall timber. The land shimmered with constant lightning flashes, thunder rolled across the sky, rain fell in tumbling sheets and it seemed to Stryker that the whole world had gone insane.

As he rode nearer to the shelf of lava rock, the unearthly wailing grew louder and seemed to originate from the rock itself. He saw the reason immediately. The wind was forcing itself through tunnels in the lava caused in ancient times by gas bubbles. When the wind gusted, it howled through the cavities and sounded like human wails.

Stryker felt a slight pang of disappointment. He'd been open to the possibility that supernatural forces had helped him kill Dugan. But it had been no such thing . . . just holes in rock.

He rode on, his eyes scanning the way ahead.

Pierce was out there, maybe waiting, and the man was better with the rifle and revolver than he could ever be.

Thus Stryker faced the reality of his situation. It was a truth not calculated to build a man's confidence.

Chapter 41

Despite the torrential downpour, Pierce had left signs of his passing: a broken branch here, a scuffed rock there, a hoofprint left in deep mud.

Stryker wondered at the man's clumsiness; then it dawned on him: Pierce was not being careless; he was leading him on . . . to a place of the renegade's choosing.

Drawing rein, Stryker scanned the terrain ahead of him. Visibility was down to fifty yards or less, and that deeply shadowed. The wind somersaulted through the trees, stripping branches of needles, and the thunder and lightning raged, as dangerous and threatening as a rabid wolf.

Through the steel veil of the rain, Stryker made out a towering parapet of rock cut through by a notch about sixty feet wide, created during some ancient earthshake. The bottom of the cleft was thick with lodgepole pine and tumbled boulders, one of the larger rocks carved into the shape of a skull by centuries of wind and rain.

Stryker's newfound superstition made him look on the rock as an omen—it was where Pierce could be waiting to bushwhack him.

He pulled his Colt, dismounted, and led his horse into the shelter of some oaks. Keeping to as much cover as he could, he moved carefully toward the notch, pausing now and then to wipe rain from his eyes.

The notch was thirty yards away and there was no sign of Pierce.

Thunder blasted. But this was the thunder of a rifle. Stryker felt a powerful blow slam into his left shoulder. He spun around and dropped, a movement that saved his life. Pierce's second bullet split the air inches above his head.

Like a wounded animal, Stryker sought the shelter of the trees, burrowing into the wet, mossy earth behind an oak. He lay on his back and touched fingers to his wound. They came away red. He'd been hit hard, maybe so hard he might never be able to get to his feet again.

The thought panicked Stryker. He could not lie there and let Pierce slaughter him.

Struggling against waves of nausea, his head spinning, he rose on one knee and stole a look around the tree trunk. Pierce's bullet chipped bark an inch from his face, driving wood splinters into his forehead.

Stryker ducked back, breathing hard, and laid the back of his head against the tree. Rain ticked through the branches and the oak talked to the wind in a rustling whisper. The land around him flickered from dark to sizzling white as lightning flashed and made the air smell of a distant sea.

His back against the trunk, Stryker painfully pushed himself to his feet. He turned his face to the rain, mouth open, glorying in its coolness. The oak leaves traced shifting, lacy patterns against the angry sky and he studied them for long moments, wondering at their fragile beauty.

Consciousness was ebbing from Stryker with his blood. Now was the time. But if he was to die, he'd meet his God on his own terms: standing on his feet.

He raised his Colt to shoulder level and stepped from behind the tree and walked into the open.

Rake Pierce stood six feet away, straddle-legged, his gun in his hand, his thick body haloed by rain.

"Stryker, you damned freak," he said, "now I'll finish what I started."

His gun came up, very fast.

Stryker heard a strange, flat *click!*, the sound that always precedes a close lightning strike. A split-second later, even as Pierce's gun roared, the oak behind Stryker was hit. The bolt stabbed out of the sky like a column of living fire, briefly enveloping both men. They stood like statues bathed in terrible light for an instant, then were blasted to the ground.

The lightning split the oak in half, entirely stripping it of bark and leaves, and a few scarlet roses of flame bloomed briefly before they were pounded into darkness by the rain.

Stryker lay stunned, his face in the mud. He

turned and saw the death throes of the oak and realized what had happened. But he had escaped one death, only to face another. Just two yards away, Pierce was on his hands and knees, struggling to get to his feet.

Stryker pushed his Colt in front him, grasping the butt in both hands. He had no hope of rising before Pierce did. Rain battered into his face, ribbons of yellow and scarlet from the searing lightning flash danced in his eyes and the day had darkened into a grim, gray gloom.

He rested the butt of the gun on the muddy ground, pointed it at Pierce and fired.

His bullet crashed into the man's ribs and Pierce screamed and toppled over onto his right side.

Rake Pierce was not a brave man. His only strength was an ability to put the fear of God in others, women, children and men who knew they could not match his gun skill.

But now hate drove him, not courage.

And it was also hatred that motivated Stryker, binding him to Pierce, as firmly as if they'd come out of the same womb and as unbreakable as the steel shackles the man had used to destroy his face.

Drawing on their last reserves of strength, both men climbed to their feet. They staggered toward each other, shooting as they came. Stryker took another hit, but kept upright. His bullets found Pierce twice, but the man would not die.

Snarling like wolves, they closed on each other. Stryker grabbed Pierce's gun hand, and found the man had little strength left. He viciously rammed the muzzle of his Colt into Pierce's right eye and pulled the trigger.

Pierce let out another shriek, then fell on his back, pulling Stryker with him.

That was how Clem Trimble found them at first light the next morning, locked in an unholy embrace, snarls of hatred still on their faces.

Trimble pulled Stryker off Pierce and clucked like a mother hen over his wounds.

"Cap'n," he said aloud, with only himself to hear, "I reckon if you survive, you'll have used up all nine of them cat lives o' your'n."

Chapter 42

The officer's mess at Fort Apache was decorated with swaths of red, white and blue bunting to honor the visit of Senator Otis Henry Nelson and his lady. The distinguished legislator was on an inspection tour of the Southwest, "to show," he was fond of saying, "that Washington cares about our boys who wear the blue."

Above the rock fireplace, beside a black-draped portrait of the gallant Custer, but at a respectful distance, the calendar tacked to the wall proclaimed that the date was February 16, 1899.

"So, Lieutenant Colonel Stryker, I hear you're shipping out for the Philippines tomorrow with the valiant Seventh."

"Not the entire regiment, sir, only a company. The rest of the Seventh will follow later."

"Give them hell, Colonel," Nelson said. He was a small, thin man with a few wisps of dry, mousy hair combed across a bald pate. A pair of pince-nez glasses, attached to a cord, were perched at the end of a pointed and permanently red and sniffling nose. "Keep the saber sharp, I say, and give those savages the keen edge of it, like we did the Apaches. Huh, Colonel Stryker, is that not the way?"

"Apache warriors never let a soldier close enough to hit them with a saber, Senator," Stryker said. "As for the Filipino rebels being savages, I don't think—"

His voice trailed away. Nelson was no longer listening. The man was staring over Stryker's shoulder, his eyes searching for the really important people.

"Yes, yes, Colonel, very interesting," Nelson said absently. "If you will excuse me . . ." He stepped around Stryker and raised a hand. "Ah, General Funston, a word with you . . ."

"You look well, Steve. Even taller than I remembered, if a little grayer."

Stryker turned toward the woman's voice.

"And the full beard becomes you so," she added.

It took Stryker a few uncomfortable moments before he remembered the face. "It's wonderful to see you again," he said. "After all these years."

He was taken aback. Still dressed in a mourning gown of rustling black two years after her father's death, to call Millie matronly would have been a compliment. Major Birchwood, less courteous but more accurate, would say later, "Hell, her ass is an axe-handle wide."

"I heard about your father, Millie, or should I say

Mrs. Nelson?" Stryker said. "I'm so sorry for your loss."

"We are old friends, Steve. Millie is just fine." The woman's eyes, made small by the upward pressure of her chubby cheeks, misted. "Papa gave his all to Washington and our great nation, but in the end it was just too much for his poor, noble heart."

Millie dabbed at her eyes with a small lace handkerchief. "However, the senator has been a tower of strength, supporting me in my time of great need. The senator and I have three sons, all made in his image. Two are destined for the clergy and the oldest will follow his dear papa into politics." She added, with some pride but little affection, "The senator is a remarkable man."

"A remarkable man, indeed," Stryker said, saying nothing at all.

"And you, Steve? You never wed?"

"No."

"Then you have not been blessed with children."

"Oh, but I have. My adopted daughter, Kelly, is over there, surrounded by that gaggle of admiring young officers. She was orphaned when her"—he hesitated a heartbeat—"parents were killed by Apaches."

"How perfectly dreadful."

Birchwood stepped beside Stryker and briefly reported on some minor matter concerning supplies. Stryker listened, then said to Millie, "Please allow me to introduce my adjutant, Major Birchwood."

"At your service, ma'am," the man said, smiling, bowing over Millie's hand.

A red-faced corporal, uncomfortable in his dress uniform, offered a tray of chilled champagne. Millie took a glass, as did Stryker.

"You are not indulging, Major?" the woman said.

"Alas, no, ma'am. I promised my betrothed that my lips would ne'er touch whiskey or other ardent liquors."

"La, a soldier who doesn't imbibe is indeed a rarity." Millie's attempt to mimic the speech of the young Washington belles was an abject failure. "And when will you wed the lady to whom you have pledged your troth?"

"We are in no hurry to enter the bonds of holy matrimony, ma'am. Soon, perhaps, after the regiment returns from the Philippines."

He turned to Stryker. "Will you excuse me, sir? I have duties to perform."

Stryker nodded. "Of course, Major."

Birchwood bowed over Millie's hand again and left, leaving behind a silence that Stryker made no attempt to fill.

Finally the woman said, "Steve, I'm sorry everything turned out the way it did. If I had it to do all over again . . ."

"What's done is done, Millie," Stryker said. "We can't change the past."

The woman nodded. "No, I guess we can't," she said, recognizing the finality of Stryker's statement. "Well, I must join the senator. I see him looking for me." She held out her hand. "Good luck, Steve."

Stryker took it. "And you too, Millie."

That night, in his quarters, Stryker lay on his cot, staring at the ceiling.

He remembered what Birchwood had said, and whispered it aloud, "Her ass is an axe-handle wide."

He smiled . . . and the smile became a grin . . . and the grin became a laugh.